MONSTER JUICE

Sickening Secrets
from Raven Hill

GROSSET & DUNLAP
Published by the Penguin Group
Penguin Group (USA) LLC, 375 Hudson Street, New York, New York 10014, USA

USA | Canada | UK | Ireland | Australia | New Zealand | India | South Africa | China

penguin.com
A Penguin Random House Company

The Library of Congress has cataloged the individual books under the following Control Numbers: 2013017784, 2013017785.

ISBN 978-0-448-48911-7   10 9 8 7 6 5 4 3 2 1

The Guts:

Pages 1-183

Pages 185-375

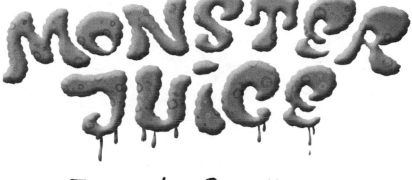

Fear the Barfitron

by M. D. Payne

Grosset & Dunlap
An Imprint of Penguin Group (USA) LLC

To Lady Payne and
our little monster, Molly

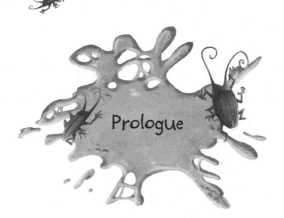

Prologue

Three mysterious figures sprinted through a dark, overgrown forest.

"We must be swift," a well-dressed pale man in the lead yelled. "We mustn't risk Percy's safety much longer!"

"We're close," a short woman in a white uniform and a hairnet yelled back. "The boy's house eez just past the creek." She struggled to push along a man nearly twice her size. His sprint slowed to a stumble. Something was wrong. He appeared to be sick, or even worse—wounded.

"Meeee wwwaaa," moaned Percy through his crooked black teeth. "Wwwant go hoooome!"

"Soon, old friend," the well-dressed man gasped. "We just need you to do one thing."

All three jumped into the creek, pushing through the cold, sandy water. Their shoes and pants legs quickly became drenched, but they had to keep moving. Percy wouldn't survive another attack.

Halfway across, the hairnetted woman lost her footing. "*Ay Dios mío!*" she yelped as she slipped face-first into the icy water.

"I've got you," the well-dressed man yelled, and helped her to her feet.

Rising out of the creek, the hairnetted woman didn't even notice the freezing-cold uniform that now clung to her. All she could do was scan the darkness for their friend.

"Percy!" she yelled. "Percy!!!"

Slumped on a log at the edge of the water sat Percy. His huge head slouched over his wide, lifeless chest. They couldn't see Percy's eye, but both were almost sure it must be closed.

"We have to wake him!" the well-dressed man yelled.

They both shot out of the water toward Percy.

And that's when they heard them . . .

Loud, slurpy growls coming from the other side of the creek.

They both froze.

Turning, the well-dressed man's eyes widened in fear. Coming toward them, through the darkness, were dozens—maybe hundreds—of spitting and screeching mouths. More than either of them had ever seen in their lives.

He grabbed Percy's wrinkled face and lifted up his head. Percy's eye popped open in surprise.

"Percy!" he yelled. "They're here. We must run. Now, Percy."

"NOW!" The well-dressed man and woman yelled together.

Percy jumped up, using what life he had left, and the three ran even faster now. Behind them, the sound of the vile creatures was deafening.

"Eet's just up ahead," said the hairnetted woman over the hungry screeching. "Soon after the clearing!"

They burst through the edge of the forest. In the moonlight, it became evident how old and weak Percy looked, despite his massive and once-powerful frame. The old man huffed and wheezed as he did his best to keep up.

Halfway from the forest to the house they were met by a fresh batch of the evil creatures.

"Nooooooo!" Percy yelled.

"We're surrounded," the well-dressed man said.

"There must be three dozen or more," screeched the hairnetted woman. Now she *was* shaking, but not from the cold creek water.

She was shaking from fear.

The well-dressed man pulled a Taser out of his jacket pocket as fast as he could, but his enemy moved swiftly.

"Waaaaaahhhhh!" Percy yelled. He swatted at them weakly, but soon they were upon him.

They scrambled all over him, dozens upon dozens, slurping and chewing. He fell to the ground, lost under the swarm.

"Noooooo!" the well-dressed man yelled, zapping as many of the hard shells as he could with his Taser.

The hairnetted woman ripped off her hairnet, stretched it out, and captured one creature at a time. She tied them up in her net so the well-dressed man could more easily kill them.

But there were just too many.

Before they could destroy even half a dozen of the disgusting beasties, the swarm left as quickly as it had come. They scurried off of Percy, leaving a trail of monster juice. He had been drained. Percy didn't have much time left.

"Percy!" the well-dressed man yelled. "Hang in there, old man."

The well-dressed man and the once-hairnetted woman worked together to lift Percy's massive body off the ground and drag him as fast as they could toward the house in the distance.

"Gwwwwaaaaa!" Percy moaned through a mouth filled with black slime.

"Shhhhh," said the once-hairnetted woman. "You're going to be okay."

But they both knew that Percy wouldn't be okay. They just needed him to hang on long enough to answer the question that burned through their minds.

After an exhausting effort, they were able to make it to the window at the back of the house.

"This is Chris," the once-hairnetted woman said to Percy.

They turned Percy's head so he could get a better look. His eye was starting to lose its glimmer. He was fading fast.

They could see a young boy on his bed, counting a large pile of money. He seemed upset by the amount, counting it over and over again. He pulled over a laptop, opened it up, and tapped away at the keys.

"Is this the one, Percy?" the well-dressed man asked.

"Guuuuhhhhh . . ." Percy groaned.

"Percy!" the once-hairnetted woman hissed in his ear. "Percy, you must tell us! Please!"

Even though he hated to, the well-dressed man slapped Percy across the face as hard as he could.

He got the reaction he was looking for.

"Yesssss!" Percy's voice gurgled up through his broken body. "Chris. Is. The."

His body spasmed, and as he slipped to the ground, his last word was:

"One."

Tears escaped the well-dressed man's eyes for Percy. He feared for the rest of his residents as well.

"Now we need this young boy more than ever," he said, "but how can we draw him to us?"

"I have an idea," the once-hairnetted woman said, and she held up her hairnet, which contained one of the vile beasts, still alive. It hissed and screeched.

"Perhaps this evil little theeng can help. . . ."

1 Summer ×
1 Zillion Lawns
= 0

Chris.Taylor.02: My dreams are destroyed.

S'whts da prb? :**karate247**

Chris.Taylor.02: Shane, please use vowels!

Thts yr prb? I dstryd yr drms w/ n vwls? :**karate247**

Chris.Taylor.02: No, you didn't destroy my dreams.
But use your vowels.

:**karate247**
Thanks, teacher. SO WHAT'S YOUR PROBLEM?

Chris.Taylor.02: Do you remember that amazing
telescope I wanted to buy?

Y! Did u get it?!? :**karate247**

Chris.Taylor.02: NOOOOOOO! I don't have enough money! What am I going to do?

Mow more lawns? :**karate247**

Chris.Taylor.02: It's almost fall! I have 2 more lawns and that's IT! I'm never going to get that telescope.

I'll ttly loan u csh. How much? $25? $30? :**karate247**

Chris.Taylor.02: $484.99 more.

I give u 99 cnt. :**karate247**

Chris.Taylor.02: Ha ha ha.

K, $4.99. I evn round it up $5. :**karate247**

Chris.Taylor.02: I still need 480 bucks.

$479.99. Huge difference. :**karate247**

Chris.Taylor.02: Whatever. I can't believe school is Monday. ARRGGHHH!

:**karate247**
Since when do you hate schl? That's my thng. You luv schl.

Chris.Taylor.02: I don't love school. I love STUDYING.

Same thng. :**karate247**

Chris.Taylor.02: No, it's not. If I had it my way, I'd get my mother to homeschool me. When you're smart, the teachers always pick on you. They think I like answering questions.

But u r always right! :**karate247**

Chris.Taylor.02: That doesn't mean I should have to stand up in front of class and give every bully in school a reason to pick on me. All the kids in our school are idiots.

Xcept 4 me? :**karate247**

Chris.Taylor.02: Well . . .

:(:**karate247**

Chris.Taylor.02: Just kidding. You, Ben, and Gordon are the exceptions. OF COURSE.

:**karate247**
Tnx. OK, now I shall reward your good behavior with vowels and amazing advice.

Chris.Taylor.02: Bring it on.

:**karate247**
Become Middle School Honor Society President! U'll rake in the dough!

Chris.Taylor.02: What?

They pay the prez, don't they? :**karate247**

Chris.Taylor.02: Last time I checked, no. Plus, I already declined an invitation to the Honor Society. I can't handle that kind of pressure.

:**karate247**

Go back and say yes! Don't they have fund-raisers?

Fund-raise for yourself!

Chris.Taylor.02: I'll keep that in mind. I should go. I've got to spend the rest of my summer cleaning my bedroom. Maybe I can get Mom to give me 10 bucks.

:**karate247**

Demand 15! I'll think of more amazing ideas, although that last one was pretty good. LTR.

The pile of money on my bed made me as depressed as the collection of dirty, funky piles in my room. I slammed my laptop shut.

My eye went from the pile of laundry with my "Mars or Bust" T-shirt on top, to a pile of comic books, to a pile of old horror movie DVDs and video games. In one disgusting corner of my room, a comb sat on top of a moldy piece of pizza. Pieces of my short blond hair mixed with goopy pizza grease.

What did I have to show for an entire summer of lawn mowing? Grass-covered legs that itched like crazy, a messy room, and an empty space by the window where my dream telescope should have been.

Hanging next to my Star Wars poster was a picture of the Super Infinity Space Gazer—positioned so that it pointed at the Death Star. The state-of-the-art TRQ92 Super Infinity Space Gazer would show me the craters of the moon! It would show me stars in distant galaxies! It would be my first step toward becoming an astrophysicist—my life's dream!

I scooped up all of my money and shoved it back into the shoe box. Crouching down low, I started to slide it under my bed, when a sound made me stop.

A very quiet crunching sound.

Reluctantly, I turned toward the pizza. Sitting in the middle of the old slice, a large black cockroach enjoyed snack time.

It had just polished off a scabby pepperoni, and was starting to munch on my hair!

"Ugh!" I grunted in disgust.

Grabbing a stinky tattered shoe, I cautiously crept toward the roach.

It saw me almost right away, let out what sounded like a tiny belch, and ran behind the piles.

I jumped down onto my hands and knees to see it scurry into a small space between the wall and the floor.

Its legs scrambled and scraped. It was so full of pizza I wasn't sure it was going to make it.

Just when I thought I'd have time to grab a can of Raid, it slipped through and was gone.

I picked up the pizza, plucked off the comb, and tossed both in the garbage.

By the time I finished cleaning my room, summer vacation was over.

The First Day

When Shane and I arrived at school the next day, it was like we had never left for summer break—a feeling worse than anything in the world.

"Ah, the smell of cafeteria mashed potatoes," Shane said as he inhaled deeply.

He texted me the night before that he planned on wearing his karate uniform "2 mk a statmnt." I'm glad he changed his mind. He showed up in a ratty T-shirt and a stinky old pair of jeans instead. It made my black pants and green collared shirt look like formal wear.

"I'll catch you later," Shane said as he gave me a quick thumbs-up and headed down another hall toward his locker. I gave him a weak thumbs-up back and kept walking.

As I walked, I daydreamed about pointing the

TRQ92 at the moon on a clear night. This helped me ignore all the idiots that surrounded me as I made my way toward my locker. I was so deep in thought that I didn't even notice the huge figure towering in front of me until it was too late.

"What the—?!" I whooped as I bounced off the massive kid and hit the ground.

I lifted up my head to see a pair of sneakers on the most monstrous feet in middle school.

"Chris!" a voice boomed.

I looked up, terrified. . . .

"We didn't mean to run into you like that. We thought for sure you'd see us!"

A beefy, tanned arm reached down to help me up.

"Gordon!" I said, happy to see my friend. "Hey, man. What did they feed you at summer camp? You're like a wrestler."

Gordon chuckled as he said, "Lots of lean meats. Protein shakes. A whole horse. You know, stuff like that."

Gordon pulled me up and I could see another friend, Ben, was with Gordon.

"What were you thinking about?" Ben asked.

"I was thinking of the moon," I said.

"Huh?" Gordon said.

"Never mind; I'll explain later."

"Okay," said Ben, a much smaller dude, with pale skin and messy reddish blond hair. "How do I look? I got a brand new suit for the first day of school!"

I didn't know what to say. His blue suit and red tie seemed really nice, I guess, but he still looked as ratty as Shane did in his jeans and T-shirt. Plus, Ben always looked like he was about to hurl.

"Um," I said slowly. "Ah . . . the SUIT looks great, man!" At least that wasn't a lie.

I turned to Gordon in his new jeans and a T-shirt two sizes too small. "Isn't that shirt a little tight?" I asked.

"Naw, dude," Gordon said. "I gotta make sure the ladies can see how much I trained this summer. Check out these GUNS!"

Gordon flexed, and I thought I could hear a bit of T-shirt rip. He turned to show his muscles to the kids walking up and down the hallway. A few giggly girls stopped and pointed. Gordon flexed again, harder this time.

RIIIIIIIIIIIIIIIIIIIP!

His shirt split up both sides, revealing his slightly hairy armpit. The warning bell rang, and there was a sudden rush in the hallway. No one wanted to be late to the first class of the year.

Gordon's face went from surprised to horrified. "Aw, man. What the heck am I gonna do?" he practically whined.

Ben and I started laughing like hyenas. His muscles didn't look so big anymore.

Ben, between laughs, said, "Come on over to my locker. I have an extra T-shirt. It might be a bit tight. Just promise not to flex in it!"

That made Ben and I laugh even harder. At least my friends had made me forget about the telescope situation.

"Man, this line is huge," Ben said as we waited for hot lunch.

"What's your rush?" I asked. "The food probably hasn't gotten any better. Everyone's just forgotten how bad it is."

"What's the special today?" Ben asked. "Icky Nuggets? Salisbury Snake?"

I looked to see what the lunch lady was scooping out. She was so short that even when I craned my neck, all I could see was the top of her hairnet. But I could see the food through the glass. She dug deep into a pan with her skinny, hairy arm and out came—

"Chicken Not-Your-Mom's," I said.

"It's chicken parmesan, but it's definitely not your mom's!" Ben and I chirped in unison.

We laughed our way to the lunch lady, who stared us down as we got closer to her station. She furrowed her wrinkly brow, but didn't say anything as she plopped a rubbery and cheesy piece of chicken onto Ben's plate. I decided to get the Blandburger with Cheese.

The lunch lady fussed behind the counter for a bit and then handed me my burger with a wink.

We made our way through the tables and found Shane and Gordon.

As we sat down, Shane said, "Welcome back, gentlemen!"

"It's almost like the summer never happened," I said. "Thanks for grabbing the regular seats."

"I think I can feel an imprint of my butt," Ben said as he wiggled his rear on the bench. "Feels good."

I grabbed my Blandburger and took a huge bite.

There was a loud crunch and something squirted out of my burger . . . right onto Gordon!

"Dude!!!" he yelled. A yellowish wad of goo slimed its way down his shirt.

"Is that some kind of sauce?" Shane asked as he poked at his dry burger. "I didn't get any sauce."

The burger was totally funky, but I didn't care. I was starving. I took another bite—so what if it was a little crunchy?

"Arrgh, this is the worst day ever!" yelled Gordon as he wiped off the goo. "Two of my shirts are ruined— "

"One of your shirts," interrupted Ben.

"And Coach Grey has gone crazy!"

"Wait," said Shane. "I thought you and Coach Grey were besties."

"Yeah, well not after today," Gordon continued. "I just found out that everyone on a sports team has to 'volunteer in the community' or we're off the team."

"So," Shane asked, "what are you going to do?"

"I guess I'm gonna have to do it. Coach said that even if we didn't care that it was our 'civic duty,' we could do it for money."

"What money?" I asked.

"He said the local Rotary was giving away five hundred dollars to the Rio Vista Middle School student who did the most hours of volunteering for the first half of the school year. But I have to spend time perfecting my technique! ARRGH!"

"Wait. Is it just jocks who can win the Volunteer of the Year award?"

"No, it's the whole school. Which is why there's no way I'd win it!"

My brain buzzed at the idea of winning the money.

"Okay, wait. No, really, last question!" I was so excited I almost burst. "Where do you go to sign up to be a volunteer?"

"Mrs. Gonzales is the volunteer coordinator. Sign-up starts tomorrow. Why do you care?" asked Gordon. "Volunteering isn't your thing. It doesn't involve books or studying or writing papers."

Shane raised a questioning eyebrow.

"Yeah," Ben asked. "What's the deal?"

I stood up for dramatic effect. A few kids looked over from other tables. "I'm going to be Volunteer of the Year. I'm going to win the five hundred dollars. I'm going to buy the telescope of my dreams!"

The Light at the End of the Classroom

BUZZZZZZZZZZZZZZZZZZZZZZZZZZ. . . .

The alarm clock buzzed and buzzed and buzzed. I set it for extra early the night before so I could get to school before all the other volunteers. The best volunteer assignment—and the TRQ92—would be mine!

My bed was so hot, I felt like a slug. My eyes refused to open. I reached over to the alarm clock to shut it up, and then yawned. And yawned three more times. My eyes felt like they were glued shut. When I finally opened them, I couldn't see anything.

I rolled over to the window at the foot of the bed and threw open the curtains. Barely any light came in—it was almost as dark outside as it was inside. Large black birds circled below huge dark clouds. I opened the window to let some fresh air into my slug cave, and I could smell rain. Thunder boomed somewhere far off.

Blindly, I stumbled over to the light switch and flipped it on. My head felt as hazy and cloudy as the sky. The lights flickered slightly as lightning struck. A boom echoed through town. My head throbbed, and my stomach hurt. I burped a little burp, and I could taste the Blandburger from the day before.

The storm continued to rage on. It was still pitch black outside when I got to school. My wet shoes squeaked loudly as I walked to Mrs. Gonzales's classroom. Each squeak echoed up and down the empty hallways, and I suddenly felt very alone. Half of the lights weren't on yet. The thunder still rolled outside. I felt like I was walking deep into a ghost town.

When I got to Mrs. Gonzales's classroom, I peeked through the window in her door. The lights were still off and the room was empty. *I'll just wait for her inside*, I thought as I pushed open the door. That's when I saw it: a strange green light coming from Mrs. Gonzales's desk.

There was a flash of lightning, and I swore I saw someone in the back of the room. I twisted my head around the door and searched the shadows. Nothing. As the thunder faded, I couldn't hear anything but the rapid beating of my own heart. My stomach squirmed with fear.

I stepped inside and closed the door.

The mysterious green light glowed stronger with each step I took toward it.

As I reached the desk, I saw that the glow was coming from a letter—

Almost as if the words were written with some kind of glow-in-the-dark ink.

I picked it up. It felt extremely old. I remembered reading a letter that my grandfather had kept from his first job in 1965. It felt exactly like that—thin, from a different time. An older time. It smelled moldy. It looked like it had been written on a typewriter instead of a computer!

I read the letter:

Dearest Students of Rio Vista,

Volunteers are needed to tend to our geriatric patients' every want and need. Many of our residents suffer dementia, necrosis, and many more rare and vexing ailments. Toward that end, discretion is very much necessary, as is a strong stomach.

Volunteers who are able to tend to

these dear, suffering wretches, for as many hours as possible and as soon as possible, will be most welcome!

All interested parties should favor us with their company at our facility on Saturday next at nine o'clock in the morning.

If you find the time and opportunity to visit, we shall be extremely glad to see you.

Yours ever,
The Staff of Raven Hill Retirement Home

As I finished reading the letter, Mrs. Gonzales's door creaked open!

I scooped up the letter, dropped to the floor, and hid under Mrs. Gonzales's desk. There was nowhere else to go.

The lights came on in the room. I held my breath and crouched down extra tight, hoping that I would just disappear.

Footsteps slowly made their way toward the desk. Huge, banging footsteps.

CLOMP. CLOMP. CLOMP.

A monstrous pair of boots, caked with black goo, appeared in front of the desk.

I clutched the letter and thought, *Someone is coming to get me because I saw this freaky old letter!*

Two massive, hairy hands came reaching down toward the desk . . .

. . . and grabbed the trash can!

The janitor tipped the can into a trash bag, and then left the room.

I jumped up and scurried out through the door before Mrs. Gonzales could catch me under her desk.

That day at lunch, I sat at our table munching a nasty, cold Ick Stick with a huge smile on my face. Gordon noticed.

"Thinking about the moon again, space boy?" asked Gordon.

"Yeah," I said, dreamily. I put my hands on my cheeks, looked up at the ceiling, and sighed for comic effect.

"What a difference a day makes," Ben said.

"I got a really sweet volunteer assignment," I said.

"Yeah, where is it?" Shane asked.

"Raven Hill Retirement Home," I said. "I just need to show up Saturday, and I'll be able to volunteer as much as I want."

"Raven Hill?" asked Ben. "I heard Tami Evans went up to Raven Hill and never came back . . ."

"What?" I asked.

Outside the lunchroom someone screamed, and I jumped. I turned my head toward the doors.

"Did you guys hear that?" I asked.

"Hear what?" Shane asked. "That Tami disappeared? I heard she moved."

"No, did you hear—" I started, but Gordon cut me off.

"You're out of your mind, volunteering there!" Gordon said. "Don't you know what old folks in retirement homes are like?"

"Well," I said, "I seem to remember visiting my Nana once when I was five. But, I don't remember much."

"Well, remember this . . ." Gordon leaned into the lunch table. Shane gave him a look that meant *Shut it, dude*, but Gordon wouldn't shut it.

"They smell totally funky. They mumble and moan. Some of them drool and shake. You'll have to do all sorts of crazy things for them, like change their bedpans, wipe drool off of their mouths, even—"

Now Shane cut Gordon off.

"Don't sweat it, dude," said Shane. He glared at Gordon across the table. "Old folks take care of themselves at these places. Well, actually, the nurses take care of them. You've got nothing to worry about!

Just play a couple of games of poker or Mario Kart or whatever it is old people play now and you're IN!"

But it didn't matter what Shane said. All I could think about was what Gordon and Ben had said. And that scream!

Welcome to
Raven Hill

Saturday arrived before I knew it. I felt like I'd been on a roller coaster ever since finding the mysterious letter—and I wanted to throw up. I spent all night thinking about what my friends had said, and I still wondered if someone else was in Mrs. Gonzales's room when I found the letter. But I just *had* to go to Raven Hill. It was the volunteer opportunity of the century.

The drive to Raven Hill felt like a dream. No, worse . . . a nightmare. Unable to focus, I just stared out the window as my mother drove us to the other side of town. Neither of us spoke.

The sign for Raven Hill sat just off the road. It was so overgrown with creeping ivy that we nearly missed it . . . almost as if it didn't want to be found. The car made a sharp left, cutting off a huge tractor-trailer, and we shot up the hill.

The farther we went up the hill, the darker it got. I looked through the windshield to see a thick forest blocking the sun.

The trees leaned down and tried to hit our car as we whizzed past! I looked up through the sunroof, and could see branch after branch just barely missing our car: WHOOSH, WHOOSH, WHOOSH!

"Mom, do you see that?" I asked, pointing. "Maybe you should speed up."

"See what, dear?" she asked.

Clearly, she didn't see anything, which made me feel even more panicked—and crazy!

I looked down the hill through the rear window and saw no road—just forest where the road we had driven on used to be. The forest was moving in from all sides!

When I looked through the windshield again, I could see a small bit of sky ahead. But the closer we got, the smaller the sky got—the forest was closing in on us.

"Mom!" I yelled.

"Honey, I'm getting you there as fast as—"

"Just floor it!" I yelled.

"Okay, okay, fine!" she said, and then . . .

VROOOOOOOM!

We reached the end of the forest at the top of the hill, but not before a branch hit the windshield! For the split second before we came out into the sunlight, it looked as though the branch had left a slimy green glow, just like on the letter from Raven Hill.

I looked over at my mother, who was yawning.

She hadn't seen anything.

The blacktop turned into a dirt road. To our left, a huge mansion loomed over the top of a hill. It was at the end of a massive lawn that looked like it hadn't been mowed since the place was built.

My mother pulled the car into the large circular driveway and stopped in front of the mansion.

"Have a nice time," she said with another yawn. "Chrissy, I'm so proud that you're doing this."

I really wished my mother would stop calling me Chrissy.

"Thanks, Mom," I said, jumping out of the car.

As the sound of the car faded, I felt more alone than I ever had in my life. Raven Hill Retirement Home looked like it should be condemned. Many of the windows were covered so you couldn't see in, pieces of the roof were missing, the paint was peeling, and most of the visible windows looked as if they had been smashed in. As I moved closer to the building, the air got cooler and had a musty, old smell, like my grandfather's leather shoes.

But that wasn't the worst part. Circling above the home were five or six of the biggest ravens I'd ever seen.

"I guess that's why they call this Raven Hill," I said aloud to myself.

One raven broke off from the others and landed on the very tip of a spire that shot out from the top of the mansion. It stared down at me with its beady black eyes.

It was quiet up on top of the hill. Too quiet.

If this were a horror movie, everyone would scream "DON'T GO IN!" Good thing horror movies are fake, right?

I clutched my volunteer form nervously. An old dude from the Rotary gave it to me with very specific instructions on how to fill it out. The most important instruction: Don't lose it! It's the only official way to track hours for the award.

The old, musty smell got stronger as I walked up the rickety stairs to the front entrance. The creaking of the wood was outrageously loud. It sounded like the whole building was going to collapse. I was sure the place had been shut down . . . probably by the health department. The creaking became louder, but I could hear something else. I stopped suddenly—the air was filled with the sound of hissing.

I turned around and that's when I saw it. The overgrown lawn . . . it was MOVING.

Something was moving through the grass.

Something big.

And it was making a loud, slurpy, hissing noise. Almost like a moan.

Before I could figure out what it was coming from, one of the ravens screamed a sharp CAW and swooped in where the grass was jiggling and shaking. Then there was a terrible scream. I couldn't tell if it was from the raven or whatever the raven was attacking, but it sounded human.

The raven flapped around in the grass. It was straining, as if something was holding it down. Soon, it was able to gain enough speed to burst out of the ground covering. It was clutching a huge brown bug—almost the size of a cat—and the bug's legs were flailing around. The screaming started again, this time not muffled by the grass. I still wasn't sure if it was the raven, but it had to be. I'd never heard of a screaming bug before.

The raven soared higher and higher and let the bug go. The bug hit the ground with a squelchy squish and the screaming stopped. All of the ravens suddenly swooped in and disappeared into the grass where the bug had dropped.

Just as I was craning my neck to get a better look, I felt a strong hand on my shoulder. I screamed.

They're All Ravin' at Raven!

I whipped my head back around. Standing in front of the open door was a huge man in a nurse's uniform. His giant round and swollen head was topped with a white hat that looked two sizes too small. He spun me around with his massive hands and then gestured through the open door. He had a look of panic on his red face.

"Inside. Safer. Now."

There was no way this nut job worked at the retirement home. The nurse's uniform wasn't going to fool anybody. I bet Raven Hill *had* closed and this escaped mental patient had moved in. My instinct was to run back down the side of the hill. Of course, massive bugs waited at the bottom of the steps, so perhaps inside was better.

"NOW!" he said again, and used a beefy arm to push me through the door. He slammed it closed behind us. Above us, a chandelier covered completely in spiderwebs swayed slightly as the Nurse locked what sounded like thirty-four locks and then muttered under his breath. I turned around to see that—for a split second—the back of the door glowed green. The same green as the letter I had stolen.

As the glow faded, the room became pitch-black. I was lost in the cold darkness with nothing but the sound of the Nurse's deep, labored breathing.

Gradually my eyes started to adjust to the darkness. Maybe it was an illusion, but on the inside the home seemed much bigger than it had looked from the outside. But just as run-down.

"Wait here," he mumbled, then turned and left.

As I waited alone in the mildewy, cavernous lobby, I could hear activity—faint voices and the occasional moan of an old person. At least I hoped it was an old person—that would mean that the crazy Nurse wasn't going off to sharpen an ax. I looked around—there were a whole bunch of rooms down on the first floor and a decrepit stairway leading upstairs. I looked down at the rug, which was threadbare and holey. Dusty old paintings of sour-looking people lined the walls.

"This is like an old old-person's home," I whispered to myself.

"Indeed," boomed a voice.

My chest tightened as a figure stepped out from the shadows. I turned to face a scrawny man with a pale, gaunt face. His jet-black hair was perfectly parted and his black eyes gleamed.

"Some of the clientele here are exceptionally old," he added, as he adjusted his amazingly crisp black suit and bloodred tie. "We want to provide them with the appropriate—" he waved his hand around the front hallway and paused for effect "—atmosphere."

As if on cue, an organ started playing from somewhere. It echoed through the house, creeping me out even more. He looked over his shoulder, toward the music, and said, "Ah, brunch will be ready soon."

"Great," I said, nervously. "I'm starvin'!"

"Oh, but you misunderstand me," said the man, with a sly grin. "You won't be eating brunch—you'll be helping to serve it. You are here to volunteer, are you not?"

"Yes!" I blurted out. I had almost forgotten why I was here, and was secretly glad that I wasn't going to be the main course. I presented my volunteer form to the slim man. "I'm ready to help day and night—whatever you need."

He took my time sheet and said, "Very well." He snapped his fingers, and the Nurse reappeared with another, equally large male Nurse. In fact, they looked so much alike that I could mistake them for each other. They were identical, down to the uniform.

"Escort this gentleman to the kitchen, and see to it that he lends a helping hand," said the man. He then turned to me and said, "Please follow the orders you are given to a *T*, and most importantly, please do not stray into any part of this facility without an escort."

With this, he pointed at the gentlemen who were looming over me.

He continued, "If you find you enjoy this kind of work once your time here is done today, please do join us again at six p.m. on Monday. We can set up a regular schedule at that time."

"Okay," I said. I wasn't sure what else to say, so rather than stand there awkwardly, I put out my hand and introduced myself. "I'm Chris. Who are you?"

The man eyed me and paused. It looked like he was trying to figure out how he wanted to answer.

"I'm the Director," he said. He then shook my hand, bowed slightly, and left, as if he had a million things to check in on.

I stood in the hallway taking in the tattered tapestries and listening to the slow, creepy organ music. I had a staring contest with a dusty old painting to the left of the hallway for a few seconds before both of my escorts, in unison, said, "This way."

We walked past the stairs and into the main hallway,

passing several rooms along the way to the kitchen. In one of the rooms, a bunch of old ladies sat around a fire, cackling. A large black pot hung above the flames, and I wondered if they were preparing brunch.

We walked past another room filled with faded and cracked leather chairs, where two very old-looking gentlemen had nodded off to sleep. At their feet were two ragged dogs.

"Hey, poochie," I said as we passed by. One of the dogs lifted his head and stared at me. His head was shaky, but he looked right at me. His eyes seemed eerily human. I felt the hair go up on the back of my neck, and was glad when we passed.

We turned left at the end of the hallway and entered a kitchen. Several more large men, identical to the Nurses but each in a chef's uniform, ran around preparing what I could only guess was brunch. Although I couldn't recognize anything, I took in a deep whiff and immediately coughed. The kitchen smelled terrible. It almost made me miss the school cafeteria. Almost.

The burly man with the largest hat approached and handed me a uniform.

"Put on," he said, and motioned over to a counter, where a number of dishes had been laid out.

I struggled to put the uniform on. It was ten sizes too large, but I could still tell that I was meant to look like a waiter. A man stood at the head of the counter. He motioned at me to come over.

Trying not to trip on my pants, I shuffled over to the massive chef.

"Special dietary needs," he said and pointed to the table in front of him.

I looked down. On the table were three bowls of what only could be described as "red" soup. Maybe it was made out of beets . . . or prunes. That's what old people eat, right? Next to the soup were three plates filled with what looked like gray mashed potatoes or grits. Its smell reminded me of the time I found a dead raccoon under the porch. And finally, two plates of finely chopped raw steak, which really just looked like a chunkier version of the soup.

"Hurry," said the massive chef. "Angry when hungry!"

He shoved a tray with the three bowls of soup into my hand.

"Table three!" he added, and pushed me out into the dining area through two swinging doors.

It was the largest room I'd seen in the mansion so far—it could easily fit fifty or more people. Groups of old folks clustered around ten small round tables that each had a number posted on a simple card. Some shuffled between tables. There were a few chandeliers strung up here and there to make the place look classy, but like the rest of the house, it was pretty tattered and torn. You could feel cold air blowing through the room.

I took a look around for table three. I saw the ladies that had been cackling in front of the fire at one of the tables in the front. I looked way in the back and saw table three near an organist, who was still tapping away at that spooky old music. He had a cape on, and was hunched over the keyboard. I wondered if he ever ate, or if they just made him play all day long.

I slowly made my way to table three, passing by tables two and four. I looked at table four and saw all three old folks staring off into space, just waiting for their food. Nobody was doing much talking.

I got to table three, and found three wrinkly and pale old men sitting there, talking to each other in some sort of foreign language. They eyed me as I sat the cold soup down. One of them licked his lips, but he wasn't looking at the soup bowl. He was looking right at me. I stared back, as if hypnotized, and he flashed a toothy grin. His incisors were rather pointy.

"Enjoy," I said meekly, and then turned around to head back to the kitchen. As I left, I heard a massive SLUUUUUUURP and looked back to see all three bowls empty and all three old gentlemen asleep with drops of red falling from the sides of their mouths. One of the old men snored very loudly. *I guess they eat fast here,* I thought.

Back in the kitchen, the chef handed me the platter of mashed potatoes or grits or whatever, and told me to deliver it to table five. I held my breath—the smell made me want to puke. That table was right near the door, so close that I hadn't noticed it before. There, at the table, sat three people with eyes that stared into nothingness and skin that oozed with open sores. *Shouldn't these people be in a hospital?* I wondered. *They need medicine, not this gray whatever-it-is.*

They swayed in their chairs and gurgled and moaned as I approached. Something smelled terrible—like rotten meat. Worse than the food. I looked around to see where it was coming from. When I brought my head back up, I noticed that one of them was eyeing me. Before I could react, it was too late. He swiped at the tray as I brought it down, hungry and clearly ready to eat. The other two came alive—a bit—once they saw their brunch-mate grab for the gray whatever-it-was. I laid the bowls on the table and got out of there quick. One of the Nurses that had been walking around the great room approached them as I left and yelled, "FORKS, PLEASE!" but I could hear from the squishy slurping sounds and grunts of pleasure that they were probably eating with their hands, as fast as they could. I wasn't going to turn around and look.

This was not what I signed up for—Gordon was right. I was serving food to cranky, smelly old mean people. Where were the sweet nanas or funny grandpas? *Is this what I am going to have to deal with on a daily basis?* I thought. These folks were really monstrous—and the staff was, too!

I walked back into the kitchen and was immediately handed the tray of soupy raw steak by the chef.

"TABLE TEN!" he yelled, as he pushed me back out into the dining room.

I headed over to table ten. Two of the hairiest old men I had ever seen in my life were sitting at the table. I laid the steak soup down on the table and turned to leave. Before I could go, one of the hairy old men looked up at me.

His eyes looked so familiar . . . but why?

I watched as both of the old men eyed the meat slop hungrily and dug in for their first slobbery bite. It was actually quite disgusting to watch, but I couldn't stop.

It was only when Shane texted me that I finally tore my eyes away from the feeding frenzy.

Hwst goin'? texted Shane.

I'm already done for today, I texted back.

I took off my uniform and slipped out of the front door. The tall grass was motionless. I moved past it quickly and then headed down the hill. The ravens watched me as I went.

I was so happy to get out of there, I wasn't sure I ever wanted to come back.

Amuse Me

At lunch on Monday, Ben, Gordon, and Shane wanted to know how my time at Raven Hill went. I told them everything as we ate Salisbury Snake.

I broke it down like this: It was insane and smelly, the residents were angry old farts, and I thought the house was haunted, but on the walk home I somehow convinced myself to keep going there.

I still just really, really wanted that telescope, and if I could survive one day there, I'd be able to again and again and again. Not to mention, I felt kind of bad for the old folks, as weird as they were.

"Hey," Ben said, "Karen said she can get us all free passes to the park this weekend. It's the last weekend!"

The park is what we called Jackson Amusement Park, a run-down collection of rides and games on the south side of town. The best thing about it, other than the awesome food, was the Gravitron, the most barf-inducing ride in the universe. Ben's older sister, Karen, had worked there the past few summers. She could sometimes be a pain, but she always got us free passes—so I guess she was all right, as older sisters go.

"Awesome!" yelled Gordon.

"Totally!" added Shane.

All the guys high-fived one another. All of them but me.

Shane looked at me and shook his head. "Really?" he asked.

"I have to volunteer," I said. "If I miss one shift, I might not win the money."

"It's your loss," Ben added. "I went to the park like ten times over the summer."

"And was there any ride that you didn't barf on?" I asked, hoping to change the subject from me bailing on my friends.

"Well . . ." Ben thought for a moment.

"I bet you even hurled on the Ferris wheel," I said.

"Yes," Ben answered. "I was way at the top, too. It was not a pretty sight."

"Even on the bumper cars?" I asked.

"Um . . . yup! Definitely on the bumper cars. I spewed right as I bumped into a little girl, and it splashed right into her car."

"Oh, that's rough!" I said.

"Well, you're the one who brought it up," Ben said.

"Actually, you're the one who brought it up," I said with a wink. "On every ride at the park."

"Ha-ha-ha," Ben fake-laughed.

Shane looked over at me. "C'mon," he said. "Do you really want to miss seeing this kid blowing chunks all day?"

"I really have to make up the hours," I said, "especially after skipping out early last time."

"Were you even there for an hour?" Gordon asked. "They'll probably laugh at you when you take your time sheet to the Rotary to get certified!"

"What?" I asked

"You have to go to the Rotary every Monday at four with your time sheet—or those hours don't count," Gordon answered.

"Aw, man!" I said. "You've got to be kidding! I left my time sheet at Raven Hill. The Director doesn't want me there until six, but I'll have to go early to get my time sheet, then run to the Rotary, then go back home to grab some food, and *then* get back to Raven Hill. UGH!"

"Whoa, dude," said Shane. "Don't sweat it! You've only put, like an hour in anyway."

"Yeah," said Ben. "You've got three hundred hours to go, knowing you!"

"That hour could be the hour that makes the

difference at the end of the fall!" I said, almost screaming. "I need every hour I can get!"

So, at the end of the day, at the exact moment that the final bell rang, I bolted up the main road from school and took a left up to Raven Hill. I bounded up the old creaky stairs, which shook from my pounding feet, and knocked on the door as hard as I could.

Nobody answered.

I knocked again, even harder this time. My knuckles hurt.

I looked at my digital watch. Thirty seconds went by.

Sixty seconds.

Two minutes.

Where were the Nurses? Where was anybody?

I leaped down the stairs and started to explore around the side of the building, hoping to find a window that I could peek into and get someone's attention.

There wasn't much of a path to follow—everything was overgrown around the old house. I slowly made my way through the waist-high grass, avoiding thorny weeds and bushes. It was dark on the side of the building, but there was one spot in particular that was brighter—a window that was hidden behind a bush. And it sounded like something was going on in the room behind it. There was a buzz of conversation and grunting. I could hear chairs squeaking on the hardwood floor.

The closer I got, the louder the commotion got. I could see through the window, but just barely—the glass was dirty. The one thing I could tell was that almost everyone from the retirement home was in there. The Director and a few Nurses were up front, at some sort of table. They were facing the old folks, who were all sitting down, looking forward. It looked like some sort of meeting.

As I reached up to knock on the window, a dark shadow suddenly rose up and engulfed the whole side of the house. The sound of something massive swooping down toward me filled the air. In a flash, I dropped into the weeds, terrified. Something was after me.

Creepy Meeting

I made my way under the bush, the wall of the Raven Hill Retirement Home behind me, with brush, scrub, and grass in front of me. Whatever it was out there was after me, no doubt about it. I could hear what sounded like claws dragging across the branches of the bush above my head. I suddenly remembered the large bugs in the grass the last time I was here, and I wondered if there was another lurking nearby. Then, as quickly as my attacker had appeared, everything went silent. I peeked my head out to see if it had gone.

Across the yard, I saw a giant black raven flapping away.

Of course, the ravens, I thought. *But why would they be after me?*

I crawled out from behind the bush and stood up.

In the distance, the raven circled around and headed straight back toward me. Then a second one joined in.

"CAW! CAW!" they screeched as they headed toward me.

I stepped back against the wall of the house and waved my hands in the air. "Stop it! Shoo!" I yelled out. "Don't you remember me?"

The lead raven looked me in the eye. We held each other's glare for a moment, and then it turned away. His friend followed his lead.

Between the bugs and the ravens, I really needed to get out of this yard.

I turned back to the house and peered through the window. There was still a crowd. In front of them all, the Director held his hands high, trying to calm the old people, who were starting to froth at the mouth and shake. The two hairy old men actually seemed to be howling.

"People, people, PLEASE!" said the Director. "There's nothing to be afraid of—everything is under control. And I'll tell you WHY if you'd just do me the favor of SILENCING yourselves."

The crowd calmed down. It again became hard to hear, as the Director was now speaking very quietly. I decided that I could wait one more minute to make myself known. This could get good.

"The lebensplasm of our new volunteer is especially

strong. It will go a long way in keeping us powered up."

A rumble of satisfaction rippled through the crowd. Through a smudge-free section of the window, I could see the old man with the sharp teeth lick his lips, as he had when he first saw me. A shiver ran down my spine.

My lebensplasm is going to keep them powered up?! I thought, panicked. *What does that mean? What in the world is lebensplasm?* Suddenly I could not care less about my time sheet.

I was looking at the Director through a particularly dirty piece of window. But through the window, I could see him hold up an old glass jar that was filled with some sort of gooey liquid.

He took a butter knife and dipped it into the jar. He pulled out the knife and spread the goo on a piece of bread.

Several old folks grunted with satisfaction. A few even leaned forward. An old woman in the front row appeared to drool a bit as she leaned in to get a closer look.

The director held the gooey bread up to his lips. All the old folks fell silent. The director took a bite. All of the old folks began to cheer, hoot, and holler. The hairy old men began howling again.

A sudden realization hit me. The goo in the jar was MY LEBENSPLASM!!! How did they get it? I didn't feel any different. That didn't matter though—the creepy old people were going to eat it to keep strong—but there were so many of them, and they all looked so HUNGRY.

What's going to happen when they drain me of my lebensplasm?! Will I die? Will they eat ME?

I didn't realize I was pulling the branch of the bush toward the window as I leaned in. I noticed one of the old folks eyeing the window, trying to figure out why a shaky branch was getting closer and closer to the window. Soon other heads turned.

The Director noticed, and turned toward the window. I could see a strange look on his face as he chewed, even through the dirty window. But I knew he couldn't see me. He turned back to the old folks.

I had to get out of there—FAST. If the old folks knew that I knew they were stealing my lebensplasm, I'd be done for. I slowly recoiled, returning the branch to its original location, making sure that it didn't snap back hard. I worked my way toward the front of the retirement home, hoping that the ravens didn't start cawing again. Once I knew nobody would be able to see me through that window, I ran as fast as I could down the road to the main street.

As I ran, I could feel my heart pounding in the veins of my neck. My volunteer time sheet—the thing that drew me to the retirement home early—was the furthest thing from my mind.

I shuddered to think of what would happen if they

used up my lebensplasm. I was pretty sure that I would die. The director had said it would go "a long way in keeping us powered up." Were they staying alive because of me? Was my lebensplasm some sort of Fountain of Youth for old people? Why was the Director eating it? He looked pretty young! How the heck did they get it out of me, anyway? I had only been there for an hour or two!

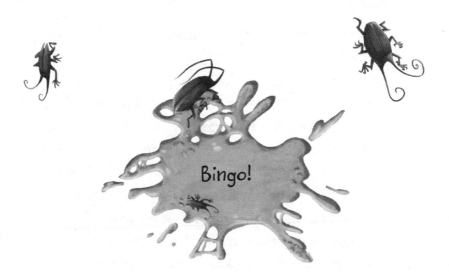

Bingo!

After thinking about it all night, I realized that there was only one way I could save my skin. I had to keep volunteering at Raven Hill and steal my lebensplasm back.

My mother dropped me off right after school. "Have fun, Chrissy," she screeched through the half-open window as she peeled away. Why does she always call me that? I guess I could have told her that Jim Kowalski always called me "Sissy Chrissy" in P.E. class. Maybe then she'd stop doing it.

I stood there in complete silence . . . feeling like a Sissy Chrissy.

Instead of running away, which was my first reaction, I looked down at the little brown bag my mother had given me to cheer me up. She wanted to make sure that I ate a good dinner, and I had already told her that the food at Raven Hill was Grade F. What I didn't tell her was that my lebensplasm was on the menu tonight. *Don't bother to pack a bag, Ma! I'm for dinner!*

I fought against my racing heart and tired mind. They wanted to run. But I knew I had to get into Raven Hill and start investigating. All I had to do was walk up to the front door.

As I moved to take my first step, a single raven darted from the sky and landed directly in front of me. It eyed me suspiciously as I walked toward the steps.

"Caw!" the raven said, and cocked his head to the side. His beady eyes locked directly on me.

There was no doubt in my mind that this was the raven that had dive-bombed me yesterday. And from the look in his eyes, I could tell that *he knew* that I knew something that I shouldn't.

"Fly outta here, dude!" I yelled. No raven was going to stand in my way. I paused for a moment, then opened up the paper bag with my dinner. Tearing off a bit of bread from the sandwich inside, I lifted it up for the raven to see. Its eyes stayed fixed on mine. I threw the piece of bread into the grass to my left.

Immediately, two other ravens appeared and dove into the grass for the chunk of bread. I turned back to the raven on the stairs.

"Caw!" it said and hopped up to the porch. The raven stood directly in front of the door now.

"Okay, I get it," I said. "You don't want me to come in. But I deserve to take back what's mine. Get outta the way!"

"Caw! Caw!" repeated the raven.

Now, I don't know how to speak raven, but the way he cawed that last time really made me feel like he was swearing at me.

I made my way over to a pile of rocks that sat just off the side of the dirt driveway. The raven's eyes followed me. Reaching down, I picked up a few stones about the size of my palm.

I held one up and looked the raven in his beady eyes. "Is this how you wanna do it?" I asked.

The raven looked right back at me and ruffled his feathers a bit. *I dare you,* I could almost hear him say.

I tossed the first rock.

The raven jumped to the right at the last instant, and the rock rapped against the door.

"CAW!" it screeched, but it wouldn't move.

I tossed the second rock.

Again, the raven jumped at the last second possible,

and the rock rapped loudly against the bottom of the door.

Before the raven could even caw again, I threw another rock, then another, then another.

CLUNK, SMACK, CRUNCH! The rocks all hit the large wooden door.

I paused, waiting.

Sure enough, within a few seconds . . .

WHOOOSH!

The door flew open quickly, and the raven was pushed off the front of the porch and rolled down the stairs, a surprised lump of feathers and anger.

I ran as quickly as I could past the ruffled raven, up the stairs and through the door that the Nurse held open.

The Nurse closed the door. "I get Director," he said, and he hurried down the hallway.

Outside the door, I could still hear the ravens squawking—they were really angry.

I turned to look through the grimy strip of glass next to the door, and saw that I had left my dinner outside in the dirt driveway. Four ravens were tearing my lunch bag apart and hungrily gobbling up the contents. Peanut butter and jelly sandwich. Chips. Cookies. One was even working on my juice box.

Oh, well, I said to myself.

Turning around, I saw the Director walking down

the threadbare carpet, past the cobwebby old portraits, and toward me. He once again looked like he was in a great rush to do very important things.

"Mr. Taylor," the Director said with a smile, "what a pleasant surprise. I must say, we were quite disappointed that you hadn't shown up at six p.m. yesterday evening. We were worried you had abandoned the residents."

He stared directly at me, awaiting some sort of reply.

"I . . . uh . . ." I stumbled for something to say. My hands were sweaty. What if he had seen me through the window after all? What if the raven had somehow TOLD HIM?!

"I . . . well . . . ," I continued, "I wasn't feeling very well yesterday, and I—"

"Ah, I see," said the Director. "It happens to all of us from time to time. I'm sure that it won't happen again, will it, Mr. Taylor?"

"No, of course not!" I said, adding, "I'm ready to work really hard here."

"Wonderful," he said. "Well, I think you'll quite enjoy what we have in store for you tonight. It's bingo night at the retirement home, and I think you would do a wonderful job of calling out the numbers."

The director slipped his arm around me like we were old friends and slowly led me deeper into the retirement home. I could hear familiar moaning and grunting sounds.

"There's just one thing, Mr. Taylor," the Director said. "Just one small thing that's nagging me that I really must ask you about."

The Director's grip tightened on my shoulder, and he said, "Nurse Jargon told me you had a bit of a run-in with one of our ravens."

I tensed up. "Yes," I said. "It wouldn't let me in."

"You know," the Director said, "we've taken much pain in training these ravens to guard our facility. They don't often defend us without reason."

As we reached the end of the hallway, the Director stopped walking and looked at me.

"I . . . well . . . I'm not sure what that raven has against me," I said.

"Well, perhaps it's because it knows that you came here yesterday."

"What?" I was flabbergasted. The Director must be able to speak with the ravens after all! "What do you mean?"

"The lead raven," answered the Director, "has his eyes on you."

I stared at the Director with my mouth wide open. I had to say something. Panicked, I reached into the depths of my brain, and came up with . . .

"Well, I didn't know how sick I was yesterday until I got up here," I said. "I'm sorry that I didn't knock on the door and tell one of the Nurses, but I wasn't myself."

The Director looked at me with his intense blue eyes. I felt almost hypnotized by his gaze and his strong cologne. His eyes squinted . . . and then he shook his head quickly. He continued walking us down the hall.

"Very well, then," he said. "I hope you're feeling splendid this evening, but do let me know if you need to leave unexpectedly. I'll need to inform the ravens."

"Of course." I almost choked on the words. I was sure that the Director would now be keeping an eye on me, and that wouldn't help the search for my lebensplasm.

As we neared the end of the hall, the Director pointed me toward the Great Room, where I'd served brunch on Saturday. Now, instead of circular dining-room tables, rows and rows of chairs and tables were set up, and all of the old folks were sitting. I could only see the backs of their heads. Some slouched to the side as if they were asleep—or even worse, dead. Some bobbed around and twitched. There were even ones covered completely in bandages. But all heads were turned toward the front of the room. A large circular steel cage filled with bingo balls sat on a table there. The cage had a handle on it so the balls could be rolled around. The table was in front of the organist, who sat waiting, staring at the Director and me.

"Horace, you may begin," said the Director.

Horace turned around and began to play. Spooky music filled the room. I didn't know what was worse—

that the music for bingo sounded exactly like the music for lunchtime, or that it all just sounded so chilling. I wondered if Horace would take requests.

"Enjoy!" said the Director, and he headed off to other business without another word or glance.

I stood stunned in the doorway of the Great Room.

"Start now?" growled one of the Nurses who was passing out bingo cards and markers to the patients. It was a question, but the way he said it made me realize that the only answer was yes. A few of the old folks moaned and gurgled in anticipation.

"Yes," I squeaked.

Moans of joy filled the hall.

"Come. HURRY," another Nurse said. I looked over to see one of the old men to whom I had fed the red soup gnawing on the Nurse's arm. His hairy, leathery arm didn't seem affected. Apparently, the old folks got really excited for bingo.

The old folks' heads followed me as I wound my way down the side of the room and made my way toward the front. I couldn't stand all of the old, creepy eyes on me, and I felt very, very uncomfortable in my skin. The old man that had been drooling all over the Nurse's arm looked up at me with razor-sharp attention. He might have been a little more excited for my lebensplasm than for the game.

Horace quickened the pace of the music—almost

like an introduction—as I stepped up to the table. I had never been in charge of a game of bingo before, but I got the concept. You roll the balls around, open up the cage, pull a ball out, and call it. Simple, right?

I looked out at the creepy old faces staring intently at me, and I knew that this would not be simple, just like it was not simple to serve food on Saturday. I sighed and looked at the cage. It looked a lot rustier up close, and there were cobwebs all around and in between the metal wiring. *Is everything in this place old?* I thought.

I grabbed the handle and began turning the cage to shuffle the balls. It moved with a terrible SQUUUUEEEEAAAAK. I wondered how long it had been since the last time they had played bingo at Raven Hill. After five seconds or so of terrible squeaking, I stopped the cage, popped open the door, and pulled out the first bingo ball. The crowd of old folks looked at me as if I was just about to reveal the meaning of life. I cleared my throat and said, "B twelve!"

A few folks in the back growled, "WHAT!?"

"BEEEE-TWELLLLVE!" I yelled back.

One person way in the back still asked, "Huh?!"

"BEEEEEEE-TWWWELLLLLVVVVE!!!" I yelled louder than I had ever yelled in my life. A gnarled hand rose up from the back of the room and gave me a twisted thumbs-up. This was going to be a long bingo game if I had to repeat every single number three times. I would have to be as loud as possible.

I gave the metal cage another spin. Spiderwebs kept falling out onto the table.

SQUUUUUEEEEAAAAK . . .

"GEEEEEEEE-FIIIIFFFFFTYYY-SIIIIIXXXXX!"

SQUUUUUEEEEAAAAK . . .

"ENNNNNNNNN-FFOOOOORRRRTTTYYY!"

SQUUUUUEEEEAAAAK . . .

"E Y Y Y Y Y Y Y Y Y Y Y Y Y Y Y Y Y Y Y Y Y E E E E E E - FFOOOUUURRRRTTEEEEEENNN!"

SQUUUUUEEEEAAAAK . . .

I pulled out a ball with no number or letter. Confused, I brought the ball closer to my eyes to see if maybe the letter and number had been rubbed off. That's when I noticed something move inside the ball!

Something black and hairy.

Something with eight spindly legs.

I let out a surprised cry and dropped the ball on the table. A few of the old folks in the front row tried to peer up onto the table to see what it was that I dropped. A few others booed me.

Before I could explain why I threw the ball onto the table, long, hairy legs exploded out of the ball and a slime-covered spider tore its way out. It scuttled to the edge of the table and jumped off into the front row, right toward the head of an old lady with a black shawl draped around her shoulders. She was chatting with the very large man with stitches on his face, and didn't even see the spider as it flew toward her.

"LOOK OUT!" I yelled.

She turned in time for the hairy creepy to land directly on her nose. She looked at it cross-eyed, but didn't seem too worried. She licked her lips in excitement as she snatched the squirming spider off her nose and began to rip its legs off, each one tearing from the body with a *sploock* sound. She put the legs in a small pile and excitedly plopped the spider body in her mouth. She chewed and chewed and chewed, and as she did, she put the legs in a small pouch that hung like a necklace from her neck.

"Thank you, dearie," she said to me with a grin.

Her teeth were covered in spider hair.

I barely had time to say "You're . . . welcome?" before the cage in front of me started shaking violently. I looked in to see that there were more spider eggs. A lot more!

I yelled and stumbled back. A Nurse came over and shoved his big hairy hand into the cage, popping the eggs he found there. Each one sounded like a really ripe cherry tomato being squished. The woman in the front row was nearing tears.

"Don't do that!!!" she wailed.

But the Nurse squished one after another as I stood

there with my mouth wide open in disbelief. He pulled the disgusting shattered eggs out of the cage and tossed them in a trash can next to Horace. The Nurse's hands were caked in hairy brown/green goo, and he looked around for something to he could use to wipe them. Not finding anything, he scraped the goo off on the side of the bingo-ball cage.

My stomach turned as I watched a glob of phlegmy goo drip off of the cage and onto the table. I took a deep breath, only to smell a putrid odor coming from the trash can behind me. I could feel something gurgling inside of me.

As I tried to hold the erupting vomit volcano back, the old folks started to grumble and moan. They were not happy that their game had been ruined. I needed to get the game going again.

I turned the handle, waiting for the familiar squeak, but it never came. I saw that some of the spider egg goop had fallen onto the joint where the ball and the mount met, lubricating the cage. As I turned the cage, the goop became warmer—and smellier. I could taste the puke rising in my throat.

The Nurse must have noticed I was about to spew. He slapped me hard on the back and I swallowed it back down.

The rest of the game went smoothly. I had called out a dozen or so more numbers when the hairier of the two hairy old men yelled, "BINGO!" and then howled excitedly. The howl took me by surprise. He looked so old that I didn't think he would be able to make such a loud noise. It filled the Great Room and shook the windows. Even Horace stopped playing the organ to turn around and see what was going on.

A Nurse headed into the back of the room to grab the old man's bingo card and confirm that he'd actually won. When the Nurse got back there, he scratched his head and looked around. That's when a few of the other old folks pointed up to the front of the room. A mangy dog held a bingo card in his mouth and limped his way toward me.

The dog jumped up on the table and placed the card in front of me, then turned around and trotted shakily to the back of the room. I noticed that he had fur missing in great patches. He was a very, very old dog—the same one I had seen the first day. Where did he come from? Was he the old man's dog?

I looked down at the card, and confirmed that, in fact, the old man had won. I announced this to the crowd, which moaned a collective, "Noooooo . . ." as they realized that they wouldn't win that round. I looked into the back of the room and saw the old man sitting back in his chair again. He waved excitedly as the rest of the crowd hissed at him.

I looked around for the dog, and I couldn't see it anywhere.

Losing Sleep . . . and My Mind

It was only Wednesday of the second week of the new school year, but it felt like I'd been in the sixth grade for two or three decades. Last night's bingo marathon seemed to last forever. The old folks just couldn't get enough. We must have played twenty or thirty games— and once it was over, the Nurses escorted me out the door. I never even got to do any investigating for my lebensplasm.

What worried me were the old folks. The more time I spent with them, the more frightened I became. It wasn't just that they were *like* monsters. I was beginning to believe that they actually *were* monsters. There was no other way to explain what I'd seen! The hairy old man who had won the first game howled and disappeared only to have an old dog appear in his place—

an old dog with very human eyes. *Werewolf?* my tired mind asked. The old woman in the black shawl who had eaten the spider was the same woman I had seen in front of the cauldron on the first day. Was she going to use the spider legs in her leather pouch for a witch's potion of some sort? And what were they planning for my lebensplasm?

Still exhausted from the night before, I shuffled into my first class of the day: Mr. Bradley's Social Studies. You could smell his breath before you even walked into the room. I don't know what was more upsetting, the stench or his huge, swollen, red, bald, spotted head. It looked like some kind overripe fruit that could explode at any minute.

I sat down next to Ben and didn't even say hi. My mind was swimming from the day before. In my mind, I could see the eyes of the dog—they looked so human. The way the old witch—I mean lady—had eaten that spider was supercreepy. I wondered if the monsters—I mean old people—ate my lebensplasm the same way.

Mr. Bradley pulled a small vial out of his jacket pocket and took a sip from it. He did this all the time, thinking that it would calm the breath down. Sometimes it worked, but then the room would be filled with a sickening medicine stench. I'm not sure which smell was worse.

"Hey, Chris," Ben said, wrinkling his nose. "You

look as bad as he smells. Are you okay?"

"They're eating my lebensplasm," I mumbled. The words just rolled out before I even realized what I was saying. The mixture of the exhaustion and stench was making me delirious.

"Did you say 'eating egg salad'?" asked Ben. "What's the matter?"

How could I tell my friend that monsters were eating a gooey extract of me to stay alive? I hardly believed it myself. At this point, I couldn't remember if I actually saw an old dog last night, or if my mind was just playing tricks on me.

"Oh, nothing," I said, recovering quickly and pretending to look awake. "If anything, you're the one who looks sick."

"Ha-ha-ha," Ben fake-laughed. "Yeah, that's sort of my thing, I guess. Which is why I'm sure there's something wrong with you."

Before I could defend myself, Mr. Bradley lumbered out of his chair behind his desk and said, "All right, everyone. It's quiz time!"

"Awww, not a pop quiz!" I yelled it before I could even stop myself.

The entire class stared at me. There were a few moments of unbelievably uncomfortable silence, and then Mr. Bradley spoke again.

"Chris, why are you joking about a pop quiz? This

quiz was assigned, covering chapters two and three. You do remember, don't you?"

I laughed nervously, suddenly realizing that I hadn't even read chapters two and three. "Well, it's still a surprise," I said. "Shocking! Ha!"

Ben gave me a look that said *Shut up*, so I shut up.

Still, I wasn't too worried. I read so much about history and culture online that I was sure to get a C.

At least I would have. If I hadn't fallen asleep halfway through the quiz.

Apparently, I snore. LOUDLY. At least that's what Mr. Bradley and the principal told me.

Ben texted me later that day:

I'm sorry I couldn't wake you up.

Dude, my mom was furious!

I know. I could have shook you more.

You should have shook me HARDER!

Are you calling me a wimp?

Maybe.

Dude, you're the one passing out from volunteering.

It's IMPORTANT lifesaving work!

They're old! How much life can you be saving?

You don't understand.

You're weird.

I know. Pls, just let me be weird.

I stared at my sent message in horror. I had just dropped all of the vowels in "please." Things were getting bad. I fell back into bed.

Put on Your Dancin' Shoes!

As a star student, I had a lot of wiggle room with my parents when I screwed up. My mother wanted to ground me for my Social Studies Siesta, but I'd insisted that I go back to Raven Hill. "But the old people *need* me," I'd explained in my most annoying, whiny voice. *If only she knew how much they need me,* I thought. After twenty minutes of begging and pleading, she let me go.

I made my way toward the retirement home. This time no ravens stood between the entrance and me. Pushing my way through the front door, I didn't even pause when the Nurse said, "Wait here."

Nothing was going to stand between me and my lebensplasm.

Beyond the entrance, the hallways were free of any Nurses or residents. I quickly got to the kitchen door and reached out to the doorknob to give it a twist . . .

"Mr. Taylor, may I help you with something?"

The voice made tiny hairs on the back of my neck stand up straight. After changing my grimace into a grin, I turned around to face the Director.

"Oh," I said, sounding completely calm, "I just needed a drink. I'm really thirsty."

The Director looked at me intently for a moment, and then said, just as calmly, "I'm very sorry, but our kitchen is closed for the night. I'd offer you some punch, but I'm afraid it's not the kind of drink meant for . . . a young person such as yourself."

"Punch?" I asked.

"Yes, punch. Tonight, we're throwing a dance for the residents, and the kitchen concocted a punch for the occasion. The Great Room has been transformed into a ballroom. All we need now is the appropriate music."

He motioned me toward the Great Room, and we stepped through the door together.

A huge, empty dance floor took up most of the space. The residents were all slouched in chairs to the side of the dance floor or growling and burping around the bloodred punch bowl. The old man with the sharp teeth avoided the crowd around the bowl by using a long straw to reach it. He slurped loudly from ten feet away.

"Tonight," said the Director, "you'll be playing

music while our residents couple up and dance. You'll find we've set up a DJ station for you where Horace usually sits."

The Director took a bow and exited.

Two old turntables and a crate of dusty old records sat on a table at the front of the ballroom. After I made sure there were no spider eggs in the crate, I shuffled through the monsterly collection, which included The Dave Boo-beck Quartet, Screamin' Jay Hawkins, The Crypt-Kickers, and a bat-shaped record that didn't have a sleeve.

I pulled out the bat-shaped record, but soon realized it wasn't a record. It was a real bat. Its leathery skin was still moist and squishy, and small wads of greasy fur fell off its rotten body. Its little bat face looked terribly squished, but I could still see its sharp fangs.

The bat reeked terribly, and I tossed it behind the organ.

"Sorry, Horace," I mumbled.

I sniffed my hand. It smelled like I had just petted a wet dog that had rolled around in week-old fish and horse dung.

"Ewww." I burped, and my stomach bunched into knots.

I'm turning into Ben, I thought, and held back another spewfest.

The old folks were starting to moan and groan, and

shuffle into the center of the dance floor. They were all well-dressed—but in really old clothes. One old man coughed and moths flew out of his holey suit . . . and his mouth!

To keep them from shuffling right up to me and making any requests (like "May I eat you?"), I grabbed a record out of the crate as quickly as I could, took it out of its sleeve, blew a few tons of dust off one side, sneezed, and then flopped it down on one of the turntables. I searched desperately for a Repeat button so I would have time to find my lebensplasm, but my only choices were Stop and Start.

I chose Start. The record crackled for a little bit, and then a spooky slow swing song started to play. After a short intro, a singer started. He sounded like he was growling.

Oh, I'm so hungry
Yes, so, so hungry for you
Dance on over to my castle
And give me something to chew

A few of the old folks went "Awww" as they recognized the tune, and shuffled into pairs. They danced a slow, slow dance. Their bones creaked.

The name of the album was *Moonlight Serenades* by Count Vlad and the Count Basie Orchestra.

The song was called "Neck Nibble Nocturne."
My skin crawled as the singer continued.

Look up at the moon
My dear
The stars are so bright
My dear
I bend down to you
My dear
And I bite you so right
Don't fear

The singer stopped and a scary-sounding trumpet started to play. My heart rose into my throat. Monsters slow danced with monsters. Banshees. Vampires. Werewolves. Witches. Swamp things. Mummies. Old monsters of all different shapes and sizes.

Two zombies were delicately nibbling each other's necks. The Nurses in the room moved in to break them up.

With the Nurses distracted, I crept out of the Great Room. I went back to the kitchen door, opened it up, and quickly slipped inside.

A Nurse stood at an open refrigerator with a big, satisfied grin. He was chewing on a large, slimy tentacle when he saw me out of the corner of his eye.

"What are you doing?" he growled.

"What are *you* doing?" I replied. "The Director said the kitchen was closed!"

Before I could even peek into the fridge, he rushed over, whipped open the door, grabbed me with both hands, shoved me back out into the hallway, and grunted, "Don't tell the Director!"

With that, he slammed the door shut, and a lock clicked into place.

There was a good chance that my lebensplasm was in the kitchen, but there was no way I could get in there now. I ran halfway down the hall to search other rooms, but stopped when I heard a booing from the Great Room.

The record was skipping!

I had to keep the music going. But I'd be so busy changing records all night, I'd never get a chance to search all of Raven Hill. I wished I could just throw on a playlist.

I rushed past the booing monsters, ripped a handful of records out of the crate, and began pulling them out one by one to find a really long track. Finally, I found a record that had one long track on side A: "Tarantella Transylvanese." I threw it down on the second turntable and pressed Start.

It started up fast, and at first the monsters were unsure of what to do. *Oh no!* I thought, *I chose the wrong song!* The monsters that were slow-dancing slowly shuffled off the dance floor, but luckily a few more came on. The song bounced along with accordions and tambourines, hoots and shouts—it sounded like it was recorded at a Gypsy camp somewhere in Europe, and the Gypsies were partying hard.

Soon most of the monsters were on the dance floor. I jumped off of the platform, and made my way back toward the door.

That's when the old witch that had collected the spider legs the day before grabbed me. Her long fingernails dug into my skin. The rest of the monsters began hooting and hollering as she dragged me to the center of the dance floor.

All the monsters formed a circle with the witch and me in the center. Their bodies flailed about wildly. They licked their lips. Drool dripped onto the dance floor.

I was trapped!

Above the music, I could hear the witch scream, "You're so precious, I could just EAT you!"

She started dancing wildly in front of me and motioned for me to follow along. I was terrified, but what could I do? I started dancing along. I looked around at the other monsters, and they looked energized. Had my lebensplasm allowed them to dance like this?

Monster legs kicked high in the air. An old werewolf howled along to the rhythm of the tambourines. An old banshee screamed with the accordions. The vampires flung their heads back—enjoying every second of the song that had come from their homeland.

The circle was slowly closing in!

Next to the witch, a zombie tried its best to dance. It slapped its knee a few times, and then its leg fell off. It kept hopping on one leg as another zombie bent over and started eating the leg, chomping in time with the music. A few of the other old monsters looked hungrily at the leg, slowed down their dancing, and headed toward the meaty treat. The three Nurses once again moved in to take care of the situation.

Now was my chance.

Great Balls of Fire

I danced my way out of the circle and toward the open door. Nobody noticed—they were either fighting over the leg or dancing like crazy.

I ran down the hallway and ducked into each room as I went. I opened drawers. I looked under furniture. I peeked in fireplaces. The rooms on the bottom floor didn't have much furniture, and there wasn't really anywhere they could have hidden my lebensplasm.

I went upstairs and into the first dark, mold-smelling room. There was a Crock-Pot with some sort of black ooze bubbling in it. All sorts of ingredients were lined up in front of it. EYE OF NEWT read one bottle; WING OF BAT read another. I recognized the contents of the third bottle—the hairy baby spider legs from bingo night. I went through all of the bottles. Not one of them was my lebensplasm.

Heading back into the hall, I heard a rattle of chains and a moan more deep and growly than anything I had heard at Raven Hill.

I froze in place, and slowly turned my head toward the noise, worried about what I would see. All I saw was a door at the end of the dimly lit hallway. It had a simple and clear sign on it.

DO NOT ENTER
Staff Only

I really hoped that my lebensplasm wasn't on the other side, but I knew that I had to check it out. As I made my way down the hall, I could hear the low growl and rattling of chains coming from behind the door. My heart beat faster as I tried to guess what kind of monster could make those sorts of noises.

"Why are you here?" someone behind me asked as a large, meaty hand came down on my shoulder. It took all my concentration to keep from piddling in my pants.

The hand swung me around to face two Nurses standing in the hallway.

"Uh . . . bathroom?" I said, only half lying.

The other Nurse pointed back down the hall toward the stairs with one hand. In the other hand, he held . . .

My lebensplasm!

"Uh, okay," I said as I walked backward.

I stared at the jar in his hand. Even in the darkness of the hallway I could see that it was ONLY HALF FULL! He didn't seem to care that I was looking at the jar—he just kept waving me away.

I turned the corner, but instead of going down the stairs, I hid in the witches' room. I got down low and poked my head out to look back down the hall. The first Nurse approached the Staff Only door. Instead of opening it, he stood to one side and grabbed a candlestick on the wall. With what looked like a great amount of force, even for the monstrous Nurse, he gave it a yank. As the candlestick pulled away, something mechanical started clicking in the wall. The second Nurse handed the first Nurse my lebensplasm, and then walked over to a statue of a screaming demon on the other side of the door. With a grunt, he dug his shoes into the ground and slowly turned the statue to the right. The heavy stone base scraped against the floor. There was a heavy clank and the Do Not Enter door swung open. Both Nurses casually entered, unaffected by the menacing growls coming from the other side. Once they'd lumbered through, the door slammed shut.

I could still hear the "Tarantella Transylvanese" playing downstairs, along with the hoots and hollers of the old monsters. I didn't think I had much longer.

But I risked waiting a little while. After about two minutes, the Nurses came out of the door . . . without my lebensplasm!

Once they vanished down the hall, I crept over to the door and gave it a cautious tug, hoping it would just swing open. But it remained firmly in place.

I reached up to the candlestick, but it was a good foot above my outstretched hand. I took a few steps back, ran forward, jumped up, and grabbed hold of the arm that connected it to the wall. It dropped slightly, but then stayed put. Hanging on with both hands like a crazed spider monkey, I tried bouncing up and down, hoping to shake it into place. No luck. Kicking my feet against the wall, I pulled on the candlestick as hard as I could. The worn soles of my old sneakers slid against the spiderweb-covered wooden wall—I might as well have tried ice-skating up an igloo.

My hands were starting to slip from the sweat. I paused for a moment, held my breath, then kicked my legs against the wall until I got some good traction. Straightening my legs, I felt the candlestick starting to move out and down. Then, with a mechanical click, it released, and my feet slid up the wall. My hands slipped back on the candlestick as I tried to hold on, but it was no use—I was headed for the floor.

Despite the pain of crashing my head into the hard floor, I stumbled over to the statue. Like the candlestick, it wasn't going to move without a fight. I grunted and pushed and grunted some more, but it wouldn't budge. Just when I had given up, I heard more clicking and clanking, like some kind of gear moving in the walls. Maybe I had done it. I ran back in front of the door to see if it would open, but as I stood there, the candlestick snapped back into place.

Looks like I'm going to have to start over.

But the clicking didn't stop—it moved from the walls to the ceiling. When I looked up toward the sound, the ceiling slid open and a giant metal claw shot down right at me. I ducked, but it was too late. I could feel its razor-sharp talons pinch into my back.

"Somebody HELP!" I screamed as the claw began to lift me off the floor. Struggling, I screamed again. I didn't care who heard me—I would rather get caught at this point than find out where this claw was taking me. As I wriggled, I heard a tear and I dropped down a bit. It was my shirt! The talons had hooked my shirt, not me!

As I rose up closer to the ceiling, I heard another click coming from the statue. Looking over, I saw its screaming face turn toward me. *How could this get any worse?* I asked myself, right as a small flame appeared in the statue's mouth.

The flame grew into a mighty fireball. I struggled harder, my shirt tore a little more, but all I could do was flail helplessly in the air. The fiery glow filled the statue's eyes, and, through the shimmering light, it appeared to almost smile as it blasted the giant orange fireball right at me.

I curled up into a ball. I closed my eyes and held my breath, trying to block out the blistering heat that filled the room. For a brief moment, I felt my body consumed by flames . . . then I felt myself falling. Opening my eyes, I could see the floor coming up quickly. For the second time in one day.

Crashing onto the cold floor, I couldn't move for what seemed like an eternity. Finally building up the nerve, I sat up and reached for my back. The whole back of my shirt been burned off—but the fireball just missed me.

I was done fooling around with Raven Hill. The next time I came, I was going to bring backup.

School Makes Me Want to Barf

I knew that I could open the booby-trapped Staff Only door with the help of my friends, but that would mean telling them everything about Raven Hill. And I knew they'd think I'd lost my mind.

When I woke that next day, I felt like a total wreck. My bones creaked, my muscles were sore, and my back felt sunburned. On top of it all, I'd barely slept—and the sleep I did get was filled with nightmares of monsters sticking their long, bloody, nasty tongues into the jar of my lebensplasm, licking it clean. But I *had* to get out of bed and rally my friends.

When I got to school, it took what seemed like an eternity for the lunch bell to ring. I shuffled down the hallways on autopilot: Take books out of locker, go to class, put books back into locker. DO NOT ENTER.

83

DO NOT ENTER. DO NOT ENTER. I cared about nothing else.

By lunchtime, delirium had set in. Maybe I had just dreamed of the fireball-spewing demon statue.

Nope, my crispy back told me. *That happened.*

I sat staring at my tray and chomped and chomped and chomped, trying hard not to chicken out of telling Shane, Gordon, and Ben about Raven Hill. DO NOT ENTER. DO NOT ENTER. DO NOT ENTER. I swallowed hard and gagged, once again holding back a Technicolor yawn.

Shane stopped talking about his latest paper route adventure, and asked the question on everyone's mind: "Chris, what is wrong with you?"

Shane and Gordon stared at me from across the table. They were waiting for an answer. I looked over at Ben. He just nodded, and I knew that I could trust my friends with my secret.

I cleared my throat. Even though I'd gone over my speech a thousand times the night before, it still felt like the words were stuck in my mouth.

What if they think I'm crazy? I thought.

I took a deep breath and said, "All of the old folks at Raven Hill Retirement Home are actually mmm . . ."

I tripped on the word.

". . . monnnnn . . ."

"Monks?" asked Ben.

"*Monsters,*" I finally said.

Gordon chuckled. Ben cocked his head strangely. Shane raised one eyebrow really high.

"So stop working there," said Gordon. "I told you not to work so hard—that volunteer stuff is wack."

"No, wait!" I said. "I don't mean that they're *like* monsters. I mean they ARE monsters."

My friends stared at me with wide eyes.

Shane, whose eyebrow had nearly flown off of his head at this point, opened his mouth and—

"AHHHHHHHHHHHHHHH!"

A scream came from the lunch line.

And this time, I wasn't the only one who heard it.

Students ran from the food counters. All the kids sitting at tables got up to get a better look.

"That thing was HUGE," someone yelled as he ran past our table.

My heart began to race. I felt as if telling my friends about Raven Hill had somehow caused the scream.

The Director is trying to get me to shut up, I thought, while looking around for a raven.

"Go on," said Shane.

Trying hard to ignore the commotion and the lump in my throat, I said, "Raven Hill Retirement Home is filled with old monsters. I've seen a few vampires. I've seen one, maybe two werewolves. I've seen, like, four witches. I actually don't know how many of them are zombies. But, they're all in the retirement home together—and I'm not sure why. But what I do know—they're staying alive by eating a jar of my lebensplasm."

"Your what?" asked Ben

"My lebensplasm!" I screamed, angry that nobody knew what I was talking about. *How do I explain it?* "I don't know what it is. My energy? My soul? All I know is they've got it in a jar, and they're eating it, and the jar is half full, and I have no idea what's going to happen when it's empty. I'm terrified that I'm going to die."

Gordon started laughing. He sounded like a hyena. Not that I was surprised. And even though he didn't say anything, I could tell what Gordon was thinking: *Oh, my friend has finally lost his mind this time. Somebody call the loony bin.*

Kids continued to stream past us and out of the lunchroom. Only a few curious kids stayed behind, and all eyes were on the lunch lady. Behind the hot food counter, she was battling something on the floor with the broom. She swung wildly and screamed in Spanish, "*¡No va a escapar!*"

"Wow," said Shane. "Lunch Lady's getting down to business!"

Ben stopped a kid that was running out of the lunchroom.

"What is it?" Ben asked.

"A HUGE cockroach, dude!" exclaimed the kid, and

he made a disgusted face before running off, leaving the four of us as the only kids left in the lunchroom.

"Ooh, a monster cockroach," Gordon said. "Maybe he's come to Rio Vista to eat your *blebenfleben*."

"See!" I said pointing toward the hairnetted head of the lunch lady zooming around behind the counters. "I saw a huge bug like that at Raven Hill that first day. I think it's here for me."

"I was just joking," said Gordon, who started laughing hysterically again.

"This is serious," I said, slamming my fist down on my tray, which made Gordon laugh even harder. "I need your help. I know where they're keeping my lebensplasm—behind a booby-trapped door. If you guys help, we should be able to get it."

Ben looked at me. I could tell he didn't believe me. But he looked like he wanted to so badly.

Shane also looked like he thought I was crazy—but he was just too good a friend to say anything. He clapped Gordon on the back, which stopped his hyena laugh.

"We'll help you get your lebensplasm back. Just tell us what we need to do," Shane announced.

"Yeah," said Ben. "I'm in."

"Fine," said Gordon. "Let's have a crazy adventure! Why not?!"

I gave the guys the scoop on everything. The ravens. The Nurses. The Director. The Great Room. I went over every detail of the Creepy Meeting. I described the layout of the retirement home. I described the monsters I had seen. Most importantly, I told them about DO NOT ENTER and the booby trap that almost fried me like chicken.

If they hadn't thought I was crazy before, they sure did now. I couldn't believe I was talking about things like lebensplasm and monster dance parties in the middle of the school lunchroom! It helped that there was nobody else there but the lunch lady, and she was a little too busy to notice anything at the moment.

Behind the counter, she had finally cornered her prey.

Smack, smack, CRACK.

I swore I heard a grunt come from the floor, and then the lunch lady dropped the broom and grabbed a bucket. She slammed it on the ground, upside down, over her prize. She bent over, and pushed the bucket back into the kitchen with a SCCCCCRRRAAAAPPPE.

She returned to the counter and yelled, "What you waiteeng for? Geet eet while eet's hot."

Students started streaming back into the abandoned lunchroom. If the Director had sent a huge cockroach to shut me up, his plan had failed. I breathed a sigh of relief.

"So," I said. "Let's head up there tonight, and—"

"Whoa, wait a minute," said Gordon. "I've got practice tonight."

"Yeah," said Shane with a shrug. "I've got karate."

"Come on guys," I pleaded. "I'm being serious here! Did you already forget about the Fireball of Death?!"

"It can't wait one more day?" asked Ben. "I have oboe practice tonight. Sorry."

"Fine!" I said, exasperated. "How about tomorrow night? The Director said I could come back Thursday *or* Friday, and I could use a day off anyway."

Shane let out a long hissing sound and scrunched up his face.

"WHAT!" I was yelling now. "What is it now?!"

"Dude!" said Gordon. "You might have forgotten— because you bailed on us—but we've got those killer passes to the park this weekend, and this weekend starts tomorrow night."

"All right," I said, "look. Just come with me to Raven Hill after school tomorrow, and as soon as we're done there we can spend the whole night and the entire weekend enjoying Ben barfing on every ride, over and over and over again."

"Perfect!" said Ben.

"Fine by me," said Shane.

"Whatever," said Gordon.

After lunch, Shane, Gordon, Ben, and I all had Mr. Stewart's chemistry class.

Although I was relieved that my friends hadn't abandoned me at the lunch table, my energy was completely drained after having told them my insane tale.

I stared down at the stained stone-top lab station, nearly falling asleep on my feet. I leaned on Shane—my partner for the day's experiment—for support.

The bell rang for the start of class, and Mr. Stewart was still nowhere to be seen. Shane turned to me to say something when the door on the side of the classroom exploded with a puff of smoke. Everyone gasped, and I must have jumped two feet, imagining a huge cockroach creeping toward me through the haze.

Instead, Mr. Stewart stumbled through with a cough, running into a skeleton set up next to the door. The smoke was superfunky—a mix of burned bacon, burned hair, and burned fart. Some kids started coughing. Others laughed as Mr. Stewart did a bit of a dance with the skeleton to keep it from falling over.

"Whew," Mr. Stewart said. "Guess I should have tested the ventilator system in the lab before I tried that experiment."

Mr. Stewart tried to straighten out his disheveled, slightly scorched mop of hair, but it just wouldn't behave.

My heart continued to bounce around in my chest as Mr. Stewart started his lesson.

"Today," said Mr. Stewart, as he walked behind his lab station, "we are going to learn about the relationship between acids and bases, starting with one of my favorites—butyric acid—which is found in the stomach." He erased a small patch of blackboard that still contained notes from years past, and wrote B-U-T-Y-R-I-C A-C-I-D in huge, crazy block letters.

I heard a small, wet burp escape from the lab station behind me. I couldn't see his face, but I could tell that Ben probably wasn't too excited to learn about stomach acid.

"To start"—Mr. Stewart spoke louder now, comically pointing a crooked finger in the air—"I will ask Chris to come up and assist me."

Mr. Stewart locked eyes with me, and raised his bushy eyebrows. I felt my cheeks turn red. Apparently the teachers had been talking in the break room.

Mr. Stewart was testing me.

"Mr. Stewart," I squeaked, "I'm not really feeling up to it today."

"Yeah, his *fleegerlosen* is a bit low," I heard Gordon mutter from the back of the classroom.

"Come on up!" Mr. Stewart yelled like a game-show host.

I hated going up in front of class even on my best day. And today was not my best day. I was still shaken. My hands were sweaty, and my mouth was dry. I looked at Shane for support. He gave me a feeble thumbs-up and a smile.

The room spun as I headed up to Mr. Stewart's lab. He awaited me with a crooked grin. I turned around behind the lab and could see everyone staring at me.

"Now, Chris," Mr. Stewart began, "can you please open that large flask in front of you and tell me what it smells like?" I pulled the flask toward me and yanked at the stopper. My hands were still sore from pulling on the candlestick. I struggled with the stopper until I let out a little grunt. The class giggled.

Mr. Stewart motioned to me to pass him the flask. "Let me try. It's been in the lab all summer, and the stopper may have melted slightly on to the flask."

I held up my hand and said, "No, I've got it!"

I didn't want to give Mr. Stewart anything but an amazing performance. I didn't want to give him any reason to talk to the other teachers or call me up here again. I twisted and pulled with all my might, and finally the stopper came out, but the flask slipped out of my sweaty hand.

"Oh no!" Mr. Stewart yelled.

Mr. Stewart lunged to grab the flask, but he

couldn't reach it. The entire class watched in horror as it slowly slid to the edge of the lab station, slipped off, and crashed onto the floor. A huge puddle of acid and glass slowly oozed past the first row of lab stations. Students lifted up their feet and stared down with wide eyes. When it didn't explode or start melting student's faces, we all breathed a sigh of relief, only to smell . . .

"Barf!" said a few students at once, and then, "EWWWWWW!"

The room smelled disgusting. It was the most powerful smell any of us had ever experienced. Overwhelming. Eye-watering. BARFY. Kids in the back started scooting out of their seats while holding their noses.

"WAIT!" Mr. Stewart cried. "It's fine. Remain calm. It's a very weak solution. Try not to think of vomit. Relax and think about Parmesan cheese. That stuff is filled with butyric acid."

Ben, upon hearing that any food was filled with vomit acid, barfed over his lab and onto the stool I had just exited. Shane jumped to avoid the splash.

All the kids ran, leaving a trail of butyric acid and barf down the hallway.

I stood there dumbfounded, until Mr. Stewart tapped me on the shoulder. I turned around slowly, ready for a huge scolding. Instead, I was surprised to see he already had an old army surplus gas mask on. He handed me one as well. "Let's clean this up," he said.

I put on the mask . . .

. . . and promptly puked all over the inside.

I had made it through rotting old monsters and deadly booby traps. It was *school* that finally made me barf.

A Crazy Adventure

We spent all night and the next day trying to figure out how to enter DO NOT ENTER.

Creating a diversion with fireworks in the front yard. Or holding a Jazzercise class. Or having a cooking class with garlic as the main ingredient. Finally, Shane came up with the best, but by far, craziest idea.

Friday afternoon we jumped on our bikes and powered up the road to Raven Hill. As we approached the retirement home, the flapping of our karate uniforms in the wind was the only sound that could be heard. When we arrived, not even the ravens seemed to be around.

The plan was simple. We would pose as elite karate masters and offer to teach all of the residents basic self-defense. The monsters would get worked up, and when the Nurses were distracted, everyone but Shane would slip out and make our way to the Staff Only section of the retirement home.

Elite karate masters we were not. We were three inexperienced dudes with karate uniforms following an elite karate master. And that master was crazy.

We parked our bikes.

"Let's hurry this up so we can get to the park," said Gordon.

"How can you think about that right now?" asked Ben, looking up at the retirement home with wide eyes. It looked like he was starting to believe me.

We walked up to the main entrance. The stairs had creaked terribly when I had gone up alone, but with four of us, the stairs groaned and shimmied. Dust started falling from where the handrails met the porch.

When we heard the creaking turn to cracking, we all rushed up to the porch just before the stairs crumbled into a heap.

"That's a good sign," joked Shane.

I brushed some dust off of his uniform and said, "If that's the worst thing that happens to us today—"

Before I could say any more, the door opened wide, revealing a rather upset-looking Nurse. Well, more upset than normal, anyway. He eyed the pile of wood beneath the porch that used to be the stairs, and grunted.

"I must fix. Ugh!" he cried.

"WOW," said Gordon. "That guy is HUGE. He should be a linebacker."

The Nurse didn't seem to get the compliment.

"INSIDE," he barked.

We didn't wait for him to ask twice.

After closing the door, he lumbered off to get the Director (and probably a hammer and a thousand nails).

"Let me do the talking," I said, looking at Shane. "Once we get into the Great Room, you're in charge. But not until then."

"Got it," said Shane.

Ben and Gordon were inspecting a vase of dead flowers.

"This reminds me of the haunted house they have on the other side of town during Halloween," said Gordon. "Cooooool."

"I dunno, Gordon; this seems pretty real," said Ben.

Ben shuddered as he looked up at the painting of a withered old woman above the vase.

"I think she's looking at me," said Shane.

"Me too," said Ben and Gordon at the same time.

"You'll get used to that," I said.

"Oh, I don't think so, Mr. Taylor," said the Director, as he entered the front of the house. "I've been working here for many decades, and I can assure you that this portrait and I do not get along. I do not like people who stare."

The Director looked up at the painting and we followed his gaze to see that the woman had turned her face away in disgust.

"Wait!" yelled Ben. "Wasn't she looking right at us? Man, this is really creeping me out."

"What is it, Director dude?" asked Gordon. "A huge video screen made to look like a painting? A projector?"

The Director looked at Shane, Ben, and Gordon with an upturned nose.

"Who exactly are you?" he asked.

"These are my friends," I said to the Director. "Shane is a black belt in karate, and I thought it would be good for the old folks to learn some basic moves. You know— to keep them . . . fit."

"I'm not sure that is such a good idea," said the Director.

Shane was dying to say something, but he kept to his word that he'd let me do the talking.

"Why not?" I asked, as innocently as possible. "The residents seemed much happier at the dance than at bingo. I really think they need more exercise. Just because they're old doesn't mean they have to rot."

The Director stared at me. I stared back. The painting stared at Ben again. Ben stared at the carpet.

"All right, then," announced the Director. "I do think the residents would benefit from a little physical activity. I will have them all brought into the Great Room."

"Thank you, Mr. Director," I said. "Shane's a great master."

"I'm sure he is," said the Director, eyeing Shane suspiciously. Shane bowed deeply to the Director.

The Director turned back to me and smiled widely. It took me by surprise, and I stumbled backward.

He said through his clenched, smiling teeth, "Do know, Mr. Taylor, that the ravens aren't the only ones who have their eyes on you around here. We *all* have our eyes on you, and you would be extremely wise to make sure that you don't do *anything* to compromise the security of this facility or its residents."

"But of course," I said, as calmly as I could, and then I bowed deeply to the Director, just like Shane had.

Before I stood up straight, the Director was gone and we were alone in the lobby.

"That guy gives me the creeps," said Ben.

"I dunno," said Gordon. "He's just like any other stupid adult."

"He's not stupid," I said. "He knows we're up to something. Our plan might not even work." I turned to Shane and asked, "What do you think?"

"Let's shake things up and see what happens," he replied and busted a smooth karate move, a big smile on his face.

Shane was always happy to teach people about karate.

The four of us stood at the front of the Great Room. All the tables had been moved to the side, just like at the dance. Word must have spread about what was happening, because all the residents were wearing loose-fitting clothes like sweatpants and T-shirts. The werewolf guy looked even hairier now with his tank top.

All of the old folks shuffled nervously in place, moaning and grunting as usual.

Shane cleared his throat. "Thank you so much for joining us today."

A few weak "You're welcome"s floated up into the room, but for the most part, the moaning continued.

"Today we will learn the ancient art of karate," Shane began.

Gordon walked over to Shane holding a small wooden board with both hands. He held it up to Shane, who came at it with a karate chop.

"Yuhhh!" Shane grunted and broke the board.

A bit of weak applause floated up from the crowd. Shane bowed.

"With months of training and focused discipline, you too could do the same thing," Shane said. "But let's start with the basics."

Shane reached his arms up to either side, and pointed to the left and right.

"Let's work out bad posture by stretching out our shoulders."

Ben, Gordon, and I demonstrated the stretch. The monsters lifted up their arms. Some of them had quite a hard time. Cracking, creaking, and popping filled the room. So did small yelps of pleasure.

"Awoooo, that feels GOOD," howled the werewolf.

Instead of stretching them out to the side, all the zombies held their arms in front of them, as if reaching for brains. Big surprise. A Nurse pulled each of their arms out in the right direction.

"Now, don't be afraid to stretch a little harder," said Shane. "Point your fingers as if you're pointing to something far off in the distance. Look from side to side. Work that tension out."

The monsters all seemed to be enjoying themselves. But suddenly, one of the zombie's moans turned to a screech. He was stretching as hard as he could when his arm flew off his shoulder and toward a witch. The outstretched palm slapped her large witch-butt with a sharp SMACK.

Her screams made the other monsters turn. She stomped at the rude arm as it flapped around on the ground. The zombie shuffled forward to try to save it.

Ben, Gordon, and Shane stared, disgusted, at the scene before them.

"His arm . . ." Ben hiccupped.

"What the . . . ," Shane started to say, but he just swallowed hard and turned white.

Gordon scratched his head.

The old monsters were agitated. Growls rose from the crowd. The Nurses realized that something was going on and looked at one another. They headed into the crowd of agitated monsters to break things up before they got out of hand.

But things had already gotten out of hand.

Just as we hoped they would.

Just as we had planned.

"Now's our chance!" I yelled.

I ran for the door with Ben and Gordon. As planned, Shane stayed behind to keep the lesson going when things quieted.

"All right," yelled Shane. He eyed the crowd nervously, trying to act normal. "When everyone settles down, I will teach you a basic low kick."

But nobody wanted to settle down.

We flew through the door and were about to turn down the hall when another scream made us stop.

This time, Shane was screaming.

We turned to see all of the zombies surrounding Shane!

His eyes bugged out with fear! He held his arms high above the circle of zombies, waving to get our attention, and then fell to the floor.

"Shane!" Gordon yelled, and rushed back through the door.

He was quickly pushed back into the hallway by a Nurse.

"Not safe here!" the Nurse yelled, and then slammed the door in our faces. With a loud CLICK, he locked the door.

Gordon pounded on the door. Ben and I joined him, screaming for the Nurse to let us in.

We pounded until our knuckles were sore.

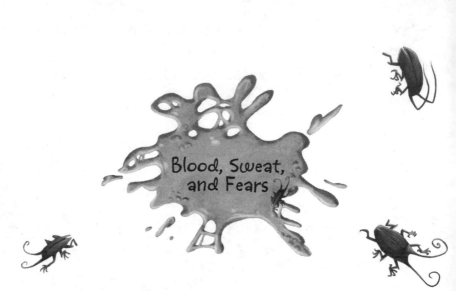

Blood, Sweat, and Fears

"There's nothing we can do here," I said, frustrated. "Let's get upstairs and find my lebensplasm!"

"But Chris—" Gordon said.

"But WHAT?" I snapped. "The door's locked and we're losing time. Of all of us, he's the best prepared for what's going on in there. He's given us an amazing distraction. Let's use it."

I looked at Ben and Gordon with pleading eyes.

"Okay," Ben said.

"Fine," said Gordon.

We sped down the hallway and my heartbeat quickened.

"I hope we don't see the Director," I said as we made our way into the lobby.

We headed up the crooked staircase.

"I forget—what exactly are we looking for again?" Gordon asked.

We rounded the corner at the top of the stairs and down the long hallway.

"A small jar of gooey stuff," I said. "My stuff."

"His lebensplasm," Ben said.

We stopped in front of the door marked

DO NOT ENTER
Staff Only

"Leg spasm? Wha?" asked Gordon.

"My soul, my life, I dunno. I've already explained twenty times, dude," I said. "But we need to get it and it's in here."

"Look," he said, "I thought you were playing a joke on us this whole time—I wasn't exactly paying attention."

"Did you forget our plan, too?" I asked Gordon.

"No, no, no, I got it!" he roared back.

"We have to hurry," I said. "The Nurses will have things under control soon."

Ben sprang into action. He hopped down on his hands and knees below the candlestick. I stood on his back and got a good hold on the candlestick, then placed my feet on the wall. Ben jumped up and held my feet into place.

"Ready?" I asked Gordon.

"Ready!" said Gordon, who crouched in front of the screaming demon.

I pulled down as hard as I could, and the candlestick popped right out of the wall. The sound of clicking filled the hallway.

"NOW!" I screamed.

Gordon rushed at the statue.

"Huuuuuuuuhhhhhhh!" he grunted as he pushed. The statue slowly, slowly scraped to the right.

"You've almost got it!" I yelled.

"Help . . . me . . . Ben," Gordon gasped. "I'm . . . pooping out!"

Ben rushed over to Gordon as I hung in place. I could feel the candlestick begin to rise.

"Hurry!" I screeched.

Ben and Gordon grunted and groaned and . . .

CLICK!

"Yeah!" Gordon yelled, and high-fived a nearly-passed-out Ben.

"Wait!" I yelled. "The candlestick is going back into the wall! Pull my legs, pull my legs!"

Gordon and Ben each grabbed a leg, and tugged as hard as they could. The candlestick was still being pulled back in to the wall.

"Harder!" I screamed.

They tugged so hard it felt like my spine was snapping. I didn't care.

The clicking turned to grinding.

"Moooooooore!" I moaned in pain.

The candlestick slowly pulled back out of the wall and the grinding slowed down until . . .

CLICK!

The door flung open. Cold air blew through the doorway. It smelled a little like a hospital—sterile and bleachy.

I let go of the candlestick.

It was pitch-black and eerily quiet inside.

"You first," said Ben. I could hear the fear in his voice.

I felt exactly the same way.

We held our cell phones up as flashlights and headed in. Ben followed close behind me and Gordon. We slowly made our way down the hallway. With every step I took, I expected something to spring out at us.

"Don't they have any lights around here?" Ben asked.

"I dunno," I said.

We flashed our cell phone lights along the wall. There didn't seem to be any switches anywhere. The doors in the hall were all closed, and had small windows in them, like in a prison or a psych ward.

Gordon flashed his light into the first one.

"Dudes, you gotta see this," he said.

"I can't look," said Ben.

I came over to look. It was hard to see through the glass, since a lot of light reflected off of it. But inside was a room without any furniture. It looked like a jungle inside—with trees and vines. It was moist, and the light that did get through appeared foggy.

"What's in there?" I asked, and we looked at one another.

We could see a slight movement in the leaves, but couldn't tell what it was.

"Do you think that your lebensplasm is in there?" asked Ben.

"I hope not," I said. "Let's keep looking."

We headed down the long dark hallway. Gordon and I peered into the next door. This room seemed normal, with a few pieces of furniture and a bed. There was something large on the bed. Something human? Perhaps not—it was hard to tell. We peered in as close as we could.

"What is it?" asked Ben, and he pushed in between us to have a peek.

I was about to turn away when the something jumped up and practically flew over to the window. In an instant, a huge grinning face with razor-sharp teeth—but skin where eyes should be—was in the window. Hot breath fogged the window up, as the creature let out a high-pitched growl-squeak.

We yelled and jumped back, our sneakers squeaking

on the cold linoleum floor.

"Do you think it can get through the window?" Gordon whined.

The blind monster lifted up a gnarled, slimy hand and pointed behind us.

Ben covered his eyes.

Gordon and I turned to see one of the old vampires. It was the vampire that had been licking his lips at me ever since I started at Raven Hill.

"Chris?" Ben whimpered. "Can we go now?"

In the pale light of our cell phones, I could see that the vampire was drooling a little. A wad of drool fell off of the left corner of his mouth and PLOPPED to the floor.

The vampire was hungry.

He backed up toward the main entrance to the hallway. The monster in the prison cell behind us giggled a high, piercing giggle. It didn't sound human.

We were cornered.

What's for Dinner?

"I've had enough of this. Outta my way, old man!" Gordon yelled.

He stomped toward the doorway and the light beyond. I grabbed Gordon before he got too close to the old vampire.

"That's not just any old man," I said. "He's a vampire."

"What?" Ben said, and finally looked up from his hands.

As if on cue, the old vampire bared his teeth for us to see.

They looked remarkably pearly white and healthy for a vampire of his age. And his incisors looked very, very sharp.

"RUN!" I yelled.

I grabbed Ben and Gordon by the belts of their karate uniforms, and turned down the dark hallway. I had no idea where it led, but I knew it led away from the vampire. That was good enough for me.

We ran past another half dozen doors and the medical/hospital/bleach smell got even stronger. At the end of the hallway, there was a small room with beakers and vials—a laboratory. We ducked inside.

"Look for a door on the other side!" I screamed.

"He's halfway down the hall," Gordon yelled.

Gordon sounded terrified.

Ben slammed the door shut, but there was no lock. We scrambled around the room, looking for a door to anywhere but here. But there was no door, and there was no window. The old vampire would be here any second, and he looked ready to feast.

I looked around for wood to make into a stake, but there was nothing but steel and stone in the laboratory.

"How are we going to defend ourselves?" I asked.

"I dunno," said Gordon. "How about this?"

He held up a beaker labeled ACID.

"It's worth a try," Ben said.

I rummaged through a drawer of rusty old medical tools and found a scalpel.

The door slowly creaked open, and the sound of laughter filled the laboratory. The old vampire was *giggling*.

"Ready for dinner?" asked Gordon as he stepped forward.

He flung the vial of acid at the vampire. It broke and the vampire started smoking, but it didn't slow him down. He giggled even more and lunged forward. Gordon backed right into a cabinet, and the vampire pounced and held on tight.

"GORDON!" Ben screeched.

"Get him off me!!" yelled Gordon.

I jumped forward and stabbed the old vampire in the throat.

The scalpel just stuck there as the old vampire leaned in to bite Gordon. He didn't even seem to feel it.

"Chris! Ben!" Gordon yelled. "Help me out! DO SOMETHING!!!"

But it was too late. The vampire opened wide and let out one more drooly, excited giggle.

And then, right before I closed my eyes—

FWACK! CRACK!

The old vampire's dentures fell out of his mouth, bounced off of Gordon's neck, and rattled to a drooly stop on the linoleum floor of the laboratory.

The old vampire let Gordon go and slowly leaned down to scoop up his dentures. Gordon ran out into the hall. I leaned down to grab the dentures before the vampire did.

Neither of us would get the dentures, though.

They started clicking . . .

And took off down the hallway!

"Gordon!" I yelled "WATCH OUT!"

"Don't worry, Mr. Taylor," said a voice that was not Gordon's, "your friend is just fine. Grigore's dentures are just heading back to his coffin."

"The Director?!" I yelled.

Sure enough the Director came through the door, dragging Gordon by his ear.

Grigore started crying as soon as he saw the Director. He rushed over and grabbed a hold of his suit, weeping into his perfectly pressed shirt. The Director let Gordon go and he came over to stand next to Ben and me. Gordon rubbed his ear, which was beet red.

"Mr. Taylor," the Director said, cradling Grigore in his arms, "you have broken into the private wing. You've soiled my laboratory, most likely ruining weeks of research. But, most despicably, you have frightened Grigore."

The old vampire cried louder at the sound of his name.

"I'm extremely disappointed in you. You were the perfect candidate. But I see now that I should never have trusted you. Certainly not today. Most likely from the beginning. I let you in after the raven tried to block you. You've been up to something the whole time you've been volunteering here. What is it?"

"I'VE BEEN UP TO SOMETHING?!" I yelled. "What have you been up to? Sheltering monsters!"

"Well, I don't really think of them as monsters," the Director said, patting Grigore's head. "Just elderly with special needs."

"Very special needs," said Gordon.

"But," the Director continued, "I will agree with you that I've been sheltering them. It is my duty to shelter and protect them. They have nowhere else to turn. And you gentlemen have stuck your noses far too far into our affairs."

An intercom next to the door crackled and a voice said, "Great Room secure." It sounded like one of the Nurses.

"Very well," said the Director. "Meet me at my office."

"Yes, sir."

"Follow me, gentlemen," said the Director, "or I'll lock you in this wing and open up all the doors."

He didn't have to tell us twice.

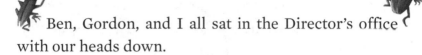

No Escape

Ben, Gordon, and I all sat in the Director's office with our heads down.

Shane was nowhere to be seen.

"I can't believe this is happening," whispered Ben. "They killed Shane! I think I'm losing my mind."

"It's okay, Ben." I patted him on the back.

I had absolutely no idea if it was okay.

"Where's Shane?" I asked the Director.

The Director paced behind his desk and stared at us. And stared at us. And stared at us. He looked very, very angry. And still he didn't say anything.

Two Nurses guarded the door. The office itself was actually quite warm and inviting—books on the shelves, a small fireplace, a nice view of the hillside. The furnishings were all wood and leather, and there was a rug that looked like it could have actually been manufactured in the last twenty years.

"If this is your idea of a joke . . . ," Gordon started to say to the Director.

But then Shane came into the room—with the zombie who had lost his arm!

Shane gave the arm, which had been reattached, a shake.

"It was great talking with you, too, Billy!" he said as the zombie turned to leave. "If they ever let you out of here, you should check out the dojo I go to. Remember— start slow—ease your body into it."

Shane sat down next to us. We all just stared at him.

"What's up, guys?" he asked casually.

"Wait," Ben said. "You made it! We thought you were done for! This is crazy! Was that really a zombie?"

"The zombies are actually pretty chill dudes," said Shane. "You just have to talk to them on their level, you know what I mean?"

The Director sat down behind his desk, sinking slowly into his chair. He clasped his hands together, but still said nothing.

"So . . . ," Gordon said, "can we go now?"

"No," the Director said, "you cannot go now. Nor can you go . . . ever. I've made up my mind—you can never leave this place. You've seen too much, and . . ."

The Director hesitated for a moment.

". . . and I need your help with the residents."

"Wait!" I yelled. "You can't just keep us here!"

"Actually, I can," the Director said. There was not a hint of joking in his voice.

"What are you going to tell our parents when they come looking for us?" I asked.

"Oh, your parents will never come looking for you," the Director said.

"Don't you dare hurt them," I said.

The Director grinned and said, "I'm not going to hurt your parents. I have some rare monsters—"

Gordon interrupted the Director with a loud snicker.

"Yes, monsters—in the very same wing where I caught you. One of them is a jungle worm that can crawl into the brain of its victim through the nose and eat their memories. We'll introduce a few to your parents, and they'll soon forget they ever had children. We'll do the same to your teachers. To your principal. To your grandparents, if in fact they still exist. Your friends might miss you, but who will believe a kid who talks about imaginary friends? The worms hurt terribly, but your parents won't remember that, either. So I won't, technically, be hurting them."

"That's disgusting," said Ben, and let out a little burp. "Oh, man, someone get me out of here!"

"What an idiotic plan," I said.

I stood up, crossed my arms, and looked right into the Director's eyes. He looked genuinely surprised.

"Excuse me?" he asked.

"That plan would never work," I said. "You'd have to erase too many memories *and* official records. Do you think the whole school district is just going to ignore all the records of missing students? What about our IM screen names?"

There was a moment of silence as the Director and I stared at each other.

"Good point!" whispered Shane.

"Yeah," said Gordon. "This is a bunch of baloney! Where are the cameras, Director Dude? You've certainly got enough actors around. That old vampire bit was a hoot."

Now I turned to Gordon.

"Wake up dude; this is for *real!*" I said.

"For real. . . ." Ben curled up into a ball on his chair.

"You have seen too much," snapped the Director. "You know about the vampires. The werewolves. It's hard *not* to notice the zombies, and I presume you've seen a few of the banshees. We have a swamp thing. And a monster pieced together from the flesh of the dead. We used to have a Cyclops . . ."

The Director looked distracted for a moment and then continued. "The witches are actually quite helpful with potions and spells to calm some of the residents that suffer from dementia. But, they, too are losing their minds.

"So, that's that. You'll be helping us here until the end of your days. Rewrapping mummies, checking the werewolves for ticks, cleaning the vampire's dentures, sewing on lost zombie parts. The list goes on and on. There's a lot to be done.

"However, I will warn you. Don't think these old monsters are harmless. Had Nurse Uwt actually applied denture cream to Grigore's dentures today as he was supposed to, Gordon would not have fared as well in the laboratory. They are very, very hungry, and it is only because we tell them to behave that they do."

I couldn't stand it! The Director acted like he was going to keep the old monsters from harming us, but I already knew what he had planned. Now he had three more sources of lebensplasm!

"You don't want us to help!" I screamed. "You're just going to feed us to all the old folks. They'll all eat our lebensplasm. Where have you put mine?"

The Director looked at me strangely. He opened his mouth to reply, but before he could, it began raining.

Yes, it began raining *inside*. A light drizzle quickly became a steady pitter-pitter-pitter of rain. It wet the documents on the Director's desk. It wet the rug. I felt it soak through my hair and onto my scalp. I touched my hair, and it felt . . . slimy.

We all looked up to see where the rain was coming from.

And then we saw them.

Dozens of them.

There were dozens of the same cat-size roaches I had seen the raven kill that very first day. And this time I could see them clearly. They looked exactly like huge roaches except for one special feature.

They had big-lipped, snaggletoothed human mouths. And they were all drooling.

It was raining drool.

The rain ended and the roaches started to hiss and moan with their twisted, puffy-lipped mouths.

I looked at the Director. He looked even more terrified than I did.

"SUSSUROBLATS!" he screamed. "ALARM!!!"

And that's when all of the roaches screamed and dropped off the ceiling.

Attack!!!

The roaches plopped down one by one, like massive ugly brown drooly raindrops. The Nurses squealed and bolted out through the door into the hallway. The Director followed.

"Let's get outta here!" I yelled.

We ran into the hallway and turned right to get back into the lobby, and the exit beyond.

"Move it, y'all!" yelled Shane.

We ran so fast, the house shook.

We got to the end of the hallway and saw the Director and the two Nurses frozen in front of the door.

"Get out of our way," Gordon yelled.

The Director and the Nurses didn't move an inch. And I could see why.

They were surrounded on all sides by the massive roaches!

We turned back to where we had run from, and saw a few zombies being chased into the lobby with the large roaches at their heels. They looked terrified.

"Sussuroblats," cried the Director. "Sussuroblats!"

"Sussuro . . . what?" asked Ben.

"I guess that's what they're called," I said.

The sussuroblats closed in, forcing the zombies into the same small circle with us and the Director and the two Nurses. The crawled over one another, hissing, screaming, and drooling as they got closer.

"I think I smell their breath," said Shane.

"Ugh, you're right!" I said.

"GRELCH, GROWWWLCH, GRUUUUG!" cried the sussuroblats. They sounded like they were burping and screaming at the same time, and when they weren't screaming, they were gnashing their snaggleteeth together, making wet, snapping sounds.

They were getting closer and closer. Shane took a karate stance. One of the old zombies tripped over another, and fell back into a pile of them. Almost as soon as he hit the floor, they swarmed him, latched on, and began slurping up his juices with their nasty mouths.

"Oh, man!" cried Ben. "We're roach meat!"

The zombie was drained fast. Just as they finished their meal, one of the old witches appeared at the top of the stairs. She had a small vial of potion in her hand.

"Helllooooooo!" she cried, and for a moment, the roaches stared up at her. She flung the vial down into the pile of roaches that were sucking on what was left of the zombie, and they exploded!

The witch disappeared, and a cry of "Go, Go, GOOO!" could be heard from the hallway beyond the top of the stairs. A group of Nurses, clad in SWAT gear, spread out through the retirement home. There were still at least three dozen roaches left after the witch had worked her magic. Half of them headed up the stairs and the other half closed in on us!

The Director reached one hand into his suit, and pulled out a Taser. He zapped a sussuroblat that jumped toward him, and it fell on the floor. One of the Nurses stomped on the bug, and it grunted one last moan as green goo oozed out of it. Its nasty roach legs twitched.

Shane was kicking like crazy, stopping the roaches with big, squelchy hits. He kicked some of them just as they were jumping at him to bite. Teeth were flying out of screeching roach mouths.

The roaches that had gone upstairs scurried into bedrooms. Old monsters poured out of the hallway, trying their best to shuffle away. Many already had roaches stuck on them, slurping away! The monsters flailed about, trying desperately to get them off. Nurses were ripping roaches off old monsters left and right, but more disgusting bugs came out of nowhere to latch on to the moaning monsters.

But the old monsters weren't completely defenseless. A few of them were actually performing the karate chop that Shane had demonstrated before, and a few of the chops actually landed, sending roaches over the banister and down into the lobby.

For all of the Tasing, kicking, chopping, and stomping that was going on, there seemed to be more and more roaches, and our circle was getting smaller.

A half dozen roaches were closing in on Ben, Gordon, Shane, and me. We backed slowly onto the stairs.

"I can't keep this up," yelled Shane as he kicked another roach in its ugly mug. "There are too many."

"I've got an idea!" I said. "Follow me!"

I sprinted up the stairs, dodging downed old monsters and roaches. My friends followed, and we turned down the dark hallway to the Staff Only section of the retirement home.

"Ben!" I yelled. "I need to pull the candlestick out of the wall again. Shane and Gordon, just hold them back for a few seconds."

Ben dropped to the floor. I jumped up to the candlestick, planted my feet on the wall, and pulled just as Ben held my feet in place.

Gordon grabbed a tattered, cobwebby painting from

the wall to help Shane hold back the roaches that had gathered at the end of the hallway.

This had to work, or we'd be roach meat!

Sure enough, the candlestick moved back into the wall and the clicking moved from the wall to the ceiling.

"Squeeze your backs against the door," I said.

The roaches snapped and spat and screamed. One jumped up and took a bite out of the painting. We stared at a dozen more through the hole in the canvas. Another tried to jump through, and Shane karate-chopped it down. Gordon stomped on it for good measure.

The ceiling opened with a *whoosh*, and the metallic claw came swooping down inches in front of our noses.

It scooped up all of the roaches. They screamed even louder, knowing they were trapped. Their drool rained down on the tattered carpet as the claw lifted them higher.

As soon as the claw was above our heads, I yelled, "RUN!"

We sped down the hallway, the light from the growing fireball throwing our shadows on the floor. When we reached the end of the hall, we turned around to see the claw engulfed in flames. The roaches' drooly screams slowly died out and a few of their bodies exploded in the heat. POP. SNAP. SPLOP. The claw disappeared into the ceiling, and we were back in a dark hallway once again.

By the time we got downstairs, most of the roaches had been cleared out. One of the vampires was still passed out on the stairs. The old werewolves had turned into dogs, and were chewing on a few roaches. A Nurse in SWAT gear kicked a roach, which flew over the banister . . .

. . . and right onto me!

And it wasn't dead!!

I screamed as the roach knocked me over. I was amazed at how strong it was. It had pinned me to the floor, its spiny legs scratching all over me. It crawled up my stomach and chest before I could lift my arms up and stop it right before it lunged at my throat.

"Ben! Gordon! Shaaaaane!" I screamed in a panic.

Now I could REALLY smell bad breath. It was inches away from my face as I tried to lift it off of me, to push it far enough away so I could scramble back up.

"GRELCH, SHMELCH, BRALCH!!" the sussuroblat mouth, so human and disgusting, spat and yelled at me.

"SOMEONE HELP!!!" I yelled, as the hideous mouth got closer and closer. I could feel the heat of the roach's breath on my cheek. I turned my head, and the smell of rotten flesh came pouring out of its mouth. I could hear it snapping at my ear, when suddenly—

"Get over here!" yelled Gordon.

He lifted the roach into the air, and turned it toward

the Director. The Director plunged his Taser into the roach's underbelly, and—

Click. Click. Click.

"Drat," said the Director. "The batteries."

The roach squirmed its way loose, right up Gordon's arm and—

CRUNCH

It bit right into Gordon's neck. Gordon screamed a phlegmy scream.

A Nurse tossed the Director a fresh battery pack. He ejected the old pack, smashed in the new one, pulled the roach off Gordon, and slammed it face-first into the floor.

Gordon clutched his neck, but blood bubbled out from between his fingers. It wasn't a lot, but he was unsteady on his feet.

The Director knelt down in front of the roach and jabbed his Taser onto its belly. He zapped and zapped and zapped.

"I. Despise. You. Nasty. CREATURES," he growled.

Zap, zap, zap . . .

POP!

The sussuroblat's head exploded in a shower of hot green guts.

The Director rose up slowly, calmly straightened his rumpled suit, wiped down the Taser with a handkerchief, and placed it back inside his suit pocket.

No Chance for Recovery

The lobby looked like a war zone. The Director was staring through the glass next to the front door. His face was blank with shock. The Nurses looked upset. One looked down at what was left of the dead zombie and then punched the wall angrily. Ben looked like he was going to be sick. Gordon, who was now slumped at the bottom of the stairs, had stopped bleeding, but the area around the bite was starting to turn a shade of green. Shane, who still had a large cockroach leg twitching in his hair, was cleaning guts off his face with a rag one of the Nurses had handed him.

I had to find out from the Director if we should be worried about Gordon's bite. But first, I had a much more pressing question.

"Where is the jar you're always dipping into?" I screamed.

"Why?" the Director, still shocked, said.

"Just give it to me," I said. "You owe me that much."

"Fine," the Director said. "Nurse Inx, go get the jar." The Director waved one of the Nurses off to fetch it.

I turned to Gordon, who was looked like he was going to pass out.

"How are you doing?" I asked.

"Not so good, dude," Gordon said. His voice sounded like he needed to clear his throat of the biggest loogie ever. "I feel really hot. And nauseous."

I helped him over to one of the leather chairs in the lobby and sat him down.

Nurse Inx came back into the lobby holding the jar. He handed it to me, and I could see at once that there was nothing in it. Scared, I unscrewed the top as quickly as I could.

"It's all gone!" I looked at the Director in horror.

"Yes, it would appear that someone put it back in the fridge after finishing it," said the Director without any emotion, adding, "How cruel."

"WHAT?!" I said, completely freaked out. "Where's all of my lebensplasm? It was in the fridge this whole time?!"

"What?" asked the Director, raising an eyebrow.

"Would you expect it to be in the pantry? I prefer my marmalade cold."

"Marmalade?!" I screamed so loud that Nurse Inx jumped. He headed up the stairs to help the old vampire, who had finally woken up.

"Yes," the Director said. "What did you think it was?"

I locked eyes with the Director. I still wasn't sure I could trust him. By the look on his face, I don't think he trusted me, either. But, if it wasn't in the jar, it had to be somewhere. He did say that my lebensplasm was keeping the monsters alive.

"Where is my lebensplasm?" I asked.

There was a pause. The Director stared strangely at me. He cocked his head like a dog would when you whistle at it. Shane, who had finally realized there was a cockroach leg in his hair, tossed it to the side and came to stand next to me, ready for whatever happened next. Ben was tending to Gordon.

"Why . . . your lebensplasm . . . ," started the Director slowly, "is inside you. If it weren't, you would be dead."

"The day after I started volunteering at Raven Hill, you held a meeting with all of the mon—"

"Residents!" insisted the Director.

"You held a meeting with all of the residents," I continued. "In that meeting, you said that my lebensplasm was going to go a long way in keeping them alive. Then you pulled out that jar, spread that goo on a piece of toast, and started eating it like it was the best thing you'd ever tasted."

"I see you were spying about earlier than I thought," said the Director. "Nevertheless, your lebensplasm was not in that jar of marmalade. I just happened to need a snack after such a long day."

"Okay, fine!" I said. "I get that the marmalade isn't my lebensplasm, but what about the comment? You know—that my lebensplasm is helping to keep the residents alive?"

"You believe that the residents are 'monsters,' as you like to call them, yes?" the Director asked.

"Yes," I replied.

The director looked at Shane, who was still standing next to me.

"And you?" he asked.

"Definitely," said Shane.

"You believe in the supernatural, where others do not. It is that belief, that lebensplasm, that keeps my residents . . . well, *alive,* for lack of a better word. So you see, I haven't stolen your lebensplasm and hidden it somewhere—it's always flowing out of you and all around you."

"So, they're just feeding off of positive brain waves," said Shane. "Theta brain waves most likely—what the ancient Asian warriors call *zanshin*."

"What?" I asked, totally confused.

"Exactly!" said the Director.

"But why do you need lebensplasm?" asked Shane. "Y'all are old monsters. What's happening here? The old vampire's dentures fall out. The zombies are falling apart. The werewolves are losing their fur . . ."

"'We all' are not old monsters. The residents are monsters. I am not a monster, nor are my Nurses, otherwise we'd be just as weak as our residents. My residents are under attack. The Nurses and I are doing the best we can to defend them."

"You're under attack from the cockroach thingies?" Shane asked.

"Yes. Those 'thingies' that just attacked us are called sussuroblats, and they've been draining my residents' energies. All of the residents here are vampires, witches, mummies, the living dead, and the undead, yes, but unfortunately, they are all dying. Their monster powers are being drained at an alarming rate by these horrific sussuroblats."

"So . . . these sussuroblats are draining all the *monster juice*," Shane said. "And you're trying to keep them from the supply."

"Precisely," said the Director. "We've put up a charm around the house and the grounds, but it's been working less and less as their monster powers diminish."

"That's the green glow I keep seeing!" I said.

"Indeed," continued the Director. "We have other defenses. The ravens can pick off a random sussuroblat here and there, but when an army, like the one you just saw, attacks us, we're helpless. We're trying to figure out a way to defend ourselves, but until then, we need a constant supply of lebensplasm to keep the residents from slipping away completely."

"That's why you were looking for volunteers from Rio Vista Middle School?" I asked.

"That was one of the reasons, yes. There are many types of lebensplasm, and the positive, belief-filled brain waves children put out is a strong variety. There are other things—food, rituals, gathering energy from sussuroblats that the ravens kill—which help to supply lebensplasm. Aside from the lebensplasm, however, we really do need a good bit of help around here. My Nurses are wonderful for defense, and for controlling out-of-control monsters. They're not so good, however, at giving my residents the 'tender loving care' that they also need."

I could see that the Director was truly concerned for his residents. He looked up the stairway. The Nurses had cleared all the monsters (and monster body parts) out and were starting the process of cleaning. One Nurse wept as he mopped the bloody hardwood floor.

"Bwaaarrrrggghh!" Gordon cried out from his chair.

He sounded like he was drowning in his own spit. Shane, the Director, and I ran over to Ben, who was doing what he could to help. Gordon was drooling and shivering. Snot was pouring down his nose. He was turning green/brown.

"I don't think he's doing very well, guys," Ben said with a look of horror.

"You don't look well, either," said the Director to Ben. "Did you get bit?"

"Nope, this is just how I normally look when participating in a sussuroblat battle," Ben said.

"Ben is always sick," Shane explained.

"I see," said the Director.

"What about Gordon?" I asked. "What's happening to him?"

The Director grabbed Gordon's face and looked him in the eyes. Gordon shook and shivered. The Director didn't seem to mind. He held Gordon's face as green goop poured out of Gordon's nostrils.

"This is the first time I've seen a sussuroblat bite a human, so I'm not sure how long it will take," the Director finally said.

"How long what will take?!" Shane, Ben, and I said together.

"As with vampire bites and werewolf bites, a sussuroblat bite can change a human into a sussuroblat."

"What?!" Ben said.

Shane and I looked stunned. Apparently Gordon heard the director, because he stopped shaking for a moment to start moaning and crying.

"There is very little research on the subject, because the chance a sussuroblat will bite a human is very low," the Director continued. "But, from what I know, most likely Gordon will soon have a cockroach mouth, and will have an uncontrollable urge to eat garbage."

"What can we do to stop it?" I asked.

"There is no chance for recovery," the Director said. "There is nothing that can be done. The only thing that will reverse the effects of the bite is if every last sussuroblat is destroyed, and that is not going to happen anytime soon. I will keep him here at Raven Hill. You'll have to think of some story to tell his parents. I've decided to let you all go—we would have not survived that attack without you—but I must keep Gordon here."

Before we could argue, a Nurse came storming down the hall and into the lobby.

"More!" he said, breathless. "Soon!"

Invasion of the Sussuroblats

The Director ran over to the Nurse for more information.

"How many?" asked the Director.

"All of them," gasped the Nurse, still out of breath.

In the leather chair, Gordon let out another moan. But this time his mouth was closed. It looked like his lips were sealing up!

"When?" asked the Director.

"Not sure," the Nurse said. "Hour? Two?"

"Let's get everyone up into the attic," said the Director.

The Nurse just stood there.

"Quickly!" the Director yelled.

The Nurse gave a small salute and rushed out of the lobby. The Director turned back to us.

"I'm sorry, gentlemen, but it will soon be very dangerous for you to be here. I must insist you leave at once. Gordon is in good hands."

"NO," I said. I couldn't bear the thought of leaving Gordon behind like this.

"What did you say?" asked the Director

"NO," said Shane.

"NO," said Ben. Although, he was so sick, it came out "Nuh."

"We have no time for argument, gentlemen," said the Director, clearly upset. "I need to get the entire retirement home up to the attic and secured, possibly in just one hour."

"We're not leaving Gordon," I said. "Plus, we might be able to help you like we did before."

The Director stared at me, trying to figure out whether to let us stay or kick us out.

Shane spoke up before the Director could give an answer. "You're gonna have to drag us out of here if you want us gone. You got time for that?"

The Director was angry, but he knew he had no choice. "FINE," he said, so loudly that the windows shook. "Go downstairs to the crypt to fetch the vampires. Grigore is scared of you now that he lost his dentures in front of you, so I'm hoping he'll trust you enough to lead the other two up without the Nurses' assistance. We've got too much to deal with on the ground floor and the second floor."

"Thanks, Mr. Director," croaked Ben.

"You may not be thanking me later, when you realize what you've gotten yourself into," said the Director.

The Director walked over to where Gordon was drooling, snatched him up, and threw him over his shoulder like a bag of potatoes. He was really strong for such a scrawny, pale dude. Gordon groaned, and sniffed wads of brown/green snot onto the Director's finely pressed suit. The Director saw us staring at him in disgust as slimy snot just rolled down his back.

"Believe me," he said as he turned around. "I've seen much worse. Gordon will be safe upstairs with the rest of us. GO GET THE VAMPIRES."

And then the Director ran up the stairs, leaving a trail of Gordon's snot behind him.

"All right," I said to the other two. "Let's do this!"

We headed behind the stairs and toward the door to the crypt.

I swung the door open, and we stood there for a moment. Shane and Ben stood to my right, waiting. In front of me were dozens of steps spiraling down into darkness. A funky cool basementy smell blew up the stairs. It was that regular mold smell you get with basements, but mixed with something else. It was the kind of smell I had only smelled at the zoo.

Upstairs, the old monsters howled as the Nurses tried to force them all up to the attic. In the panic, furniture was being destroyed, glass was breaking, and the Nurses were suffering bite wounds. There was chaos above us, and who knew what down below.

I turned to Shane and Ben. Shane gave a nod toward the stairs—he was ready to go. Ben looked scared about the whole situation and stared off into space. Despite the fact that I was scared, too, Gordon was in trouble and we had to move fast. I needed all the help I could get!

"Hey! Ben!" I screamed over the noise. "Ben!"

"Huh!" Ben's face snapped back to life. "Wha?"

"I really need you to help us, man!" I yelled.

Ben tried to pull himself together. "Okay. Yeah, all right, I'm ready for anything. LET'S DO THIS!!!" He didn't look so convinced, but I didn't have much time for any more pep talks. I had no idea how long it would be before the sussuroblat army made its way to Raven Hill, or if Gordon would be a part of it when they got here. We had to move!

We were about five steps down the stairs, and it was already as dark as midnight. We whipped out our cell phones to use them as flashlights.

Down we spiraled, for what seemed like forever. I was starting to get crazy dizzy. The farther down we went, the more it smelled like zoo. And when I say it smelled like zoo, I mean it smelled like the monkey cages hadn't been cleaned for a week, and when they finally decided to clean them, they used year-old hippo water. Already, I could hear Ben gagging behind us. He was starting to slow down and I feared I'd soon have a barf hat on my head.

I turned around and whispered past Shane, "Just keep moving! Put your shirt over your nose!" Shane and I did the same thing.

The air was getting smellier but cooler. The coolness almost made the stench bearable. But the staircase just wouldn't stop. I wondered what would be worse—an eternity of spiraling down a dark staircase wondering when a sussuroblat would bite me with its drooly mouth, or death by vampire. I was starting to think death by vampire might be the better choice.

Finally, we reached the very bottom. A moist layer of dirt and funk had piled up on the floor. I'm pretty sure it was a thousand years of dust. We held up our cell phones to try to see ahead of us, but it was pitch-black. To the right, water was dripping into a puddle. To the left were a number of half broken, half opened coffins. The vampires had apparently gone through a number of beds before picking one with "the right feel."

We all stopped, and even though these guys could barely gum us without their dentures, I was afraid to move forward.

"Grigore?" Shane called out tentatively. "Griiiiigooooore!?"

Ben, meanwhile, looked one tap away from a full-on vomitous explosion thanks to the spiraling stenchfest our bodies had just suffered.

"GRIIIIGORE?! Oh, GRIIIIIIIIGORE?" Shane's voice didn't echo much. The crypt must have been tiny.

"Come on, guys," I said, snapping out of it. "Let's go."

So, we went. Away from the safety of the bottom of the stairs, deeper into the stank, cold, wet crypt. We held our cell phones as high as we could, and after about ten steps, we found what we were looking for.

Shane silently pointed ahead, and I squinted to see Grigore lying halfway out of his coffin. He snored loudly. I could hear snores from the other vampires deeper in the crypt. Clearly we had nothing to be afraid of. It looked like Grigore didn't even have the time to get into his coffin before he passed out after his adventure today. His huge knobby feet stuck out of the end of the coffin, his toes taking in the cool crypt.

"Whoa. That's disgusting!" Shane yelled into the dark. He pointed his light at Grigore's feet.

Grigore's toes were not only crusty with toe jam— several bats hung sleepily off of his feet. Below the bats and the toe-jammy toes was a pile of bat poop almost two feet high. I guessed this was the normal sleeping arrangement in the crypt. And, apparently, what I had taken to be moist dust before was in fact . . .

"GUA—GUAN—GUANO!" Ben blurted out. A small bit of drool left his lips and he gagged. The floor was covered in a millennium's worth of bat dung.

"Oh no!" said Shane, stepping back.

At first I thought Shane was stepping away from Ben to avoid a chunky shower. But Shane was pointing under the coffin, and we saw a flash of wet, drooly mouths as soon as we pointed our cell phones down.

There were three sussuroblats crawling out from under Grigore's bed!

Heading for the now-screaming Shane, they started to hiss and spit.

They rushed forward, but before they could attack . . .

BAAAAAAARRRRRRFFFFFFFFFFF!!!!!

Ben blurted out the vilest volley of vomit ever known to man.

He covered the sussuroblats!

Their hissing turned into sizzling . . .

. . . and they quickly disintegrated before our eyes!

"Barf!" I cried out. "Their weakness is BARF!"

Buckets of Barf

When we got up to the attic, the Director and Gordon were nowhere to be found. It was pure chaos up there—the old monsters were restless and scared. The Nurses were trying to calm them down, but were ending up with a lot of teeth marks on their beefy arms. I wondered why—with all of the biting—none of the Nurses had turned into vampires, zombies, or werewolves yet.

We handed the three stunned old vampires over to a Nurse, and then took a minute to brainstorm what we were going to tell the Director about Ben's barf.

"We should just get to barfing!" said Shane. "And we should find out if the Nurses and the old monsters could work up some barf as well."

"Do monsters barf?" asked Ben.

"Even if monsters barf, which I'm not sure they do,

143

we'll never have enough barf!" I yelled. "There's only so much lunch everyone can lose. Not everyone's as good at it as Ben, and his massive spew only killed three of the sussuroblats."

"Good point," said Shane. "How can we get people to barf even more?"

We stood listening to all of the monsters howl, growl, and moan. I tried hard to think of all the barfy things that had happened to me in my life. Suddenly, it hit me.

"WAIT!" I yelled so loud that one of the banshees nearby let out a scream. "Parmesan cheese!"

"What?" Shane asked.

"Oh, right!" Ben said. "How could I forget! The same acid found in barf is also found in Parmesan cheese! Buh . . . byuh . . ."

"Butyric acid!" said Shane.

"YES!" all three of us yelled.

"We just need a whole bunch of Parmesan cheese!" I said.

"But how?" asked Ben. "How are we going to get enough Parmesan cheese? We don't have time to go door-to-door asking for Parmesan-cheese donations. And there's no way we'd be able to buy enough of the stuff. I remember my mother saying that it's superexpensive. I've got, like, five bucks and a few pennies."

"Let's see . . . ," Shane said as he stared off into the distance.

"We'll have to ask the Director for money," I said, and ran over to a Nurse to see where the Director was.

"Busy!" said the Nurse.

"But this is important!" I said. "If I get money from the Director, a few hundred dollars, we might be able to fight the sussuroblats."

"No money at Raven Hill," said the Nurse. "Barter system. Donations."

"What about the kitchen?" I asked. "Do you guys have Parmesan cheese in the pantry?"

"One canister," said the Nurse.

He held one hand five inches above the other to indicate that the canister was quite small.

"That's it?!" I screamed.

"Too expensive," the Nurse said, and then started walking over to check on the elbow of the vampire that had fallen on the stairs earlier.

"Wait!" I yelled. "How long until the next sussuroblats arrive?"

"Sunset," he said.

"How many?" I asked.

"Ninety or a hundred."

As I walked back over to Ben and Shane, I knew what I had to do.

"I'm sorry, man," Shane said, "but we got nothin'."

"That's okay," I said. "We can use the money I was saving for my telescope."

"What?!" both of my friends yelled at the same time.

"It's okay," I said. "Gordon's way more important. If he hadn't saved me, I would be the one turning into a cockroach. Now, we don't have much time. Shane, find out when sunset is. Ben, you and I need to figure out where we're going to find the most Parmesan for our buck."

Fifteen minutes later, Ben, Shane, and I left my house with my five hundred and twenty dollars. Ben had come up with the genius idea to head to the local Italian restaurant, Mama Francesca's, and see how much Parmesan cheese we could get for the amount of money we had. Shane was pulling his younger brother's little red wagon behind him, and we all had our biggest backpacks, in the hope that we could fill everything up with cheese.

"We've got forty-five minutes left until sunset," said Shane.

"All right," I said. "Let's just get as much as we can, and then we'll figure out what to do with it. But start thinking."

I wondered what could be done with the Parmesan, and I just couldn't figure it out. Did we melt it and pour it over the side of the retirement home? Did we feed it to the ravens and have them poop on the roaches? It really did depend on how much we got, and how much time we had when we left the restaurant.

We walked up to Mama Francesca's, which was

packed for dinner. There was a huge line coming out of the front door.

"We should just go in the back," Shane said. "There has to be a door into the kitchen. You know, for deliveries. Deliveries of huge wheels of Parmesan cheese."

We started to walk around back.

"It comes in wheels?" asked Ben.

"I don't care which way it comes," I said, "I just want as much of it as possible."

"Cross your fingers," said Shane. "We could get booted out of the kitchen before we can even ask."

Less than five minutes later, my five hundred and twenty dollars had bought us admission to the walk-in refrigerator. We could walk out with as much Parmesan cheese as we could carry. Mama Francesca herself pointed over to an eight-foot-tall rack that was filled completely with Parmesan. Grated Parmesan. Chunks of Parmesan. Parmesan wheels. Our eyes bugged as we gazed upon what must have been the largest collection of Parmesan cheese in the universe.

"Okay," I said, "Let's get as much as we can and get out of here!"

"Yeah, let's get goin'," said Ben. "It smells a little like . . ."

"BARF!" Shane and I said.

"Yep," said Ben.

"Forty minutes!" yelled Shane.

Eat That, Roaches!

Fifteen minutes later, Ben, Shane, and I headed up the road to Raven Hill Retirement Home. We were weighed down by our backpacks, which were completely full of cheese. We also had to move slowly so that the mountain of cheese on top of the red wagon didn't crumble and spill over the sides.

"I don't think I can make it," wheezed Ben. "We should have called your mother, Chris!"

"We wouldn't have had time for all the explaining," I huffed.

"Carrying a hundred pounds of Parmesan cheese is a normal rite of passage for any middle-schooler," said Shane. "I'm. Sure. She. Would. Have. Understood."

Shane stopped, breathing heavy.

"Here, let me take the wagon," I said to Shane. "It's my turn."

"Okay," said Ben. "We're almost there! How much time is left, Shane?"

"Twenty-five minutes!" Shane yelled.

"It's going to take us five more minutes to get up the hill. What are we going to do in twenty minutes?" Ben asked.

"Well . . . ," I said.

"What?" asked Shane.

"Wait, I'm thinking!" I yelled back.

We crept up the side of the hill in silence for a minute, while I thought so hard that my brain hurt.

"I think the most important thing to do is to keep the roaches from coming inside the retirement home," I finally said.

"Why?" asked Ben.

"Because once they're inside, they can crawl around wherever they want—through cracks, up walls, even on ceilings. If we can keep them from getting inside, then we'd have a little more time to figure out how to defeat them."

"Well," said Shane, "why don't we just lay down one big circle of cheese, all the way around the retirement home? They'd creep up to the house, but not be able to crawl up to the door or through any windows."

"But we know a few of them came in through the crypt," I said.

"That's fine," said Shane. "We just have to spread some cheese at the bottom of the stairs."

"This just might work!" I yelled.

We got up to the top of the hill, and were greeted with the excited caws of the ravens. I cupped my hands around my mouth and screamed out a message that I knew the ravens would deliver to the Director.

"We're back with Parmesan cheese! If we spread it around the retirement home and in the crypt, we should be able to keep the sussuroblats out. We have chunks of Parmesan cheese for each of the residents to hold for protection!!!"

Sure enough, one of the ravens flew away to deliver the message.

"Twenty minutes!" yelled Shane.

A shiver ran through my spine. Twenty minutes to sunset. The light was fading, and it was getting cold outside. I wondered if this crazy idea would even work. Whoever heard of Parmesan cheese defeating monsters? *Oh, well,* I thought, *Dracula hated garlic and giant cockroaches hate Parmesan cheese. I guess monsters just don't like Italian food. . . .*

There was no time to think, or to be scared.

"All right!" I barked orders. "I've got the backpack of cheese chunks! I'll head into the home and get the

Nurses to distribute them to the residents. You guys start laying a trail of Parmesan cheese around the building. It's got to be deep enough to keep the roaches away, but I'll still need enough to fill up a backpack for the crypt! HURRY!"

I ran into the retirement home and upstairs to the attic. The Director was waiting for me.

"How sure are you that this is going to work?" the Director asked. He looked completely scared—more scared than I was.

Terrified monsters huddled in small groups around the large, open attic. Gordon was nowhere to be found.

"Where's Gordon?" I asked.

"I asked the first question," said the Director.

"WHERE'S GORDON?!" I screamed. Grigore started crying again.

"He's in a private room in the back of the attic, but—"

I didn't even let the Director finish. I walked past him and handed him the bag of Parmesan chunks.

"Pass these out!" I ordered him.

I walked into the back of the attic, looking for a door.

"Mr. Taylor, I really don't think you should see Gordon," said the Director nervously.

I opened the door.

"MR. TAYLOR!" the Director yelled.

I walked inside. Gordon was slouched over in a chair in front of a small table. His back was toward the door, so

I ran up to him and tapped him on the shoulder.

"Gordon?" I asked.

Gordon slowly turned around, and that's when I saw . . .

HIS MOUTH WAS NOW A COCKROACH MOUTH!

He looked up at me and his eyes filled with tears. He tried to talk, but his cockroach mouth just chattered and drooled a brown substance onto his karate uniform and mixed with the green snot stains from before. He smelled terrible.

"Gordon!" I yelled, and jumped back. I couldn't help it. My friend looked absolutely disgusting!

From the door, the Director called for me one more time.

"Mr. Taylor," he said, "I'm dreadfully sorry. The witches tried a few potions, but nothing worked. All we can do is keep him comfortable, and feed him garbage."

At the sound of the word "garbage," Gordon nodded his head enthusiastically and rubbed his stomach.

"I have to secure the crypt," I said. "I'll grab some garbage on my way back up."

Gordon gave me a thumbs-up.

I walked with the Director back out of the room and toward the stairs.

"There should be enough Parmesan chunks in that backpack for every resident and Nurse," I said. "I'll be back."

The Sussuroblats MUST DIE!

As the sun faded, everyone—monster and human alike—waited in the attic silently to see what would happen next. The residents clutched their chunks of Parmesan cheese as if they were the most precious things in the world. The Director paced continuously back and forth along the creaky attic floorboards. The Nurses tended to the residents that had been wounded in the last attack. Everyone looked upset and scared.

Ben, Gordon, Shane, and I were in Gordon's room. Gordon had just eaten some coffee grinds and a banana peel that I had brought up from the kitchen.

"Good stuff?" asked Shane.

Gordon gave a big thumbs-up and patted his belly.

"We'll need to take you to New York City," said Shane. "I hear that the garbage there is great!"

"We're not going to New York City!" I yelled. "Because we're going to kill those sussuroblats and get Gordon's mouth back!"

"Sorry," said Shane.

Ben had stuck his head out of the window to get some fresh air. He couldn't handle Gordon's smell, and I didn't think he or anyone else from school would hang with him much if the cockroach mouth became permanent. Ben pulled his head back into the room for a minute.

"Is it time?" he asked.

Shane looked at the time on his cell phone.

"One minute until sundown," he said.

Shane and I went over to the window to look out with Ben. It was eerily quiet as usual. I tilted my head up and looked to see the raven's nest at the top of the retirement home. One raven sat in the nest. It was looking to see what happened next, just like we were.

"And . . . sundown!" said Shane.

Off in the distance, the GRELCHing of the sussuroblats could be heard. At first it echoed faintly through the night, but soon it grew louder and louder.

"There!" yelled Shane, and he pointed down the road we had just come up. Sure enough, a handful of large, drooly cockroaches were on their way up the side of the hill.

"And there!" yelled Ben. His head was tilted all the

way to the right, and he was looking around the side of the building.

Butterflies bounced around in my stomach. I knew that this was the moment of truth—the moment we would see if our shield of cheese worked.

"GRELCH, GROOOOLCH, BLULCCHH!"

The sound of the sussuroblats was overwhelming. The grelching began to terrify the old monsters. I could hear stomping feet and squeals of panic through the door to Gordon's room. Gordon started panicking as well. His roach mouth let out little whispers of grelching and grolching.

"They're almost up to the Parmesan cheese that Ben and I laid down," said Shane.

I could see it from the attic window. My friends did a good job of laying the stuff down—too good of a job. All the cheese we had left now was the chunks that the old monsters were holding. The zombies had already eaten theirs.

"Look, one's run up front to check it out," Ben said.

There was a single sussuroblat—a really drooly one—that was now chewing into the protective ring of cheese.

At first, it sounded like he was enjoying it, almost like when they were dining on the zombie in the lobby. Then, its "yum yum" slurpy sounds turned to screeches of pain. Its lips burst into flames, and it screamed even louder, its drool unable to put out the flames no matter how hard it sputtered.

"YES!" Ben said. "It works!"

"Yeah," yelled Shane at the sussuroblats. "EAT THAT!"

Shane's remark angered the sussuroblats, and they all began to shout and grelch and snap their snaggleteeth even more. They were all close to the ring, but none of them would go over it. They just got angrier and angrier, snapping and screaming and spitting.

"All right!" I said, pulling my head back into the room from the window. "That's Phase One, gentlemen! We've secured the retirement home!"

"Phase One?" asked Ben. "What's Phase Two?"

"We've got to get Gordon's mouth back," I said. "And the only way to do that is to destroy every last sussuroblat."

"Ah, Chris . . ." Shane said. "We might have a problem."

"What is it?" I asked, and looked down.

"Over there . . ." Shane pointed. "It looks like all of the sussuroblats are gathering in one spot, and taking turns to . . . drool."

Dozens of sussuroblats spat huge juicy wads of drool and phlegm onto one section of the Parmesan ring that we had built.

"Their drool is going to wash it away!" I yelled.

I jumped away from the window again, and paced the room nervously.

"We have to think of a way to destroy these things!" I yelled. "I can't believe they're going to make it through the cheese! Maybe we do need to throw up buckets of barf after all. Or figure out another way to get butyric acid. From Mr. Stewart?"

"No," said Ben, "I think you knocked out his supply!"

"All right," I said. "We have to think of a way to create as much barf as possible. Quick, Ben, you're the expert. When you think about bucketloads of barf, what do you think?"

"Uhhh . . ." Ben started. "Cafeteria food. Speaking in front of people. Talking to girls. Eating too much ice cream. Brussels sprouts. The Gravitron . . ."

Suddenly, Ben's face lit up.

"The GRAVITRON!" Ben yelled. "Oh, man, I never barfed more than on the Gravitron! That would be perfect!"

"And we've got weekend passes from Karen," I yelled. "Let's get to the park!"

"I don't think we have time to get over to the Gravitron and back," said Shane. "Plus, I don't think there's any way we can get off of the hill without the sussuroblats noticing."

"No, we *need* the sussuroblats to notice," Ben said. "In fact, we need to lead the sussuroblats there. They're

157

the ones that need to go into the Gravitron. They're the ones that need to barf—all over themselves."

"Oh, man, that's genius," I said. "But how do we get them into the Gravitron? We could use some sort of bait, but . . ."

"But then they'd eat the bait," said Ben.

"Unless the bait could fly away," said Shane.

"What?" Ben and I said at the same time.

Shane took another peek outside of the window.

"It looks like we've got about five, maybe ten minutes at the most before our cheese barrier is broken," said Shane. "So we need to work fast."

Ben and I still had our hands up like *What?* Shane just kept on going.

"Follow me."

A Batty Plan

The old monsters were still panicked in the main section of the attic. They knew their doom was near. The ones that could stand up shuffled over to Shane and me as we met the Director.

"The line of defense?" asked the Director.

"It doesn't look good," I said.

The director nodded to the Nurses, and they started putting on their SWAT gear and unpacking different types of clubs.

"But we've got an idea," said Shane.

"Let's hear it," sighed the Director.

I could tell he thought Raven Hill was finished. A few more of the monsters shuffled over to listen. They still gripped their Parmesan cheese chunks.

"We're going to take the sussuroblats to the

Gravitron at Jackson Amusement Park," I said.

"You're trying to get them to vomit on themselves?" the Director asked.

"Exactly," I said.

"And how do you propose to get them there?" the Director asked.

Shane turned to the Director.

"We need to lure the sussuroblats into the Gravitron," said Shane. "But whoever we use as bait to draw them in would be eaten in seconds. So, we need one of the vampires to be the bait. They can turn into bats and fly away, right?"

Shane looked around to find the vampires. The three old vampires made their way over to us. Two of them held their heads down.

"No," one croaked. "It's too hard. Ve're too old."

The third stepped forward. Grigore.

"Vait," he said.

Grigore had a bizarre look on his face. He gritted his dentures and started concentrating. The veins popped out of his bald head. He grunted. With a POP, two bat wings sprang out of either side of his head. It was really quite ridiculous, but he didn't find it funny—in fact it seemed to startle him. He jumped back and let out a small "Huh?" before reaching up to his new headgear.

We kept staring, waiting, barely able to breathe.

"He's too old," said Ben. "He just doesn't have the power."

"VAIT!" growled Grigore. He shook his head violently, and the bat wings disappeared. He steadied himself, then took on the same look of concentration. He grunted even harder this time—turning a dark shade of red-purple. But it was starting to work! He shrank, his feet came up off the ground and disappeared into his body, his body shrank into his head, and this time the wings came out large and perfectly formed. His face grew hairy; his nose and his ears took on a pointy quality, and soon he was a small vampire bat, flapping in the middle of the room.

Shane held out his hand. The bat fluttered past Ben and me, and hung itself upside down on Shane's hand.

The bat squeaked a wheezy squeak. Upon closer inspection, I could see that his fur was gone in certain places. His ribcage, heaving from all of the hard work, could be seen clearly through what was left of his hair. He had a small hole on his left wing. Ben bent down and looked through it up to Shane.

The wheezy squeak took on a human quality.

"How's that?" squeaked Bat Grigore.

"Perfect!" I said. "Now, how do we get out of here?"

The two hairy old men stepped forward, along with

the monster that had been stitched together.

"We've got an idea," said the werewolf that had won bingo.

The two old werewolves transformed into their shabby dog forms and raced downstairs—they were filled with energy.

We followed.

RUN!!!

The old green stitched monster, the Director, Ben, Shane, the old werewolves, Grigore, and I gathered just in front of the porch. The sussuroblats were frantically slurping and drooling, and the cheese barrier neared its breaking point. The Nurses turned on the flood lamps and stood on the porch, clubs raised, in case any of the sussuroblats were able to make it over the barrier.

The old green monster stepped forward.

"I will zap them!" he screamed. "You run."

"Zap them?" I asked the Director.

"Frederick came to life thanks to a huge bolt of lightning," said the Director. "And he still retains a small charge that he can use from time to time. I've seen him power a smartphone, but I'm not sure how he intends to create a strong enough 'zap.' Nevertheless, you should get ready to run."

I turned to Grigore, who had changed back into vampire form.

"Are you ready to run?" I asked.

"Ready," he said. "Must. Destroy. These terrible creatures."

"Are you guys ready?" I asked, looking at Ben and Shane. "Do you have all of the cheese?"

"Yep," said Shane. "We collected it from the monsters in the attic."

"All right!" I yelled. "I'll help Grigore along. You guys toss the cheese behind us to slow them down."

The werewolves howled, and a few sussuroblats looked up at us.

The huge old green monster spread his legs apart, unsteady at first.

Then the werewolves began circling around each leg.

Faster and faster and faster.

I could hear a crackle and smell ozone in the air.

"Static electricity," I said, astonished.

"Well," Shane said, "there's one good thing about being a stinky old werewolf with a mangy, dry coat. Charging up monsters!"

Sure enough, the tall green monster began glowing. Brighter and brighter.

"Aaaaaarrrrggghhhh!" He let out a yell that shook the trees. The sussuroblats stopped for a moment.

And then . . .

CRACK!

A huge bolt of lightning blew a hole in the seething pile of sussuroblats, creating a path down the middle of the huge, stunned bugs.

"HURRY!" the old monster screamed, and then fell back onto the ground. The old werewolves licked his face and the Nurses ran down to help him.

"GO! Don't worry about him!" yelled the Director.

We ran through the sussuroblats.

Grigore was slower than I had hoped—I was practically pushing him along.

We hit the forest and headed down the dark, dark road.

Halfway down, we heard them.

BLARFFFF, BLLLLLLARBB, BLURBB!!!

Ben yelled, "They're right behind us!!!"

"Come on, Grigore," I yelled. "You've got to do better. They're going to suck you dry!"

We ran down to the bottom of the hill, and as we burst out of the twisty steep drive and onto the main street, the sussuroblats were practically on top of us.

We turned right and ran for our lives!

Shane and Ben began lobbing hunks of cheese behind us. Most were just bouncing off the drooling field of massive roaches with a small thump.

We ran and ran and ran.

They got so close that I could smell their disgusting breath.

GRELCH! GROLCHHH! BLARFFF! BLURRFF! BLAAAARRRR!

Shane lobbed one more chunk of cheese, and he must have thrown it right into the mouth of one of the sussuroblats, because it exploded with a POP like a squishy, thick water balloon.

"Wooo-hoo!" yelled Shane.

The other sussuroblats slowed down for a second to munch on their fallen friend. But not for long.

"Shoot!" Ben said. "They're still really close."

"Grigore," I yelled, "come on!"

We ran into Belle Aire, a quiet little neighborhood on the south side of town. Jackson Amusement Park was just on the other side.

"All right, lawn-mower master!" Shane yelled to me. "I know this neighborhood like the back of my hand from my paper route, and it's going to take us forever unless we can cut through it! Any smart ideas?"

I yelled, "The Joneses' backyard connects with the Forsythes's. And the Forsythes live on the same street as the park! Follow me!"

Ben threw the last chunk of cheese at the

sussuroblats, which were now just five feet behind us. Another sussuroblat exploded and the gruesome pack of drooly bugs slowed down once more. We were running as fast as we could, but we were still pretty far from the park, even with the shortcut.

We turned left, up the Joneses' driveway. We rushed around their garage and into their backyard.

The sussuroblats followed quickly.

We rushed through a gap in the bushes that lined the backyard, and burst into the Forsythes' backyard.

The sussuroblats slowed down even more as they scraped and scrambled their way through the bushes.

Within seconds, we were on Smith Street. We rushed down the street toward the park.

We were breathing heavily, and out of cheese. But we just had to push as hard as we could and get there.

Grigore was really struggling now as we made the last sprint down Smith Street.

"They're getting really close again," yelled Ben.

"We gotta move!" Shane yelled.

"Grigore," I yelled. "You've got to push it just a little harder."

He shook his head back and forth in an exhausted NO motion.

"We'll just have to pick him up," I said.

Shane, Ben, and I lifted Grigore up. He let out a surprised "Oof!"

"Go, go, go!" I yelled, and we burst forward with newfound speed.

We entered the huge amusement parking lot. Up ahead, we could see the entrance, the rides towering behind it.

The roaches were now only a few feet behind us. I looked over my shoulder to see their teeth flash in the dark.

Their teeth.

Teeth!

"Grigore," I yelled, "spit out your teeth!"

PLOP!

Out came the teeth. They clattered ahead of us toward the entrance for a moment, and then turned around.

ZOOM!

"Whoa!" Shane screeched, and jumped up to avoid the chattering fangs.

They shot behind us and out of the parking lot.

MUNCH, CRUNCH, GRIND!

The teeth made their way through the sussuroblats as they raced back to the retirement home and Grigore's coffin.

The sussuroblats stopped to munch on their wounded. This time, there were more tasty treats, but they were fast eaters—we had to rush.

We ran up to the entrance. We put Grigore down

and shoved our way to the front of the shortest line, annoying everyone.

"Hey!"

"Watch out!"

"What's the big rush?!"

"Old man coming through," Shane yelled. "Respect your elders, people!"

In the parking lot, the sussuroblats screamed and hissed—their snack break was finished.

I threw our passes in front of the sour-looking woman in the ticket booth, and didn't even wait for her to hand them back.

We ran into the amusement park.

"HEY!" she yelled. "Is that old guy okay? I'm not sure he should go on any rides."

We pushed our way through the crowd toward the Gravitron.

Behind us, we could hear screams at the entrance.

"That's disgusting!"

"Are those roaches?"

"I'm outta here!"

The sussuroblats had invaded Jackson Amusement Park.

We ran past the Ferris wheel. We ran past the Haunted House. As we did, a vampire jumped in front of us and yelled, "Welcome to my castle!"

"Vlad?" Grigore asked, confused. "Is that you?"

"Keep moving!" I yelled.

We ran past the bumper cars. The Gravitron loomed in front of us. It must have just finished a ride, because it spun slower and slower.

"Perfect timing," Shane said.

"Let's wait here," I said, panting. "We need to make sure the sussuroblats are right behind us. We have to make sure every last one of them follows us onto the Gravitron."

Shane walked toward the concession stand.

"Wait!" I yelled. "What are you doing?"

"Grabbing some cotton candy," he replied.

"WHAT?!" I screamed. "I said 'wait' not 'hang out.'"

"I don't know why you're so mad," said Shane, walking back. "Isn't cotton candy your favorite? I would have shared."

"I love all carnival food," I replied. "But *we'll* end up as carnival food if we don't stay on our toes."

"Tired," Grigore said. "I'm so tired."

"Just a little while longer, Grigore," Ben said.

Behind us, there was more screaming. We turned around to see the crowd run and the sussuroblats gather in front of us.

"Goooooooo!" I yelled, but Grigore stayed put.

"I . . . just . . . can't," he gasped. "Barely have enough energy to be a bat."

"Grab him!" I yelled.

We snatched Grigore up and ran as fast as we could. As we approached the Gravitron, riders were stumbling off, giggling. And helping them off was . . .

"Karen!" yelled Ben.

Karen, Ben's older sister, was working at the Gravitron!

"Karen!" Ben yelled again. "KAAAARENNN! Don't let anyone else on. WAIIIIIT!"

We jumped into the line, carrying Grigore along with us. We shoved and pushed our way past everyone.

"Hey, no cutting!"

"Ugh, that old man smells terrible!"

"What are you doing?"

We made our way to the front of the line.

"BEN!" Karen screeched. "What are you doing?! I can't just let you cut. Who is that old bum?"

"Hey," said a short, angry girl at the front of the line. "I've been in this line FOREVER!"

Her unibrow furrowed and she gave us an angry scowl.

"Trust me," said Shane, "you are not going to want to get on this ride."

There were more screams, and the kids who were yelling at us just seconds before abandoned the line. The sussuroblats had almost reached us.

"We need to get on NOW!" I yelled.

"I'll explain later," said Ben to his sister, "but you

have to trust me! And make sure all of them are in before you close the door."

"What?" she asked.

But there was no time for any more explanations.

We pulled Grigore into the Gravitron and got as far from the door as we could.

"Grigore," Shane asked as we put the old vampire down, "are you still able to transform?"

The sussuroblats poured through the door, snarling, scuttling, and drooling over one another. They headed straight for the old vampire. Ben, Shane, and I jumped out of the way, hoping that Grigore could make the transformation happen.

Grigore scrunched up his face, grunted, and was able to POP into a bat just as the sussuroblats lunged at him. He fluttered to the center of the Gravitron, and all of the sussuroblats followed, snapping their snaggleteeth hungrily.

The doors closed and Ben, Shane, and I strapped ourselves against the wall.

The monster roaches hissed and snarled at the bat that teased them. Bat Grigore flew just above their drooly mouths, and then shot up higher if any of them pounced. A few sussuroblats tried to scurry over to us, but Grigore would quickly draw them back to the pile by flying right in front of their faces.

The ride slowly started turning. At first, the

sussuroblats didn't notice. When the turning quickened, the sussuroblats were pulled slowly from the center. As much as they scurried and scraped to stay in the center and snap at the bat, they all ended up pressed against the wall. Some had their backs against the wall, their legs flailing wildly.

The Gravitron spun faster and faster and faster.

"Oh, man!" yelled Ben. "Oh, maaaaarrrrrrffff!"

Ben spewed the juicy contents of his stomach all over the two sussuroblats closest to him.

They started to sizzle and smoke.

Shane and I were next, barfing in almost perfect unison. The sussuroblats that had slid over to us began to melt. I'd never been happier to lose my lunch, and only wish I had eaten more before coming to Raven Hill.

The sussuroblats' screams turned to whimpers as they realized what was happening.

Then their whimpers turned to gagging.

They were getting sick!

BAAAAAARRRRRFFFF! BLUUURRP! BLAAAAP!

The sussuroblats were barfing all over themselves—and us!

Huge, drooly wads of barf flew around in the Gravitron. Brown barf. Green barf. Bucketloads of barf.

And the barf melted any sussuroblat it touched.

The Gravitron slowed down, and the barf oozed into the center. The sussuroblats that had survived the barf-splosion rolled into the center and were eaten alive by the barf puddle.

Up above, Bat Grigore giggled and let out a wheezy, "YES!"

Steam rose up from the pile of barf and roach parts. Popping and sizzling, every last sussuroblat was coming to a disgustingly stinky end in the Gravitron.

The Gravitron stopped, and we unstrapped our barf-soaked bodies from the wall.

We could hear Karen call out, "Now get out of there!"

She poked her head in and gagged out the words "What . . . happened . . . in here?!"

We stumbled out of the Gravitron, past Ben's sister, and out into the fresh air.

The few kids who hadn't been scared out of the line by the sussuroblats took one look at us and ran.

"Aw, man!" someone called out. "They turned it into a *Barfitron*. GROSS."

"You guys smell absolutely terrible!" Karen said, holding her nose. "Where did those massive roaches go? Why did you want them in there with you? What happened to that old man?"

A small bat fluttered out of the open Gravitron door and circled Karen's head with a squeak before heading off to Raven Hill. She let out a squeal.

"There he is," said Shane. "Safe and sound."

"BEN!!!" she screamed. "I need answers. NOW."

"Sis," he said slowly, swaying on his feet, "I'll tell you everything, I promise. I just need a minute to pull myself together here."

Ben gagged a little, still overwhelmed by the wild ride.

"And you guys?!" she asked. "What do you have to say for yourselves? What just happened here?"

"Look, it's a little complicated," started Shane, "but . . ."

Shane was interrupted by a hiss coming from the open door. One sussuroblat, smoking, but still very much alive, scurried out of the door and to the top of the Gravitron. It let out an angry GRELCH.

"What IS that thing?" asked Karen, a disgusted look on her face.

The sussuroblat turned toward Karen—and jumped right toward her face!

She screamed. Shane and I froze.

Ben steadied himself, opened his mouth, and . . .

WHHHHAARRRRFFFFF!

He spewed all over the sussuroblat . . . and Karen . . . knocking them both backward. The sussuroblat was good and dead by the time it hit Karen's face.

"Oh, man, now that's *talent*," Shane screamed, and gave Ben a high five. Ben smiled and promptly passed out.

Shane laid Ben out on a bench while I reached down to help Karen up. Once she was on her feet, I grabbed the melted sussuroblat at her feet and tossed it back in the Gravitron.

"Oh, MAN!" Karen said. "I think I'm having a nightmare. I should get janitorial to clean this mess up."

She held a walkie-talkie up to her mouth and was about to press the button.

"WAIT!" I said as I grabbed the radio. "I'm not sure that would be a good idea."

"Where are the cleaning supplies?" asked Shane.

Karen pointed past the entrance to the Log Flume to a shack.

"We'll explain everything while we help you clean the Gravitron," I said.

All's Well That Ends . . . Uh-oh

That night, we returned to Raven Hill and found Gordon back to his old, nonbuggy self.

"Took ya long enough," he said.

Leave it to Gordon to insult us for our hard work. I was just happy to hear words coming out of his normal, human mouth.

The Director looked truly happy when he saw us.

"Gentlemen, you did an amazing job," he said. "I can't thank you enough."

The Nurses all came around and shook our hands. By the last shake, our hands were practically crushed.

"Well," I said, "we couldn't have done it without everyone's help."

And it was true. If it weren't for these kooky old monsters coming through in the last minute, our plan would have failed miserably!

"Just wait until I tell the other Directors about you!" beamed the Director.

"Other Directors?" Ben asked.

"We're not the only facility," said the Director. "There are many, many more around the world. There are a lot of residents to tend to, but everyone will be getting a boost of energy with the demise of that sussuroblat pack!"

After the Battle of Raven Hill, Ben, Shane, Gordon, and I came back to volunteer at the home.

Shane continued training the residents in karate.

Gordon helped the Nurses with out-of-control monsters when they needed someone who was quicker on his feet.

Ben's trivia night was the highlight of the week, and he was slowly building up a tolerance to all the funky smells found at Raven Hill.

I worked closely with the Director on special assignments.

It seemed our lebensplasm really was helping the monsters along! As their monster juice was replenished, they all got a little stronger and a little less demented. Except for the zombies. They'd be forever brainless.

Although they still got along great with Shane.

One night, about two weeks after the battle, I was rewrapping a mummy in its pyramid-shaped room.

The Director knocked and entered the room.

"Hi, Director," I said. "I'm almost wrapped up here," I said.

"Actually, I'm the one who's wrapped up," said the mummy.

The Director and I laughed.

"What's up?" I said.

"This is what is 'up,'" the Director said. "I wanted to thank you. I realize that it was a group effort, but we really couldn't have done it without your leadership. Anyone else would have shied away from such a massive task. You took it on without question. Just as we always knew you would."

"What do you mean, you always knew I would?" I asked.

"Perhaps I should let someone else explain," the Director said, and he motioned toward the door for someone to come in.

Rio Vista's lunch lady walked into the room.

"Huh?" I said.

"Hi, Chrees!" she said, and gave me a big hug as if she knew me.

She squeezed me hard. I was completely confused.

"We always knew you had sometheeng special een

you," she said. "Your lebensplasm is strong, you are so smart, and you never brag. You see, I keep an eye out for keeds like you at Rio Vista—keeds who can help Raven Hill out. If there's a keed I think can help, I whip up a special concoction and feed it to them."

"It was her concoction," the Director continued, "along with the volunteer letter that she planted, that drew you to Raven Hill. That combination gave you the feeling that you should help us. Do you remember how angry I was when you snooped around our home? That was never supposed to happen! But that was really the only snag. You were merely supposed to strengthen the residents before the attack happened."

"Wait!" I asked, my stomach suddenly upset. "What *did* you put in my food that first day?"

"It was quite seemple, really," said the lunch lady. "In order to prepare you to do battle with thee sussuroblats . . ."

The lunch lady paused.

"Go on," I said.

"I ground up a few sussuroblats, and put those een your hamburger on thee first day of school."

The Blandburger! That weird crunch! The nasty yellow wad. That funky taste. It was a sussuroburger the whole time!

The room spun around me.

"A sussuroburger," I moaned. "You fed me a sussuroburger?!"

"What's thee problem?" the lunch lady asked. "It's a low-fat protein source."

"It was quite harmless, I assure you, at least once its initial effects wore off," said the Director. "And very necessary to prepare you for our world. I hope you don't take offense."

I stood there for a minute, not sure if I should run . . . or barf. I was disgusted, but I was also proud that I had been chosen. I had so many questions.

"What about the sussuroblat that attacked the day I told my friends about Raven Hill?" I asked her. "I thought for sure the Director had sent one along to get me."

"That was a deeversion I created," the lunch lady said. "We had just gotten word the sussuroblat army would come that day. I was so happy that you were goeeng to bring friends to fight, and I wanted you to have privacy when you told them. We can't have everyone know Raven Heel's secret, can we? So, I cleared out the lunchroom!"

"Of course," said the Director, "you thought you were fighting the residents of Raven Hill—but your timing couldn't have been better. You were ready to fight something, and fight bravely you did!"

"Thank you for that, Chrees!" shrieked Lunch Lady.

She gave me one more tight hug and left.

"That must have been difficult for you," said the Director.

"Not as difficult as the Gravitron," I said.

"Nevertheless, I have something for your troubles," said the Director.

The Director waved a Nurse in. I think it was Nurse Inx. It was so hard to tell.

The Nurse was holding a package, wrapped up in old newspaper with a silver bow on the top.

"Wow!" I said. "What is it?"

I ripped off one section of paper and saw a lens pointed at the sky. A telescope! Finally, after all of this, my dream had come true! I thought I'd never, ever see the telescope once I paid for all of the Parmesan! I quickly forgot about the sussuroburger.

"That's amazing!" I said, and finished tearing open the package.

"I hope it's what you were looking for," said the Director. "I heard from your friends that it would be the best gift for you."

It wasn't the TRQ92 Super Infinity Space Gazer. It was the TRQ2000—the top-of-the-line model!

"Oh, man!" I said. "This is great. Thank you, Director."

"Call me Zachary," said Zachary.

"How about Director Z?" I asked.

"As you wish," Director Z said. "There's just one small condition for keeping the telescope."

"What's that?" I asked.

"I need you to keep an eye on the sky," he said, suddenly serious.

"Why?" I asked.

"Because the next batch of supermonsters could come from anywhere. We'll need you and the other gentlemen to be on watch. This was just one battle. But we still have to win the worldwide war on these vile new creatures that are after the residents. We will need your help again."

"You can count us in!" I said.

Ben, Shane, Gordon, and I kept volunteering at Raven Hill, and we went about school as if everything was normal. But we knew we could be called into action at any moment.

What monster juice-drinking evil would come next?

MONSTER JUICE

Fartsunami

by M. D. Payne

Grosset & Dunlap
An Imprint of Penguin Group (USA) LLC

To Major Payne and Mummy,
for all their love and farts

Prologue

The fat man in the suit fell to the floor, writhing and drooling.

"*Der Schmerz!*" he moaned in his native tongue. "*Nein! Ich kann es nicht kämpfen . . .*"

His assistants—even larger, almost identical men—rushed into the man's office. They were dressed in casual tropical clothes.

He kicked wildly as he fought his invisible attacker. His huge figure shimmied and shook. He knocked over a lamp that smashed into his aquarium, spilling piranhas onto the plush carpet. They flopped around wildly, splashing in the thin layer of water that was left. The fish bounced over to the writhing man,

189

and bit his twitching body.

CRUNCH. CRUNCH. CRUNCH.

But the crunch wasn't the sound of the man's flesh—it was the sound of the piranhas' teeth shattering!

The assistants kicked the piranhas off of their boss and bent down to help him up. Sweat poured down his contorted face.

"Aaaaaahhhhhhhh!" he moaned.

It was hot in the room—as if the air-conditioning had failed.

"The window," said one of his assistants, "is open."

"Close it," said the other. "Now!"

He jumped up to do so, when a large sucking noise stopped him in his tracks.

The sound came from the man.

SLLLLLLUUUUUUUUUUUPPPPPPPPPPP!

The suited man twitched a few more times . . .

SLLLLUUUUUPPP!

Gave one final yawp . . .

ZLIP!

And then he farted an intensely long, loud fart. After it stopped, he coughed violently, and then passed out, his head bonking onto the floor.

The two assistants quickly moved to cover their noses and waited for a great stench.

It never came.

The suited man snored with a look of contentment on his face.

The two assistants stared at each other, not sure what to do.

The one near the window slammed it down forcefully, locking out the hot, salty air.

Then, both assistants carefully picked up their boss and brought him to the infirmary.

Once he was placed on the table, the ancient witch doctor looked him over carefully from head to toe. He burned incense. He applied jungle leeches. He mumbled spells. He shook his staff angrily.

The boss-man's assistants wrung their hands, not knowing how to help.

"Is he okay?" asked one.

"Do you know what's happened to him?" asked the other.

The witch doctor scratched his head.

"A thing like this, I have never seen," he said in a deep and otherworldly voice. "He seems normal—healthy, even—but, alas, my leeches cannot dine upon his blood." He lifted one of the slimy black slugs to his ear. "They say that it's as if something has enveloped his body, but I see nothing. Very, very distressed I am. I will raise a few spirits tonight to see what they have to say about this."

"What can we do?" one assistant asked.

"Rest, he must," said the witch doctor. "Take him to his bed and keep your eyes on him."

The two assistants carried out the witch doctor's orders. Despite the fact that neither leeches nor piranhas could make a mark on their boss's skin, they made sure to close his netting. No vampire mosquitoes or zombie frogs could dine on him in the night.

They stood watch, but all their boss did was snore, and occasionally giggle. Outside, the jungle seethed with the sound of mysterious creatures.

In the morning, as the first light crept in through the window, their boss awoke, refreshed and renewed.

"Gentlemen," he chortled with glee. "Vhy are you in my bedroom? Are you afraid ze mermaids vill call you out to sea again?"

"Boss," one asked, "don't you remember what happened last night?"

"Vell," he said as he scratched his head, "I vas reading ze latest numbers on ze residents' lebensplasm . . ."

"And?" the other assistant asked, leaning in.

"Vell . . ." the boss said, "I can't remember. Ze next sing I do remember is vaking up here."

"How do you feel?" asked one assistant.

"Amazing!" he said. "Und I've had ze most vonderful idea!"

"What's that?" they asked in unison.

He jumped out of bed, his suit still perfectly crisp,

his leather shoes shining. The room shook and his huge jowls jiggled as he landed on the floor.

"I haff to make a very important phone call," he said.

"Boss?"

"BOSS!?!"

But, in a flash, the boss had swung the door open and run down the hall.

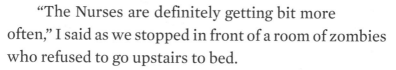

Dirty Work

My friends and I survived another very long day of helping out at Raven Hill Retirement Home. I sluggishly pushed my way past a few residents and out of the Great Room. Shane, Ben, and Gordon stumbled out after me. We had just cleaned up after a huge—and messy—Sunday dinner.

"It's really, really hard to feed the old monsters now that they're stronger," I said.

"Nobody got bit today, did they?" asked Ben.

"The Nurses are definitely getting bit more often," I said as we stopped in front of a room of zombies who refused to go upstairs to bed.

"Why don't the Nurses ever become monsters?" asked Gordon.

We all shrugged, too tired to care.

Three identical Nurses—huge, bulky gentlemen in one-size-too-small uniforms—struggled to get the residents out of the room and upstairs to bed.

"Hey!" one of the Nurses yelled as a wrinkled old zombie knocked him over.

The zombie playfully chewed on the small hat perched on top of the Nurse's swollen, red head. The other old zombies giggled.

"Not funny!" warned the Nurse, who jumped back up to his feet with a THUD.

The three Nurses were finally able to wrangle the residents out of the room and past us.

Once the zombies were out of the way, we shuffled past the room of old witches, who were, as always, cackling away over a special bedtime brew. We dragged our tired legs down the hallway, over the holey, moth eaten rug.

"I was wondering how the holes got so huge," Ben said, and pointed at a figure hidden in the alcove.

Shane smiled and waved at the figure.

Moth Man, cheerily picking carpet fibers from his blackened, slimy teeth, waved back.

"Hurry up and eat the dusty old thing," said Ben. "It's giving me allergies!"

We slunk into the lobby and past the portrait of Lucinda B. Smythe. Even she looked happy tonight as she watched us walk past.

Everyone was happy at Raven Hill. Everyone but us.

"I think I might be officially done with Raven Hill," huffed Gordon. "This has stopped being a good time."

"I feel like they don't need our help anymore," I said as I opened the door and headed for freedom.

"Oh, but I can assure you that they do, Mr. Taylor," came a voice from behind us that stopped us in our tracks.

We turned. Director Z, the man in charge of Raven Hill, stood in the center of the foyer with his hands behind his back. His crisp and perfectly pressed suit gleamed from the dull light of the old, cobwebby chandelier above him. He took a few steps toward us.

"If it weren't for you gentlemen," Director Z said, "this facility and its residents would most certainly have been obliterated from the face of the Earth."

"Well, thanks for reminding us," said Gordon as he turned back to the door. "Those were some great times. Some real roach-killin' times. But, I've got practice at five a.m., and I need to get some sleep."

Gordon slipped out into the cold December air and slammed the door behind him. The creaky old house shook for a few seconds.

"If the rest of you gentlemen could spare just one

more moment," Director Z pleaded, "there's a lot to take care of before you leave for your big trip."

"Director Z!" I pleaded back. "We're exhausted! We've been here all day. We've been working so hard."

"And that is precisely the reason that everyone is doing so well!" he said. He paused for a moment and looked me straight in the eye. "Those poor old souls need you. I really wish you weren't leaving on Tuesday."

"Allll riiiight," I said, caving in once again. "What is it?"

He brought his hands out from behind his back.

He held a plunger, liquid clog remover, and a shiny metallic bag.

"We really need your help with the werewolves' bathroom," he said.

"Yeah, maybe I have practice, too," said Ben. "I'm not sure if I can smell that much wet dog without barfing."

I looked at Shane. He nodded. Ben headed home.

"All right, we're on it," I said.

Can you believe this?" I hissed as we entered the werewolves' room. "They're totally taking advantage of us! After *we* saved them from the sussuroblats, they should be waiting on us!"

"Oh come on, they're just a bunch of helpless old people," said Shane. "Remember what kind of mess this place was before we got here."

"They seem strong enough to be on their own," I said. "I mean, what did they do before we came along?"

"Before we got here, bugs were guzzling their juices . . . and who knows what's out there now, just waiting to suck it all up," Shane said.

"Well, they're gonna have to get along without us," I said. "I don't care if Director Z begs and pleads for us to stay, I'm not missing the science-class field trip. Not for *anything*."

"Ah, sunny Florida," Shane said with a smile. "A little sun. Palm trees. Sand between my toes. Florida's still really warm this time of year."

"Dude!" I yelled, "This isn't spring break. We're not going to waste our time on the beach! This trip is all about Kennedy Space Center. The astronaut training program. Getting to *touch* a moon rock. Meeting a real-life astronaut! The only sun I get will be on the Gemini launchpad. I'm soaking up every bit of cosmic information I can."

"But my mom just bought me new swim trunks," Shane added as I stormed into the bathroom. "They have surfing sharks on them."

This Could Get Hairy

Ben was right. The room smelled like wet dog. The funkiest, moldiest wet dog ever. There were other smells too, but I didn't want to think about where they'd come from.

"Next time, I'm not giving them any extra doggie treats," Shane grumbled.

Every surface was covered in hair. On the sink. On the floor. In the bathtub. Probably the ceiling, too. I didn't dare look up. The worst of all was the toilet. It was completely clogged. Wads of hair and shaving cream floated in the gloopy water. A razor and a bottle of shaving cream sat on the rim of the toilet. Both were completely covered in hair.

"Wow," I said, "I guess they shave with toilet water."

Shane peeked into the sink. "Nope," he said. "They clogged the sink, too. I guess they just switched to the toilet after that, those dirty dogs."

"I'll never figure out why they bother to shave," I said. "I mean, it's gonna grow back!"

"I think they like to look fresh for the ladies," said Shane. "Pietro told me he had the hots for Clarice, the banshee."

"A werewolf and a banshee?" I asked. "Can they do that?"

Shane turned from the sink. "Who are you to say that two people—or geriatric monsters—can't fall in love?"

"You have a point, but we should still show Clarice this bathroom and save her some trouble," I snickered.

Shane shook his head. "Where should we start?" he asked.

After cleaning the hair off the floor and around the sink, we stuffed it all in the bag that the Director had given us. It was going pretty quickly.

Then we started on the toilet.

Shane was plunging like a madman as the moon rose and shone through the bathroom window.

"I think I'm getting it," he said. "The water's going down!"

"Dude," I said. "That's only because you're getting it all over our shoes."

"Ugh!" he yelled.

He let the plunger go.

But it kept plunging.

"Huh?" Shane gasped, and he turned to me.

It bounced and splashed around, and a growling sound bubbled up from the toilet.

Gurrble, Grrrble, Burrbble!

"Grab the plunger!" I screamed. "Plunge whatever it is out of here."

Shane and I grasped for the handle, but I couldn't hang on. It bounced around and . . .

FWACK!

The handle hit me right on the head. I stumbled back and hit the cold tiles with an *"OOF."*

Shane still had a good grip. He plunged with all his might. Pulling back, the plunger came out of the toilet with a FLOOP. Shane hit the floor, butt-first, right next to me.

"Is the water going down?" I croaked.

"Let me see," Shane said. He fumbled back up on his feet, and peered into the toilet.

The toilet started to shake and vibrate.

GURRRBLE, GRRRRR, BURRBBLE!

"I can't tell if the water is going down, but something is definitely coming up!" he said, and started to back away from the bowl.

Before we could skitter out of the room, the toilet

exploded all over Shane. He was completely covered in wet brown goo.

He turned to me, his eyes squeezed shut, and said, while trying to keep his mouth closed, "Please tell me this isn't what I think it is."

"Most of it isn't," I replied, trying to sound encouraging.

Shane stood frozen in disgust as the brown goo dripped down his body and piled up on his feet.

It formed the largest, nastiest wad of goopy hair I'd ever laid eyes on.

"Open your eyes," I said. "You have to see this."

"What!?" Shane yelled as he pried open his eyes.

We stared at the wet werewolf hair wad growing on the floor.

"Well, this is something new," he said. "It's a furwad!"

"Hairwad," I insisted. "Unless they were shaving in werewolf form."

"Are you sure," Shane continued. "I think—"

The hairwad shook violently and growled a low, angry growl.

"Forget it! The liquid clog remover!" I yelled.

Shane bent over quick, grabbed the liquid clog remover, and poured it all over the hairwad.

There was a whimper and squeal as the hair broke up and got sucked down the drain on the floor.

"Whew!" I said, and high-fived Shane. "Well done, man!"

That's when we noticed something crawling out of the sink.

"GRRRRRRRR!"

"Um, Shane?" I asked, "Did you happen to save any of that clog remover?"

"Sadly," said Shane, "no."

The hairwad slowly crept out of the sink. It flopped onto the cold, hard bathroom floor. It headed toward us, leaving behind a slimy, watery trail.

"Any bright ideas?" asked Shane.

"Um . . . uh . . ." My brain froze as the hairwad inched closer, growling all the way.

And then the hairwad pounced. It jumped amazingly high—right toward my face.

"Ah!" I yelled, and grabbed the hairwad.

It writhed and spat and growled. It smelled terrible. I couldn't see any claws, teeth, or even a mouth, but I had little doubt that it could hurt me. I struggled to hold it as far away from my face as possible.

"Hold on!" said Shane, and he waved the mysterious metallic bag in front of me. "Can you get it in here? It doesn't seem like the hair we put in earlier is doing anything."

I looked through the bathroom window and saw the moon. Suddenly everything clicked.

"Of course," I yelled. "The hair is freaking out because of the moon. This must be a silver bag. It blocks moon rays!"

"Thanks for the mad-science lesson," Shane said as he tried to position the bag under the struggling hairwad.

As I pushed the hair down toward the bag, it started whimpering like a puppy.

"Don't listen to it!" yelled Shane.

I forced the quivering, growling hair in the bag. It began to shake violently and . . .

SILENCE.

Shane quickly tied up the bag and glanced over to the sink. It was empty.

"The hair must have unclogged itself," Shane said.

"It's about time the monsters cleaned up after themselves," I snickered.

"Speaking of cleaning up," Shane said, "I'm desperate for a shower."

We headed out of Raven Hill, and the smell of wet werewolf, and worse, followed us all the way home.

We Gotta Get Outta This Place

"Can you believe Director Z made us clean the werewolf bathroom?" I groaned as I poked at the Mac 'n' Sneeze on my plate.

"You're forgetting to speak in code," said Ben, peering nervously around the cafeteria.

"Oh right," I said, lowering my voice a little. "Can you believe *the guy* who runs *the place* at the *top of the hill* made us clean *the place* where *the hairy dog men* go *potty*?"

"Yes," said Gordon, "I can believe it. That's why I left."

"How *was* practice?" Shane asked Gordon.

"Just like the Mac 'n' Sneeze today," said
Gordon. "TERRIBLE."

"Yeah, it does taste a little funky," agreed Shane. "Almost fishy."

Gordon stretched his neck and his bones cracked.

"I just couldn't loosen up," he continued. "I felt like a zombie."

"Billy and the other zombies might disagree," Ben said, "but I totally know what you mean."

"Dude, the code," I mocked Ben.

"Arrggh," Ben said, "You're right. *Random* zombies might disagree."

"Maybe we should just stop saying the word 'zombie.'" said Shane. "Oh, wait. I said it again."

"Where were you this morning?" I asked Shane. "I texted you twenty times! You were supposed to help me figure out our itinerary for Kennedy Space Center. We have to make sure we can see everything. There's a lot of stuff to do, and we're only there for a week, and we already have one whole day filled with astronaut training, and—"

"Yawn," said Gordon, which made Ben yawn. "Boooooring."

"Yawn!?" I screeched. "Guys, this is the closest we'll ever get to space! Aren't you excited?"

"Actually," said Gordon, "this is the closest we'll get to Cocoa Beach—home of Ron Jon Surf Shop. Do you think Mr. Stewart will take us?"

"Since when are you a surfer?" I asked.

"I keep up on all sports, even the extreme ones," Gordon said with a smile.

"I know Shane's excited about getting some sun," I said. "What about you, Ben?"

"I'm just worried about barfing on the plane. This is the first time I've ever flown anywhere. Speaking of barf, did the hairwads from *the hairy dog men* smell?" asked Ben. "I bet they smelled."

"Terribly!" I gagged. "You were right—you wouldn't have been able to make it very long without spewing."

"At least it wasn't as bad as *the fishy old man from the swamp's* gas," Shane said. "I wonder what his bathroom looks like these days."

"Who?" asked Gordon.

"Gil," whispered Shane.

"The cooooooooode," whispered Ben, even more quietly.

"Yeah, his farts are insanely nasty," I said. "That was a great idea you had to just cork his butt, Ben. Which reminds me—where is the cork?"

"I think it's still in my bag," Shane said. "But that doesn't mean it's my turn to plug him up. It's definitely your turn next time. The last time my thumb slipped and—"

"AHEM!"

The "AHEM" came from behind me, and I turned around to see . . .

THE LUNCH LADY.

Ben choked on his Mac 'n' Sneeze. Shane and Gordon both looked in different directions.

Lunch Lady and I locked eyes.

She had only spoken to me once before—at Raven Hill, after my friends and I saved the old monsters there from the disgusting cat-size cockroach creatures known as sussuroblats. They had been draining the monsters of their lebensplasm, as Director Z liked to call it—or "monster juice," as we liked to call it.

She had surprised me with the news that she worked with Director Z and his Nurses to keep an eye on the kids at Rio Vista Middle School. When she found a kid that might be able to help out at the home, she whipped up a special bit of food that, once eaten, led them to Raven Hill.

So far, I'm the only person who's ever gotten to taste her Raven Hill recipes.

"May I have a word weeth you?" she asked.

"Aren't you . . . ?" I looked over at the line of students waiting at the hot-lunch counter.

"Busy?" she finished my sentence. "Not at all."

A Nurse—not the school nurse, but one of the Nurses from Raven Hill—slid into place behind the hot-lunch counter. His big beefy arms were better at detaining demented monsters than doling out scoops of food. He was practically cracking the platters as he brought the scooper down.

"Come weeth me," she said.

We walked out of the cafeteria and into the hall. I didn't say anything, and just let Lunch Lady lead me down the math and science wing, straight into . . .

"Mr. Stewart's office?" I asked.

We stood in the middle of my chemistry teacher's room.

"Does he work for Raven Hill, too?" I asked.

"No," said Lunch Lady. "But the laboratory in the back is soundproof, and that's where he spends his entire lunch. So we won't be heard here."

"Oh," I said, a little disappointed.

She shut the door and glared at me.

"What are you gentlemen do-eeng?" she asked. "Are you out of your minds?"

"I'm sorry, I—" I started to say.

"Don't know what you mean?" she finished my sentence . . . again. "Yes, well, that's thee problem. You guys don't even realize how much you've been blabbing about Raven Heell. You're acting like workeeng een a retirement home for monsters iss perfectly normal. I just heard you talkeeng about werewolf hair theengies . . ."

"Hairwads," I interrupted her this time.

". . . all the way over at my counter. What iff students started leesteneeng een to your conversations?"

"So what?" I said, suddenly angry. "They'll just think we're talking about some crazy video game. We need to get this stuff off of our chest—Director Z and the Nurses have been working us way too hard. We don't even know what we're saying anymore!" I knew I was whining, but I couldn't help it. "When we agreed to help out at Raven Hill, we all thought it would be an adventure. We thought we'd get to know more about the monsters, maybe learn more about their secret powers. It was awesome when we were battling evil cockroaches together. Now it feels like they're just using us to cook and clean—while they get stronger and angrier."

"Yeah, well, you better keep your tongue at school, or I might feed you sometheeng that will make you mute," she said, wagging a finger at me.

"Fine," I said. "But since you're spying on me, tell Director Z that once we're gone, he'll see that the monsters can take care of themselves."

The bell rang, and lunch was over.

Lunch Lady opened up Mr. Stewart's door and headed back to the cafeteria. I followed her.

She was right. We *were* talking about Raven Hill constantly. But it was hard not to. They were just driving us crazy—and it would *never* be anything but crazy at Raven Hill. I desperately needed a break from the madness, the sleepless nights, the annoying grunts and moans.

I returned to my friends and my Mac 'n' Sneeze.

"I wish we were leaving for the trip right now," I said, and laid my head on the table.

Strange Visitors

That night, as usual, we slowly rode our bikes up the windy, overgrown road to the top of Raven Hill.

The ravens circled above us. One cawed.

"It's nice to see you again, too, Balfor," I said.

"Don't lie to the nice raven," said Shane.

Balfor landed on the nest on the tallest spire of Raven Hill and cocked his head strangely. "What is it?" I asked Balfor, and turned around.

Speeding up the hill was a man in a crisp, pressed suit very much like Director Z's. But unlike the skinny and gaunt Director Z, this gentleman was plump with a well-tanned face. His huge mustache bristled as he approached us. He stormed right up to me,

211

grabbed me by my jacket, and pulled me up so fast that I lost my breath.

"Hey!" I squeaked.

His face turned from deep tan to red.

"Vhat are you kids doing up here? Spying on zese poor old folks?" he demanded.

"No," I pleaded, trying to shake free of his swollen hands. "We're here to help."

"What are *we* doing?" Gordon yelled as he jumped up to grab me. "What are *you* doing? Who are you? Put him down!"

The plump man ignored Gordon and turned around to yell down the road, "Vell, vould you hurry it up! Ve seem to be haffing an issue here!"

Two identical figures lumbered up the side of the hill. They were huge—the ground shook as they huffed and puffed their way up to where we stood.

"Wait," Shane said. "Those guys look like Nurses!"

They were Nurses, although strangely, they didn't have on the usual white Nurses' uniforms. These two wore Bermuda shorts and colorful Hawaiian shirts.

Shane ran down to meet them.

"Hey, guys! Can you help us with this maniac?!" Shane yelled.

The two Nurses charged up to Shane—and pushed him into the dirt!

"This is crazy!" yelled Ben, and he ran into the retirement home to get help.

Shane jumped up and assumed a karate fighting position, but the Nurses had already passed him by. They easily dragged Gordon off me, and then yanked me from the hands of the plump man.

The well-dressed gentleman loomed over us and cracked his chunky knuckles.

"I vill ask you again," he said. "Vhat are you kids doing up here?"

Shane yelled as he reached us, "Don't you dare hurt them."

He paused nervously in front of the gentleman, not quite sure what to do.

Gordon and I squirmed, but the Tropical Nurses were strong. We weren't going anywhere.

"Who are you?" Shane demanded.

The mustached gentleman eyed us with caution and said, slowly, "I'm ze Direktor."

He leaned in closer to me. I could smell his breath as he said, "And I vant to know vhat you're up to here."

Shane ran at the Direktor, when . . .

"GENTLEMEN!"

A booming voice from the retirement home stopped everyone.

We looked up to see Director Z calmly walking down the stairs, followed by a twitchy Ben.

"I believe there's been a huge misunderstanding," Director Z said calmly.

He walked toward us and stuck out his hand.

"Herr Direktor Detlef, it's been quite a long time," he said.

"Director Zachary!" he yelled back. "It's quite good to see you!"

He grabbed Director Z and hugged him so hard that we heard bones snap.

"Yes, quite good," said Director Z, rubbing his side with a grimace. "Now, what seems to be the trouble with my associates?"

"*Your* associates?" Herr Direktor Detlef gasped. "Oh, zese must be ze *children* zat saved your facility—of course."

He waved at the Tropical Nurses to let Gordon and me go. Shane stood down.

"I'm so very sorry," Herr Direktor Detlef said.

He and the Tropical Nurses gave each of us a hand-crushing handshake as we introduced ourselves.

"Here I vas sinking you were spying on ze facility." He laughed. "And it is you who have saved it. Vait until I tell everyone at ze facility back home."

"My pleasure," I said, as I cradled my crushed hand.

"Well, then," Director Z said, "we don't have any more time for introductions, as I've gathered all the residents for a briefing, and they grow weary. What took you so long, Herr Direktor?"

"Ve parked at ze bottom of ze hill," he responded. "I alvays like to get a little bit of exercise ven I can."

He pat his large belly as if it was a beautifully sculpted set of abs.

Ben fired off a series of questions: "Facility back home? Briefing? What's going on?"

"All will be explained inside," insisted Director Z.

We stepped into the foyer, and almost immediately, the painting of Lucinda B. Smythe began to scream at Herr Direktor Detlef.

"You charlatan. Leave this house at once!" Lucinda yelled from her dusty frame.

"Lucinda, dear," scolded Director Z, "you mustn't treat our guest so rudely. He's come too far to suffer your wicked tongue-lashing. I do apologize, Herr Direktor, but Lucinda has quite a rude streak in her."

"That's all right, Zachary," said Herr Direktor Detlef. "I've heard worse from some of my residents."

"No, it's not *all right*," screamed Lucinda. "This isn't *all right* at all. Get this *thing* out of my house!"

"We don't have time to quibble, Lucinda," said Director Z as he walked by the cranky portrait. "We've got business to attend to in the Great Room."

Excuse Me

The Great Room was packed. Rows of old monsters lined up from front to back and side to side. They whispered and growled excitedly—a change from their normal moaning and groaning. I rubbed my sore body.

Director Z pointed to a couple of empty seats in the back row.

"Gentlemen," he said to us, "we've saved you these seats. Please take them quickly, as we must get started."

He and Herr Direktor Detlef rushed up to the front of the room as we sat down. Horace, the old organ player, tapped out a more upbeat tune than usual on his keyboard. The tune made Herr Direktor Detlef smile, and he began to say something to Director Z, who laughed.

Shane and I leaned in to hear what they were saying. That's when Shane noticed whose behind we were sitting behind.

"Oh no . . ." Shane said and pointed in front of him.

It was Gil, the creature from the swamp.

"Oh man," said Ben, "I think I'm going to hurl."

"What was on the menu?" Gordon asked. "You know . . . what did he eat for lunch?"

"It's Monday," I said. "So . . ."

"Mexican fiesta," we all said at once.

We didn't have any time to move.

"Ladies and gentlemen," Director Z started, "I have a very special guest to introduce to you tonight, and he comes with some very exciting news—Herr Direktor Detlef from the Paradise Retirement Island in the Bermuda Triangle."

Herr Direktor Detlef stood up. The crowd applauded loudly. Then Horace stopped the organ music and everyone stared, waiting for the Direktor to speak. Mouths opened in anticipation. A wad of drool escaped from one of the zombies' mouths and hit the floor with a PLOP.

"Ladies und gentlemen!" boomed the Direktor. "I come to Raven Hill bearing news of great significance. Ve heard vhat you vent through with sose terrible sussuroblats. Ve, too, vere once veak and now haff gained strength."

PFFFFTTT!

"Oh, sheesh!" whispered Ben. "He's starting."

Sure enough, a small green cloud of gas wafted up from the wrinkled and scaly green bottom of the swamp creature.

Herr Direktor Detlef continued, unaware of the swamp gas. "Sussuroblats haff a very hard time swimming. So, ve veren't nearly as veakened as you vere, and can only imagine how hard it vas to be at ze epicenter of ze attack . . ."

PPFFFFFTTTTTTT!

A larger cloud floated up from the swamp creature's seat. He sat happily in the cloud before it slowly drifted back toward us. The four of us blew as hard as we could and pushed it toward the front of the room. This time, a few of the residents started coughing.

"His swamp gas is outta control!" hissed Gordon.

"Hold on," said Shane, rummaging around in his bag, "let me get the cork . . ."

Shane pulled out the prized cork, and handed it to me.

"You're closest," he said. "Do the deed."

"But you're better at it!" I said while handing it back. "Just do it."

"Rock Paper Scissors?" asked Shane.

"You're on!" I said.

PFFFTTTTTSS!

"Make it quick," said Ben, who had taken on a greenish hue. "I can't take much more."

Herr Direktor Detlef kept talking, but we were too busy to notice what he said.

"One, two, three!"

I had rock. Shane had paper.

"NOOO!" I hissed, and snatched the cork out of Shane's hand. "He's sitting down. What am I supposed to do?"

Ben grabbed his cell phone and flung it under the swamp creature's chair. It landed next to his webbed foot.

"Huh?" said the swamp creature. He bent over awkwardly to grab the cell phone. I cautiously leaned forward and through my watering eyes I searched for my target. And there it was, between his frizzled green buttocks. I held my breath and started to make my move.

I hadn't quite finished when the swamp creature shuffled around and stared at me with a puzzled look on his face. I jerked my hands back to the top of his seat and gripped it nervously.

"Uhhhh . . . ," I stuttered.

"Is this crazy contraption one of yours?" he asked while holding up the phone.

"It's mine," Ben replied, grabbing his phone. "Sorry."

The swamp creature turned his attention back to the stage and slowly started to lower his backside onto the seat. I quickly tried to finish the deed.

SHHHHHRRRRPPPP

A little gas seeped out from around the cork, I could feel it like a warm breeze on my hand.

"Get out of there," Shane whispered.

"I haven't pushed it in far enough yet," I whispered back.

My hand would soon be sandwiched between his posterior and the seat.

"Oops!" Ben yelled, and dropped the phone under the swamp creature's chair again.

"You brainless buffoons," the swamp creature muttered.

The phone had slid a little farther forward this time, and the swamp creature had to hold on to the chair in front of him in order to bend over far enough to grab it. Soon, we were cheek to cheek. Well . . . butt-cheek to cheek. Not wanting to get my hands too far into a swamp butt, I grabbed my cell phone and used it to prod the cork tightly into place.

"I'm going to need to boil this before I can use it again," I said.

The swamp creature sat down and Herr Direktor Detlef rambled on.

"It really is quite amazing vhat has happened here at Raven Hill," the Direktor continued. "Ze energy gained by ze network of retirement homes is invaluable. Giff yourself a round of applause!"

The Great Room filled with applause, hoots, and cheers. The zombies moaned happily, the werewolves howled, and the witches cackled with glee.

The swamp creature stood up to applaud with the rest of the monsters.

The Direktor boomed above the applause: "Zat said, it's my distinct pleasure to announce—"

He was interrupted by a great rumble from the swamp creature.

BLLLLLUUUUUURRRRRRGGGGG!

"Uh-oh," said Ben.

Our chairs vibrated. Above us, a crystal chandelier dropped wisps of spiderweb as it started to sway.

"Oh no!" Gordon gulped. "I don't think the cork is going to hold."

Before we could do anything, the excited swamp creature let out the most rip-roaring raunch *ever*. The cork flew out of his fishy old butt and hit me right between the eyes. I stumbled back into my chair. Stars danced before my eyes. I stood up and tried to get out of the way, but it was no use. The green cloud surrounded me.

"We're going to need a bigger cork," Shane announced as the room turned black and I tumbled to the floor.

My last thought was *I wish I had left for Kennedy Space Center today . . .*

Three, Two, One, LIFTOFF!

At lunch the next day, we spoke about normal, non-monstery things for once.

"No, really," said Gordon, "I think that we have a really good chance at making regionals this year."

"Yeah, right," said Shane. "I'll wager you a Grilled Screams that you guys win three games—TOPS."

"We just need practice and focus!" Gordon said, "I even convinced Coach Grey to come along on the science trip so we can practice. Everyone on the team is already going to be there. Plus, all the pros train in Florida."

"Hey, are you guys practicing on Cocoa Beach, perchance?" asked Shane.

"Guys," I said, almost choking on a Chicken Linger,

"can you please just *pretend* to be excited about touching a moon rock? Or seeing a Space Shuttle?"

"I'll be excited once I survive the plane trip," said Ben as he poked at his lunch.

"We're going to have a great time at Kennedy Space Center," said Shane, "but thinking of the beach keeps me calm . . . especially when toilets explode in my face."

"Or swamp butts," Ben added.

"Look," said Gordon, "I have sports. You have space. Why do you need me to like what you like? You don't like sports, and that's fine."

"Fine," I said. "Got it. But let's not talk about monsters—the whole trip."

"Agreed," everyone said.

After lunch, almost one hundred sixth graders hovered over their luggage in the school gym, discussing how they would survive the plane ride and how much candy they had hidden in their carry-on bags. The room buzzed with anticipation.

Shane, Gordon, Ben, and I formed a tight circle.

"Wait—are there only two seats between the aisle and window, or three?" Ben asked. "If it's three, please don't make me sit alone. I hate barfing alone."

"Actually," said Gordon, while he pinched his nose and waved his hand in the air, "maybe that's why you *should* sit alone."

Gordon giggled.

"Hey!" said Ben. "I didn't make fun of you when you had a roach mouth, did I?"

"Technically, you won't be alone," said Shane. "I'm sure someone will sit next to you."

A voice from outside the circle said, "I'll sit next to you!"

"Huh?" we all said, looking around to see where it came from.

A short girl with dark hair and dark eyes walked over to our circle. She had on the thickest glasses I'd ever seen, and a fanny pack.

"I'm Nabila," she said with a grin that revealed a tangle of braces.

"Na . . . leeba?" asked Gordon.

"No, na-BE-lah," she said. "And I'd be happy to sit next to you, Ben. In fact, it would be my pleasure."

Ben looked shocked.

"Wait," I said. "Who are you? I haven't even seen you around school."

"Are you new?" asked Ben.

"Somewhat. I usually keep to myself," she said. "My family moved from Egypt this year. My dad works for the government and got transferred here."

"Sounds cool," said Shane.

"I've seen you boys around school," she said, with a smirk. "In fact, we met at Jackson Amusement Park. I was the girl at the front of the line you cut to get on the Gravitron. It took me days to get the vomit out of my hair."

"Look," I said, "thank you for saying you'd sit with Ben, but we've got him covered. Right, guys?"

"Wait a minute," said Ben. "You're more than welcome to sit next to me."

Ben bowed awkwardly.

Shane, for perhaps the first time in his life, was speechless.

Why was this nerdy girl trying to invade our group? I couldn't let this happen. I had just spent months working my tail off with my friends at Raven Hill, and I just wanted to spend a relaxing week with them at Kennedy Space Center. I didn't want an outsider coming in and ruining our fun—especially not a *girl* that Ben was flirting with.

I started to say, "Now, just wait a minute . . ."

"LADIES AND GENTLEMEN!" boomed a voice from the front of the gym.

I looked up to see Mr. Stewart holding a bullhorn.

"LET ME JUST INTRODUCE YOU TO YOUR CHAPERONES. COACH GREY . . ."

"Yeaaaaaahhhhh!" screamed all of the jocks, including Gordon.

"AND MS. VERACRUZ."

225

"Who's that?" I asked Ben.

"Dunno," said Ben.

We craned our necks to see where Mr. Stewart was pointing. An extremely familiar hairnet rose above some of the shorter sixth graders.

"Lunch Lady?" asked Shane.

The room spun. My stomach sank. *This can't be happening,* I thought.

"I *knew* I wouldn't get one moment's peace from Raven Hill," I said. "Lunch Lady is going to be watching our every move. Ugh!"

"Who cares?" said Ben. "We're not talking about monsters during the trip. What is she going to tell Director Z?"

I wasn't sure, but I had a really, really bad feeling. . . .

"LADIES AND GENTLEMEN, THE BUSES TO THE AIRPORT ARE OUT FRONT. PLEASE LINE UP AND GET READY TO GET GOING!"

Nabila sat next to Ben the whole bus ride to the airport. He was too shy to speak with her, so she just sat quietly watching him. When we finally got on the plane, she followed him on, and sat down right next to him.

Shane and Gordon sat in two empty seats behind them, so I was forced to sit next to her. Immediately, I went to work figuring out how to get her as far away from us as possible.

We were dealing with a new breed of monster.

Intruder Alert!

The flight down to Florida was a bumpy one.

I looked over to Ben and—big surprise—his face had gone green. His hands gripped the armrests for dear life. He was going to blow chunks any second. This could be the break I was looking for. If he lost his cookies all over Nabila, she'd surely ditch him. I didn't even care if I caught a little side splatter. It would totally be worth it.

Ben's chest started to spasm. He was going to erupt soon. Nabila just kept smiling at him. I didn't want her to think I was actually paying attention to them, so I ignored Ben's retching and went back to updating my itinerary for the space center.

227

Sure enough, a few bumps later, Ben was done.

WHAAAARRRFFFF!

All the kids on the plane started EWWWWWing at the top of their lungs. All but one.

Nabila wasn't EWWWWWWing.

Nabila was almost AWWWWing in amazement. She looked at Ben as if he was the most stunning thing on the planet.

She reached into her backpack and pulled out a jar. She handed it to Ben.

"Here, go in this," she said calmly and patted him on the back.

"No," he drooled. "I'm good. I think I'm okay."

Nabila yelled, "Brussels sprouts!"

WHAAAARRRRRFFFF!

And Ben threw up again.

The whole plane EEEWWWWed again—this time some of the adults joined in.

"Thanks," she said, and screwed a cap on the newly-filled jar.

I watched the whole thing in amazement, trying my best to ignore Nabila, but I just couldn't.

"What are you DOING?" I screeched.

"Collecting a sample," she said. "As far as we know, Ben's vomit is the only non-sussuroblat vomit that can actually melt a sussuroblat. It needs to be studied."

"WHAT!?" both Ben and I yelped.

"How do you know what a sussuroblat is?" I demanded.

"You guys talk about *everything* at lunch," she said. "I heard about sussuroblats from you."

Ben and I gasped.

Shane and Gordon popped up from their seats behind us.

"WHAT?!" they both yelped.

"I knew that those roaches you led into the Gravitron were not ordinary roaches. I knew something else was going on. So, the next week at school, I started listening in on your lunchtime conversations. Now that I know you're helping defend a bunch of old monsters from some force of evil," she said matter-of-factly. "I want in."

"In?" I asked. "In on what?"

"On the action," she said. "I want to help you guys out. Most of all, I want to meet the monsters."

We were stunned.

Before we could even ask why, Lunch Lady appeared out of nowhere. I almost jumped out of my skin!

"What eeesss going on here?" she asked.

I stammered to get out a reply when Nabila said simply, "Ben threw up."

"All right," she said, eyeing me suspiciously. "I'll geet a flight attendant."

She turned to leave, and we all stared at Nabila again.

"Yes," she said, "I know she's part of Raven Hill, too. And I'm not about to let her know I heard everything from you . . . if you guys cooperate."

"If we . . ." Gordon started, ". . . cooperate? Are you threatening us?"

"It doesn't matter," I said. "We're on vacation . . . I mean, we're not talking about monsters this week. So, that's that."

"Talking about monsters or not," she said, "I still need your help. I'd go there myself, but I can't find Raven Hill on any maps, and I've wandered around town day after day looking for the place."

"It has a way of keeping out unwanted visitors," I said.

"Wait!" Shane said. "How did you hear EVERYTHING? We might have gotten sloppy at the lunch table recently, but in the beginning, we kept things to a whisper—and we always speak in code."

"You were speaking in code?" she asked. "I didn't even know."

"It doesn't matter," Shane said. "What I want to know is how you actually HEARD everything. I've never seen you sitting near our table."

"You never saw me because I was born without a sense of smell," she said matter-of-factly.

We all looked at each other. Even Ben.

"I have an extremely sharp sense of hearing," she

added. "My poor nose gave all of its powers to my ears."

"It looks like your eyes might have helped out as well," snickered Gordon.

Nabila eyed Gordon through her thick lenses and continued, "Do you know how some people say they can hear a pin drop?"

"Yes," we all said.

"Well," she said, "I actually *can* hear a pin drop. I can hear the flight attendant's shoes coming toward us, and I know that she has wet paper towels with her because I heard her turn the sink on, hold something in it, and squeeze out excess water."

Sure enough, a concerned-looking flight attendant came down the aisle.

"Oh dear," she said, looking at the mess.

We all forgot that Ben had barfed. We were hypnotized by Nabila's tale. Even Ben forgot he had barfed—the flight attendant had to ask him the same question twice: "Didn't you know there was a barf bag in the seat in front of you?"

"Nope," he said simply, and grabbed the paper towels as the attendant passed them over.

"Sorry. This is his first time on a plane," I explained.

There was a pause as Ben started to clean up.

"You need any more of this stuff?" he asked Nabila, holding up the dripping paper towels.

Behind us, Gordon gagged slightly.

"No," she said. "I've collected more than I possibly need to run my calculations."

The flight attendant looked at Nabila strangely as she grabbed the paper towels from Ben. But, before she could ask any questions, the intercom crackled and the captain announced that we'd be landing soon.

The flight attendant motioned to Gordon and Shane and said, "Please sit down."

"Yes, ma'am," Shane said politely as she walked away, and then turned to Nabila. "Wait! Why do you care about the monsters at the retirement home?"

"Ever since I was a little girl, I've been obsessed with American monster movies. Vampires. Werewolves. Mummies. I learned all about Halloween. Celebrating Halloween in America for the first time was amazing, but that was make-believe. What you guys are doing is *real*, and I can assist. I know things. I know a lot about mummification. I've read the ancient Egyptian *Book of the Dead*—"

"Interesting hobbies," said Shane, his eyebrow raised.

"—and I could help you guys in more ways than you can imagine."

With that, she sat down in her seat and looked forward.

My friends and I passed each other strange glances.

Wild Life

We arrived in Orlando in the early afternoon. While waiting in front of the terminal for a bus to take us to Cape Canaveral, I walked over to Mr. Stewart.

"Are we going right to Kennedy Space Center?" I asked him, trying my best to ignore Lunch Lady, who stood right next to him.

"That's the plan!" Mr. Stewart said with a smile. "We have orientation and then we will meet with an astronaut. Did you know there's always at least one astronaut answering questions there?"

"I did," I squealed, barely able to hold in my excitement.

Meanwhile, Coach Grey and all of the football players, Gordon included, were gathered at one side of the bus stop. There seemed to be a lot of high-fiving and muscle flexing going on. I've never understood athletes, but Gordon looked happy. I guess he was right—we each had our own things and that was okay.

I walked from Mr. Stewart over to Shane and Ben, who were standing alone at the other side of the bus stop.

"Man this weather is supreme!" yelled Shane. "I could totally get used to this."

"I dunno," said Ben, "this humidity is a little nasty. I'm feeling pretty clammy."

"Aren't you always feeling clammy?" I asked.

"The weather is much, much hotter in Cairo," said Nabila, from out of nowhere.

"Ah!" I yelled and jumped.

The idea of meeting with an actual astronaut had made me forget about Nabila. But here she was, walking toward us with a bottle of water in her hand and a braces-filled grin on her face.

"Is it really?" Ben asked Nabila. "I don't know if I'd make it there."

"We'll see," she said with a wink, and handed Ben the bottled water. "Here, I thought you could use this."

"Aw, thanks," he said, and blushed for the fourth time that day. (I'd been counting.)

Two buses arrived, and everyone pushed and shoved their way on board. Ben and Nabila headed onto the first bus with Lunch Lady.

Shane reached out to stop them, but I pulled his arm back.

"Just let them go," I said, and walked toward the second bus.

I headed to the back of the bus, and dropped down in the very last row with a FLUMP.

"What's wrong?" asked Shane, slumping down in the seat next to me. "This is supposed the best day of your life, Space Boy."

"I feel like we'll never get a break from Raven Hill. First Lunch Lady shows up for the trip, and now all Nabila wants to talk about are the monsters. That's the last thing I want to discuss. We all agreed, no monsters on this trip."

"Ben knows to keep quiet, and he's the only one she wants to talk to," Shane said. "As for Lunch Lady, so what if Director Z sent her to keep an eye on us? We're not going to say *anything*. It was probably just her turn to chaperone, anyway."

"She's not just chaperoning," I said. "Something's going on, I know it."

"Stop worrying," said Shane. "Even if something *is* going on, there's nothing you can do about it. Just relax—we're heading to Kennedy Space Center, remember."

Forty minutes later, we arrived at Kennedy Space Center.

"See?" said Shane. "Nothing to worry about. We made it!"

I had seen a million pictures, I had spent hours on Google Maps zooming into the facilities, but I never thought it would look like this. There were very few buildings—it was mostly swamp. But that was okay—this swampy wonderland hid the mysteries of the universe. We passed by launchpads scorched by powerful rockets. We passed by crazy-looking radar equipment. *What star system is it observing?* I wondered—just one of a billion questions blasting through my brain.

I stared out of the window with my mouth wide open and moaned, "I. Can't. WAIT!"

When we passed the huge tower that used to house the space shuttles, even the jocks stared with bug eyes.

The buses pulled into the parking lot of the Visitor Complex.

Mr. Stewart rose out of seat and turned to face us. "Please exit the bus in an orderly fashion and form a line outside," he announced.

"It better be a *straight* line," grunted Coach Grey. "I don't want to see any sloppiness out there today."

Once off of the bus, Gordon, Ben, and Nabila walked toward us.

"So," said Gordon, "are you psyched or what? This

must be like Christmas morning for you!"

"Yeah, what are we going to do first?" asked Ben.

"Moon rock," I said without hesitation. "I have to touch me some moon rock!"

"Are any of the monsters you work with from space?" asked Nabila loudly.

Lunch Lady squinted her eyes in our direction.

She walked toward us to investigate, but something stopped her in her tracks!

The front of the first bus was parked up against a swampy gulley. Something was growling and snapping in the gully. Something monstrous!

"Aaaaaahhhhhh!" a few of the girls and more than one football player screamed and headed toward the Visitor Complex.

"No, wait!" yelled Mr. Stewart. "Everyone back on the bus, immediately!"

"You heard the man," barked Coach Grey. "Get your keisters back on these buses on the double! NOW!"

A second monstrous form appeared and began thrashing around with the first. A flock of cranes standing in the gully began to flutter their wings. Suddenly one vanished in an explosion of feathers and water. Then another. These monsters were hungry. And they were coming right at us.

"I wonder if cranes taste like chicken," said Shane as he leaned forward to get a better look.

Ignoring his question, I grabbed Shane's arm and ran back to the bus. "I *knew* it!" I yelled. "I knew that the Director would ruin it for us."

Kids crammed in front of the bus doors, desperate to get on. A panicked jock pushed a girl out of his way so hard that she fell and rolled toward the gully.

The water bubbled and a slick, leathery form rose out of the muck to meet her. Now we all leaned forward to get a better look.

"Get back!" yelled Coach Grey, and he lobbed a fastball at the monster's head.

With a splash and a growl, the monster was knocked back.

Coach scooped up the girl, who moaned, "It has teeeeeth! So many teeth!"

Once we were back on the bus, we had a better view of the vile creatures.

"I'm not sure if this was Director Z's work," said Shane, pointing out of the window. "Look!"

Two giant alligators emerged from the gully and crept up into the parking lot. They stopped in front of the buses, warming themselves in the late afternoon sun.

"Well," said Mr. Stewart, "it looks like we got a little Biology instead of Astronomy today. You're looking at two North American alligators, which are common to this area of Florida."

Mr. Stewart turned to the bus driver. "Mack, can you drive us directly to the entrance?"

"Wait!" a girl screamed. "There's another alligator behind the bus!"

"We're surrounded," said Shane, pointing out of the window. "There must be a dozen of them out there."

Forty-five minutes later we were still seated in the sweltering hot bus, watching as the alligators slowly made their way back into the swamp.

"I'm losing my mind," I said to Shane. "We're so close to Kennedy Space Center—and all we can do is stare at it."

"On the bright side," added Shane, "at least no one asked us to clean up after the gators . . . or serve them lunch. That's a step in right direction."

Finally, the buses left the parking lot, drove past the Visitor Complex, and . . . headed back onto the main road.

"Wait," I said, jumping from my seat. "What?"

"Ladies and gentlemen," Mr. Stewart said, "considering the time, we've decided to go directly to our lodging and unpack."

"Noooooooo!" I screamed.

"Chris." Mr. Stewart looked at me strangely. "My decision is final. Don't worry—we'll have plenty of time to explore the facility tomorrow."

I looked at Kennedy Space Center, and had a sinking feeling that I'd never make it back.

Fart Machines

Kennedy Space Center had long faded from view by the time the buses pulled into our "lodgings."

"Way to go, Rio Vista Middle School," Shane said as he saw where we were staying . . . Zed's CraZy DiZcount CabinZ. "Couldn't you find anyplace crummier for us to stay?"

"What were you expecting?" I replied. "A five-star hotel?" I didn't care where we stayed, I just wanted to drop off my bags and head back to the space center.

"I take back what I said," Shane said, patting me on the back as we stepped off the bus. "Look, the beach is just down that path. Thank you, Rio Vista!"

In the parking lot, Ben and Gordon were waiting

for us. And, of course, Nabila stood close by Ben's side. It was a good thing she couldn't smell Ben, who still reeked of warm barf.

"I have to get to my cabin," said Nabila. "I want to freshen up before we meet Mr. Stewart on the beach for the welcome announcement. I'll see you boys later."

"Yeah, much later," grumbled Gordon. "You've got A LOT of freshening up to do."

"Whew," I said as she walked away.

"Wow, she's special, guys," said Ben. "I mean, really smart! And an expert on Egyptology. I think we should introduce her to the mummies."

"Yeah, we know what you think, lover boy!" Gordon said. "But I don't want her cramping our style."

"Me neither," I said. "We can tell her how to get to Raven Hill when we get back from the trip. Director Z will be happy we found fresh blood."

After we all tried our best to "freshen up" in our CraZy Cabin, we went down to the beach. It was cool and breezy, with waves gently lapping up against the shore.

"Man," Shane said with a sigh, "I could really get used to this. Nice."

"Yeah," I said. "It's so quiet and—"

"Hey, guys!" we heard a shout from farther down the beach.

Nabila was walking over.

"Arrrgh!" I harrumphed. "When is she going to get that we just don't want to hang out?"

"Hi, Ben," she said as she approached us. "How are you feeling?"

"Pretty good, actually," Ben said, and he got a little red in the face.

Ben was not blushing for the fifth time—he was already starting to get a sunburn.

"That's a nice fanny pack you have," he said nervously.

"Oh, thank you," she replied. "I always have it on me. I even sleep with it. I never know when I might need something!"

Mr. Stewart and the chaperones made their way up the beach.

"So," Ben shyly continued with Nabila. "What—"

"Shhhh . . ." Nabila said, and then whipped out a small notebook and pen from her fanny pack. "I think they're going to give us the outline of the week's events."

Mr. Stewart said, "Welcome to Cape Canaveral! We planned a lot of fun events for everyone, but due to today's unfortunate incident with the overgrown reptiles of Kennedy Space Center, we're going to scale back a bit. I've decided that there will be no snorkeling in the nearby springs. Nor will there be any swimming. We're just going to stick to Kennedy Space Center—"

"Yeah!" I yelled. I knew that Shane was depressed by the news, but we came for the space center, not the beach.

Mr. Stewart continued: "—with a little bit of bird-watching at Cape Canaveral National Seashore."

A whole bunch of *Aw, man*s and *No*s floated up from the crowd of kids.

He went on to talk about all of the rules and regulations and blah-blah-blah boring stuff. He ended with an announcement that we'd all have a BBQ dinner that night on the beach, cooked up, of course, by Lunch Lady.

"I'm sorry, Shane," I said, and put my hand on his shoulder. "You should wear your surfing sharks to Kennedy Space Center. Want to just sit down and enjoy the view?"

"I was really excited to go snorkeling," said Nabila. "I brought along an invention I've been working on that I hoped to test out."

"What's that?" Shane asked.

"It's a device that attracts fish," she said, and pulled a small, black rectangular device out of her fanny pack. "Someone's already created an iPhone app, but I really wanted mine to be waterproof. Since, as you know, most fish are underwater."

"How does it work?" Ben asked.

"Well," she said, "it uses natural sounds to attract fish—small fish sucking on rocks, shrimp shells rubbing together, herring flatulence . . ."

"Wait," Shane said. "Do you mean herring *farts*?"

"Yes," said Nabila. "Herring communicate by farting, and the theory is that hearing their farts could attract other fish—fish that like herring. At the least, it should attract other farting herring. I was interested to see if more fish approached me than approached others while we were snorkeling."

"Oh, man, that's hilarious!" Gordon laughed. "I wonder if Lunch Lady is going to barbecue some farting herring tonight?"

Shane, Gordon, and I cracked up.

"I think it's cool," said Ben. He gave Nabila an approving nod.

Gordon continued chuckling uncontrollably. "Wait, wait! I've got something like your device on my iPhone. Check this out."

He whipped out his iPhone and, after touching the screen a few times there was a noisy, wet, sloppy FLLLLUUUURRRRT!

He laughed and touched his screen one more time. This one was higher pitched.

FEEEEEPT!

And another.

FWWWAAAAAAAAAP!

"Wait, wait," he said, practically crying now, "let me add one more."

There was a PING as he touched the screen, followed by a countdown.

"THREE!"

Gordon moved the phone down to his posterior.

"TWO!"

He stopped laughing for a moment and concentrated.

"ONE!"

He farted a long, juicy fart. He started to chuckle near the end and it came out with a little *fit-fit-fit* sound.

I couldn't help laughing. Shane and Ben joined in.

"Oh, man," said Shane. "It almost sounded like he was saying something. Ha-ha-ha!"

Nabila gave Gordon the stink-eye and said, "Oh, no, that's nothing like my device. My device attracts fish. Yours attracts idiots."

She stormed away as we laughed our heads off, and I looked forward to a fish dinner with my friends.

Something's Fishy

After our beach BBQ, Shane, Ben, Gordon, and I all headed back up to our stuffy old cabin. I was too excited to sleep. And even if I wanted to, it would be impossible to block out the sound of Gordon snoring away on the top bunk across from me. Shane, however, was fast asleep, lying stiff as a board on his back, but with a look of content on his face. He even slept like a karate master.

Ben must have heard me shuffling above him in my bunk. "Are you awake, too?" he asked.

"Yeah," I whispered back.

"Is it me, or was the fish extra fishy tonight?" Ben asked. "It kind of tasted like that last batch of Mac 'n' Sneeze."

"Fish is supposed to be fishy," I said. "Or it wouldn't be fish. Would you want chicken to taste like cow?"

"Well, at least I got to eat dinner on the beach with Nabila," he said, and sighed.

I saw where this was going.

"She's OFF LIMITS, dude!" I hissed.

"Hey," Ben said, "she's just a special kind of girl."

"That's true," I said. "I thought Gordon's fart library would keep her away, but even after that, she sat down with us at dinner."

"Sat down with *me*," said Ben. "Even on the plane. Most girls usually run screaming when I barf. But this girl is . . . different."

I didn't know what to say next, but I knew for sure that if Ben fell for Nabila that we'd be forced to let her into our circle, and I'd lose a friend to puppy love. So, I changed the subject.

"Can you believe that fish talk by farting?" I asked. "No wonder Gil likes to fart so much. He's just saying, 'Hello!'"

Ben started to giggle.

"The way he goes at it," Ben said, "he's saying a WHOLE lot more than 'Hello!' He's reciting the Declaration of Independence!"

"*Parlez vous fartzes?*" I chortled.

"*Habla fartspañol?*" Ben countered.

We laughed until we cried, and then as we caught

our breath, we smelled something funny.

"Whew," I said, "speaking of nasty smells."

"Ugh," said Ben. "What is that?"

The smell was superfunky and overpowering. I put my T-shirt over my nose and mouth. Ben did the same.

"Where the heck is that coming from?" Ben asked.

I climbed down from my bunk and sniffed around.

"It smells fine outside," I said as I looked out the window.

"Good; I'm coming over there," said Ben.

With a snort, Gordon sat up on the bunk bed.

"Dudes, put your shoes back on," he moaned, still half asleep. "That's some serious athlete's foot I'm smellin'."

It smelled like something from the ocean had flopped into our room and died—worse than the swamp creature—but I couldn't see anything in the room.

I kept sniffing around. I sniffed Shane's feet. I sniffed the closet. I got down and sniffed the floorboards.

"Ach!" I almost choked. "It's coming from under us."

"Great," said Ben. "What the heck crawled into the crawl space and died?"

I sniffed one more time, and the smell was even worse.

That's when there was a BANG, and our cabin shook.

"What the . . . ?" Gordon swayed on his bunk.

BANG!

This time one of the floorboards cracked, just in front of Shane and Gordon's bunk.

BANGCRACKBANG!

The bunk beds swayed. Under the floorboards, a low, wet hiss could be heard.

There was a pause and then . . .

CRAAAACK!

A huge, wet worm with hundreds of slimy, squirmy legs burst through the floor and slithered out between the broken wood.

HISSSSSS!

As more of the worm slithered into the room, the stench went from overpowering to painfully eye-watering.

"Aahhh!" Shane yelled. He was finally awake. He leaped up and landed on the floor in a karate pose.

The worm towered over Shane, writhing and wet, and opened its huge, slimy hole of a mouth.

SCHLUUUUUUUCK!

It paused for a minute, and then swung over to Gordon.

"Aaaaarrggh!" Gordon yelled, and then he squeezed himself between the wall and the bunk bed, pushing it toward the massive sea worm.

The bed knocked the worm over, right onto me!

"Oof!" I grunted . . .

. . . and collapsed on the floor. The worm's limp head crashed down in my lap.

It was stunned, but just for a moment. It turned its eyeless head toward me and opened a mucus-filled mouth.

HIIIISSSSSSS!

The smell overwhelmed my senses. I was stunned. But not because it was terrible. Because it smelled so good.

"Chris!" Shane screamed. "To your left!"

I looked up to see my bunk bed coming down and rolled out of the way just in time.

SPLUNK!

With a juicy crack, the bed landed on the head of the worm-beast, and it twitched under the weight.

"Let's get out of here!" Ben yelled, and we ran for the door.

But before we could get outside, two more worms burst through the door.

We scrambled to the window.

And two more worms were waiting for us!

They shot out in a flash. The two at the door reared up in front of Gordon and Shane, opened their mouth-holes wide, and then . . .

GULP!

. . . came down on my friends so fast that I didn't even see them get swallowed.

"Nooooooo!" I screamed, and rushed at the worms, which had already turned to slither back out the door.

"Chris!" I could hear a muffled voice. "Chriiiiiiis!"

I couldn't tell if it was Shane. Or Gordon. Or both.

Before I could reach either worm, my feet were brought out from under me. I went flying forward, and bumped my head hard. I saw stars, and was too weak to fight as the worm grabbed me with its sticky mouth and started to slurp up my legs, my face dragging along the floor. I could feel its muscles ripple all around me as I was pulled in deeper and deeper.

I was able to turn just in time to see Ben, terrified, also being swallowed. He clutched two phones in his hands.

"Catch," he gasped, and tossed me mine.

I grabbed it, and wondered, why, as a soon-to-be-dead man, I wanted this. Perhaps Ben wanted to make sure we connected in the afterlife?

It didn't matter. Nothing mattered. We were worm meat. Still . . . I clutched the phone as the worm slurped me up into its hot guts.

Good-Smellin' Guts

It smelled amazing inside the worm. A. May. ZING. It smelled exactly like the roasted nuts you might find at a carnival or fair, but even sweeter. Like the roasted-nut guys were cooking the nuts in a vat of cotton candy juice.

I felt warm. I felt happy. I felt . . . safe.

I curled up into the warm guts and thought about taking a nap. I was almost off to dreamland—

When my phone rang in my hand.

The light from the screen illuminated the guts and I was once again reminded that I was not at some local fair, but inside a massive sea worm. I was wrapped in the stomach of the creature, covered in goop and black stuff. Veins pumped thick, black blood just through the surface of the stomach skin.

Suddenly I didn't feel so safe.

I acccpted the call and slowly, slimily pulled the phone up to my ear. It was difficult, and it felt like the creature's stomach muscles were trying to slow me down along the way.

Finally, I got the phone up to my ear.

"Hello?" I asked

"Hi, Chrissy!" a voice squealed with excitement on the other end of the line.

"Hi, Mom," I said as unexcitedly as I could.

"Well, sheesh!" she bubbled. "Thanks for picking up. You usually just call me back later."

I had no idea what to say to my mother, but I had to get her off the phone.

"Well," I stumbled. "We made it here just fine today, and the wildlife is really . . . wild! In fact I have to run up the nature trail real quick—someone saw a . . . um . . . hippo."

The guts were making me delirious.

"Hippo?" My mother sounded confused. "Chrissy, it doesn't even sound like you're outside—you sound like you're inside."

If you only knew, I thought.

"Okay, Ma!" I yelled. "I gotta go. Love you!"

I hung up the phone and was once again plunged

into the sweet, sweet darkness of the sea worm. I really wanted to nap, but before laying my head on the squishy stomach lining, I made a very important call.

"Huh . . . hullo?" Ben purred on the other end.

I had clearly woken him up.

"Hey!" I yelled. "It's me, Chris! We're still alive!"

"This is so weird," Ben said. "What's happening? Does your worm smell like the best brand of dryer sheets ever? Like, mixed with really, really good dishwashing detergent and body wash?"

"Well, my worm smells really good, but like the best carnival sweets you could ever imagine."

"Weird! It made me so happy in here that I just . . ."

". . . fell asleep," I finished. "Yeah, I would have too, if my mother hadn't just called me. This is really, really weird."

"It doesn't look like we're being digested," said Ben. "I'm not being burned by any acid. You?"

"Nope," I said, looking at my pale-white-as-usual arm in the glow of the phone.

"Listen," Ben said.

When we were first scooped up by the sea worms, we could hear hundreds of legs stomping along the ground, and the guts were much more jiggly.

Now all we could hear was a soft *swishhhhhh*.

"We're in the water," I said. "Oh, man, where are they taking us?"

"Do Shane or Gordon have their cell phones?" Ben asked.

"I have no idea," I said. "I'll call them and see if they answer."

"Okay," said Ben. "Enjoy your good-smellin' worm. If they'd smelled as bad on the inside as they do on the outside, I would have died in two minutes."

Ben hung up.

I tried calling Shane but before I could get halfway through his number on the third try, my fingers slipped off of the keypad and I fell into a deep, relaxed sleep.

I woke up FAST.

The muscles of the sea worm rippled around me. They pushed and squeezed—I could barely breathe. Then a light appeared above me, and I heard a retching sound.

Below, a black ooze bubbled up around my feet, and the sweet smell of roasted nuts and cotton candy was immediately erased. It once again smelled like centuries-old rotten fish.

WHHHURP!

WHHHHHARRRFFF!

The worm retched and coughed, and I slowly,

painfully made my way up toward the light, the muscles squeezing me tightly the whole way.

The smell was absolutely horrific, and I didn't know how much more I could take. The worm was trying to get me out, but it was just too slow.

The black goo had made its way up to my waist, and I was about to pass out. I had to speed things up somehow.

My arms were pinned to my side. My legs were pushed straight down.

I only had one weapon . . . my mouth.

I opened up as wide as I could, coughing and spitting, and

CHOMP!

I bit the tender stomach lining of the sea worm.

I could hear an angry hiss, and the sea worm's body rippled. It squeezed me with its guts even harder.

"Arrrrggghhhh!" I yelled.

The pain was intense.

And then, suddenly,

SPLOOT!

I shot out of the worm, and into the blinding light.

I was completely dazed and confused, but I knew two things right away.

I was rolling through the most beautiful beach I had ever seen in my life and . . .

I stopped right in front of the feet of Director Z!

Beach Bums

"YOU were the one who sent the worms!" I coughed through a mouthful of sand and sea worm gunk.

"Indeed," said Director Z.

"I knew you would do something like this," I said.

Director Z and two Nurses stood on a white sand beach, surrounded by sunbathing monsters—some in creaky wooden chairs, some on ragged, thin towels. It was bright—and HOT. It felt a hundred times hotter than it had felt on Cape Canaveral. Beyond the beach was a thick jungle, and from out of the jungle, tall, white resort towers pushed into the sky.

Behind me, I could hear the giant sea worm splash back into the water. It burped one last painful burp and disappeared under the waves.

I couldn't believe it. I closed my eyes and shook my head, but when I opened my eyes again, I still saw old monsters up and down the beautiful beach. I tried to stand, but stumbled backward and rolled toward the surf. The Nurses came down to help me.

"Hold me up to his face," I ordered one Nurse.

He gave me a strange look, but did as he was told. I was nose to nose with Director Z, covered in sandy black gunk. I shook with anger in the hands of the Nurse.

"What are you doing!?" I screamed. "You ruined my Dream Trip, just like I knew you would!!!"

"Chris, you might not feel the same, but it's wonderful to see you," said Director Z calmly. "I do *very* much apologize for the mode of transportation I selected to get you to Paradise Island."

"Paradise Island . . . in the Bermuda Triangle?" I asked. "That's where Herr Direktor Detlef's retirement home is . . ."

"That is correct," said Director Z. "The important news Herr Direktor Detlef was never able to announce—he'd be swapping facilities with us—as a congratulations for defeating the sussuroblats. We left that very same night, but you left before I could tell you. He and his residents are now at Raven Hill."

"Great for you guys, but why are *we* here?" I demanded, still staring Director Z directly in the eyes.

"And why did you send worms to get us?"

"First off," Director Z said, "I'd like to point out that it could have been worse—the witches put several spells on the sea worms, which led to a much more pleasant journey. The stomachs of the beasts were charmed with a smellgood spell and a hibernation spell. You fell asleep comfortably, I assume?"

"Yeah, I guess I took a little nap," I growled.

"You had more than a nap," said Director Z. "It's at least a six-hour journey by sea worm to this island from Cape Canaveral, and I'm sure for you it felt like . . ."

"Fifteen minutes!" I said, flabbergasted. "Why didn't you just ask us to come with you?" I asked. "It would have been a better trip than the one I just took."

"We didn't need you until now. Plus, I knew that you were fed up with Raven Hill, and quite frankly, I think you had every right to be. I've been working you hard, and despite all your efforts, the residents have been quite rude. So I let you go on your field trip, but had Ms. Veracruz keep a close eye on you in case you were needed."

"What about the fact that four students are now missing?" I asked.

"Ms. Veracruz slipped a short-term-memory-erasing serum into the breakfast of everyone in your group so that they will forget that you were even with them. Everything has been taken care of, and I'm grateful that you're here. You see, we have a major problem, Chris, and I need your help."

I was still angry I was missing out on Kennedy Space Center, but what could I do? The main reason we wanted a break from Raven Hill was because the monsters really didn't need us. Now that I knew they needed us, I felt ready to help.

"Put me down," I said to the Nurse.

The Nurse put me down and Director Z crouched down closer to my face, speaking softly. "Several of the residents have suffered a severe lebensplasm loss," he explained, "but we can't tell *how* they are being drained. They seem perfectly happy one moment, and then the very next, they're agitated and annoyed, lashing out and biting—harming others and themselves. It's like they've been given a strange strength at the same time that they've been drained."

"But how can we help?" I asked. "And where are my friends?"

"I made sure your sea worm arrived first," Director Z said, "so that we could talk. I figured you might have a few questions. The others should be along shortly. As we're not sure what we're defending ourselves against, I'm not yet exactly sure how you gentlemen *can* help. However, you helped defend Raven Hill from the sussuroblats, so I'm sure you can help us here with whatever enemy we face. And, I can assure you, I will *more* than make up for your missed trip to Kennedy Space Center."

His normally cool face became sad and tired. He headed into the crowd of sunbathing monsters.

"Please join me," he said.

We weaved our way through the old monsters. The swamp creature was applying sun cream to his scaly body. A group of witches stood up and ran toward the water, cackling in their long black bathing gowns. All of the banshees lay facedown on threadbare towels, enjoying a bit of sun on their backs.

We walked a few feet past the last sunbathers.

"Now, I don't want to alarm my staff or my residents," said Director Z, "which is why I'm trying to be as discreet as possible, but this is an extremely worrisome situation. We've absolutely never seen anything like this before. One of the mummies unwrapped himself and walked right into the ocean. A witch went mad and hexed a few of the zombies luckily she was so deranged, the effects were minimal. Flowers grew out of their ears.

"As you can see, not many of them have been affected—most are actually amazingly healthy and relaxed after only a few days here. You'll see that everyone is much better behaved. But, the ones who have been drained . . ."

Director Z stared at the crashing blue waves for a moment, his face growing even sadder.

"Yes?" I asked.

"Well, Chris, they are mere shells of their former selves. In my history as Director, I've never seen any residents drained so fast. I think we may lose the residents in mass numbers unless we can figure out what's going on here."

"Okay, okay!" I said, now just as worried as Director Z. "I'm ready to solve your mystery."

The dark frown left Director Z's face, and he straightened his suit.

"And, while you solve the mystery, you should also enjoy all the perks of a private tropical island. As soon as your friends arrive, I'll give you a tour of the facility. I'm sure you'll want to see where all the Jacuzzis are, and knowing the layout of the facility will also be helpful in piecing clues together."

We walked back toward the sunbathers.

Vacations Make Me Sick

Director Z and I walked past a group of sunbathing old vampires on the beach, their wrinkled bodies on display. They wore a stomach-churning choice of swimwear: Speedos. Their hairy chests smoldered slightly in the morning sunlight.

"Chris!" said Grigore, one of the vampires. "It is vonderful to see you here!"

He got up to say hello, grinning a sharp-toothed grin from ear to ear. He had helped us defeat the sussuroblats, but like the other monsters, Grigore was usually grumpy and hard to deal with. I was surprised to see him so happy.

"What are you doing in the sun?" I asked.

"One of the few benefits of being a weak old vampire," he said, "is that the sun affects me very little."

"But the smoke . . ." I said, smelling bacon in the air.

"Smoke?" Grigore looked confused. "I'm smoking? Sheesh. I just applied an SPF 5,000 a few minutes ago."

"Yes, you gentlemen might want to find a palm tree," said Director Z. "You don't want to overdo it. That being said, I think you're getting quite a nice tan, old man."

Before I could ask Director Z any more questions, there was a huge splash, and three sea worms crawled out of the crashing waves. They reared up, retched loudly, and spit out my three friends, before returning to the water.

"Ah," said Director Z, "right on time!"

Director Z called a few Nurses down to help my friends, who began to stir on the sand.

Ben and Shane grunted as the Nurses helped them to their feet. Gordon appeared to be asleep. His head bobbed on his chest.

I walked down with the Director to talk with them.

"Dude," said Shane, "why are we here?"

"The monster juice supply is in danger," I said. "Director Z ordered the worms to bring us here. We have to help."

"And why are *they* here?" asked Ben, rubbing his eyes in disbelief.

"They've traded facilities with Herr Direktor

Detlef's residents," I replied. "Welcome to Paradise Island!"

"Ohhhhhh," Ben and Shane said.

Gordon's head came up so quick I swear I heard his neck crack.

"Wow!" said Gordon, screaming through clenched teeth. "This place is beautiful! Is this the Cape Canaveral Alligator Refuge Thingamajiggy? How did we get here? Why do I smell like my mother's roast chicken?"

Gordon drooled a little bit and then passed out again. The Nurse held on tight.

"Shane, what did your worm smell like?" I asked.

"Oh yeah!" he said. "It was the strangest thing. It smelled like the inside of a jack-o'-lantern when you burn a candle in it—specifically, the lid of the jack-o'-lantern, when you pull it off and give it a whiff at the end of the night. I think that's my favorite smell of all time, actually."

"But of course," said the Director. "The smellgood spell the witches cast on the innards of the sea worms give them the odor of your favorite smell."

"Cleaning products," said Ben.

"Carnival food," I said.

Gordon's head slowly came up once again.

"Gordon, is the smell of your mother's roast chicken your favorite smell?" I asked.

"No, I hate my mother's roast chicken," Gordon

growled, staring into the distance like a zombie. "Where is the rest of my team? We have practice with Coach Grey tonight. Coach. Practice. We. Have. Roast . . . chicken?"

He looked at his hands and began to cry.

"Gordon?" Ben asked, "Are you okay?"

He looked at Ben and screamed. He shook and spat in the Nurse's arms, gurgling and frothing at the mouth. A few of the old monsters turned toward the noise.

"Gordon!" I yelled.

"Nurse Gigg, release him at once," Director Z commanded. "He's seizing so hard he'll break his bones if you hold on to him!"

Nurse Gigg dropped Gordon, who hit the sand and flopped around like a piranha on a carpet. He kicked sand onto a few of the sunbathing mummies, who looked up in surprise.

Shane bent down to help Gordon, but Director Z pushed him back.

"There's nothing we can do now," said Director Z. "It's up to him to fight it."

"Fight what?" Ben asked.

"He's having an allergic reaction to the sea worm," Director Z said.

"Gwaaaaah!" Gordon yelled.

He arched his back until I thought it would break, and then lay terribly still.

"Gordon?"

Trouble in Paradise

Director Z kneeled down next to Gordon, and checked his pulse. He then stared off in the distance for a long time. Almost all of the monsters got up and shuffled down to the water's edge to investigate.

"Well?" asked Frederick, the old stitched-together monster. "Is he dead?"

Ben, Shane, and I stared in shock, waiting for Director Z's answer.

"His pulse is slow," he finally said, "but it's there. We must get him to the infirmary at once."

He waved Nurse Gigg back over.

"Quickly," he commanded.

Nurse Gigg bent over, picked Gordon up, and threw

him over his shoulder in one smooth motion.

"Is he going to be okay?" asked Ben.

"Yes," said Director Z. "But we must act swiftly."

Director Z and the Nurse ran up the beach and into the jungle.

Ben, Shane, and I stood on the beach, dumbfounded. Shane finally broke the silence.

"Well, what are we waiting for?" he said, and sprinted up to the path, which was marked with a tiki torch.

Ben and I followed.

"Wow," Ben said as we ran deep into the jungle. "It's cold in here. Where did the sun go? I can't even see the buildings anymore."

"Look—Director Z is just up there," I said.

We ran up to meet him. Nurse Gigg was a few yards ahead. Gordon's head bobbed up and down as he plowed forward.

We caught up to Nurse Gigg, and kept running. Strange noises escaped from the jungle, but none was stranger than the low, deep growls that shook the leaves.

"RIIIIIBBBBBBBIIIIT."

"What the heck was that?" gasped Ben. "It sounds like a massive frog!"

"Perhaps we should move a little faster, gentlemen," said Director Z. The Nurse repositioned Gordon on his shoulder and we picked up our pace.

"RIIIIIBBBBBIIIITTTBRAINS!"

"Brains?!" I said. "Did that frog just ribbit, 'brains'?"

"RIBBBRRAAAIINNNS!"

"RIBBBBRRRAAAIINNS!"

"RIBBBBBRRRAAAIIINNNNSSS!"

"Make that four or five frogs," Director Z said.

The vegetation ahead of us shook, and a massive frog, slick with slime and covered in sores and gashes, flopped out of the jungle.

"BRAAAAAIIIINNNNS," it croaked, and flopped toward us.

Two more frogs flopped out of the jungle just in front of the Nurse. They shot their bloody tongues out of their mouths, nearly tripping him. He jumped to the side, kicking one in the head with a wet SQUISH and we ran past them.

"Almost there," Director Z said.

FLOP. FLOP. FLOP. FLOP.

"There are a bunch of them behind us!" screamed Ben.

I took a peek behind my shoulder. The frogs were bright red and green, like the poisonous frogs I've see on the Internet. But these were huge! They stumbled over each other on the narrow path, tongues lashing.

"Here we are," said Director Z.

We approached two Nurses, who stood guard on either side of the path.

"Four, perhaps five zombie frogs are right behind us," he yelled at the Nurses as we passed. "Please halt them, and arrange a frog-leg fricassee for dinner."

We spilled out of the jungle into the resort. It looked like the kind of place parents would go for a romantic getaway. All the walkways were open to a blue sky. As we passed a small open-air theater, I could see Horace, the old organ player, playing steel drums for a small audience of old monsters. We flew past an infinity pool. A zombie floated facedown in a bubbly Jacuzzi.

"The Jacuzzi better be heavily chlorinated," gasped Shane, "or I'll be sticking to the beach."

We ran farther back into the resort. The cool white adobe walls gave away once again to jungle, although this time we were in a clearing, and surrounded by the resort on all sides. There was a large hut set up in the center of the clearing, and out of the large hut came screaming and moaning.

"Oh dear," said Director Z. "I do hope the Nurses have everything under control."

We headed inside the thatch hut to find Nurses and witches frantically running around from bed to bed, doing their best to soothe demented old monsters.

"Griselda!" the Director called to one of the witches. "Please help me with this child immediately. He's had a severe reaction to your sea worm."

The Nurse threw Gordon onto an exam table, and

Griselda rushed over, opened up one of Gordon's eyes and peered inside. She then leaned down to listen to his breathing. We held our breaths.

"Hmmm," Griselda mumbled aloud to herself, "let's see . . . antihistamine spells . . ."

She held her hands high and chanted a spell.

Gordon sat up, gulped a lungful of air, and fell back in the bed.

Griselda turned to us and said, "He's going to be fine."

We stopped holding our breaths.

Gordon might have been on the road to recovery, but the others in the infirmary were not. The Director and the witch tended to Gordon while the three of us watched the panic.

"I didn't think there was any way these guys could look older," said Shane. "But, look at them—they're practically skin and bones."

"Yeah, but they're wild," said Ben. "Look at them kick around. They look old, but they act . . . possessed."

"I don't have a good feeling about this," I said.

We walked closer to Gordon's bed to have a better look. Director Z and Griselda were in a heated argument.

"Well, Zachary," said Griselda angrily, "I could probably do a better job if we had taken the time to pack the right herbs before leaving. These facilities are a mess! I'm a modern witch working with old materials here!"

"First off," said Director Z, "it's 'Boss' or 'Director.'

Secondly, I apologize for the facilities, but I'm told the witch doctor actually does a good job with the resources he has on the island. You may just need to tweak your recipes."

"Tweak the recipes?" she asked, flabbergasted. "Tweak the recipes, Zachary, dear? That's all I've been doing all day. And all I've gotten for it is a bunch of farting, angry old monsters."

Gordon stirred on the table. He moaned, but the two arguing adults didn't seem to notice him.

"Coach," he groaned. "Coach . . . am I up?"

"Um . . . Director Z." I pulled gently at his suit.

"What?!" he snapped at me.

I pointed at Gordon. Griselda continued her examination.

"Oh, yes, quite right," he mumbled. "Did you say 'farting old monsters'? Is the core issue digestive, Griselda?"

"Hmmm . . . ," Griselda said, staring at Gordon. "I believe all this one needs now is an herb-based restorative talisman."

She rummaged around every basket nearby, before grabbing a small doll made of leaves.

"Sage," she said, and held it out to Gordon. "Here, take it."

"Noooo," he whined. "I don't want that. Where's Coach?"

He looked around confused, searching for Coach Grey.

"Zachary," Griselda said one more time, and Director Z scowled. "I need to make sure this child, of his own free will, accepts my talisman before I cast a final spell. This could take a while. Why don't you touch base with the Nurses about the farting? They'll fill you in."

Before heading into the back of the hut and all of the screaming, frothing monsters, Shane gave Griselda a tip: "Put the herbs in a football, and pass it to him. He'll hold on to it tight then."

Ben snickered and we walked away.

There were three old monsters strapped to small, squeaking beds in the back of the hut. Each of them was fighting, gnashing his teeth and screaming.

"Let us go, and ve'll spare your life, beefcake," a vampire spat at his Nurse. He was practically rotting away in front of us.

"You look stringy and far too chewy," said an ancient-looking werewolf, "but we will tear you limb from limb and chew you down to your bones if you don't let us go. We need more juice—these are nearly dry!"

The werewolf howled so loud that his eyes bugged out. They popped, but didn't squirt—the juice stayed on him as if he were covered with a thin film, like saran wrap.

"What's wrong, guys?" asked Shane.

"Shut up, young one," said the dried-up zombie writhing on his bed. "You are neither ripe with the juice nor a tool worthy of manipulation. You are worthless to us. WORTHLESS."

"Nurses," said the director. "Please give me a status report."

"Boss," said a Nurse, "reason for lebensplasm drainage unknown. Residents appear to be covered by something. No herbs can help. Strange side effects."

"That's the most I've ever heard a Nurse talk," said Shane.

"This must be serious," I said. "The Nurses are talking. Director Z is freaking out. What's going on here?"

"What do you mean, strange side effects?" Director Z asked the Nurse. "Are these the digestive issues that Griselda had mentioned?"

"Not caused by drainage," said another Nurse. "Caused by herbs."

"Show me," said the Director.

The Nurse closest to him gulped and grabbed a sack of herbs from the floor. He jumped up on the bed and pinned the already strapped-in zombie with his knees. The zombie's head thrashed about and even more foam poured from his mouth.

"Look at that," said Ben. "The drool isn't dripping off his face; it's just pooled under his chin."

"It is quite bizarre," said the Director. "It would appear that he's captured by some invisible force that has sealed itself to his body. We can't even take a fluid sample to see how low his lebensplasm supply is."

"EEEEEEEEEEEEEE," the zombie screamed, and the other sick old monsters joined in, thrashing even harder. Dust rose from the dirt floor.

The Nurse took a large wad of freshly-ground herbs and shoved them directly into the zombie's screaming mouth.

"EEEEEEEEEE-gug."

The zombie swallowed, and for a minute, seemed to be calm. The other two monsters, on the other hand, went insane.

"Noooooo," they screamed, in unison, "he is ours now. We shall take him back."

The zombie's eyes blinked. He looked at the Director.

"So weak," he whispered. "Help me."

The zombie's eyes then went wide, and he grunted hard.

"Nooooo!" he wailed. "Not again!!!"

He grunted and spasmed, as if being attacked by some invisible force. He shuddered in his bed so hard that the Nurse was thrown off and onto the floor with an *"OOF."*

The zombie paused for a moment, gasped, and then . . .

BLLLLLLLUUUUURRRRRRFFFFFFFT!

Let out the most earth-quaking, neighbor-waking fart I had ever heard in my life.

His body went limp for a few moments, and the other monsters were silent.

The Nurse on the floor got up slowly, and said, "Strongest herbal remedy . . . doesn't work."

He leaned down to check on the zombie, when suddenly . . .

RIIIIIIIIIP!

The zombie's torso tore free from his arms, and he sprung forward, biting the neck of the Nurse. There was a meaty crunch as the zombie dug in deep and chewed frantically on the Nurse-flesh. The Nurse fell back with a grunt, and brought the zombie with him. The zombie's feet popped off the ends of his restraints.

"I'm free," he gurgled, and then used the stubs that were left at the bottom of his legs to run out of the hut.

The Nurse stood up, staggered, and fell back on the bed, which still had the wiggling limbs of the zombie shaking it. The other two monsters laughed and laughed.

"Is he okay?" shrieked Ben.

"Griselda! GRISELDA!!!"

Security Measures

"Should have moved," the Nurse moaned. "Was too slow."

He coughed up a wad of blood and passed out.

The other Nurses and witches immediately surrounded him and went to work.

"Wait," said Ben. "Isn't he going to be a zombie now?"

"Not likely," said the Director. "The Nurses have undergone years of medical processing to assure that they are immune to vampirism, zombieism, werewolfism, mummification, and more."

"Ooooh . . . ," we all said. Finally, an explanation for why the Nurses never turned into monsters.

"He's going to make it," said Griselda. "That old zombie just missed the jugular."

One Nurse pulled out a huge needle and twine.

"But after these stitches," continued Griselda, "he's gonna have one heck of a scar."

"On the bright side, at least one of the Nurses will finally look different from the others," said Shane.

Someone screamed in the resort.

"That sounded like one of the banshees," said Director Z.

A Nurse came running through the door. "He's run into the jungle."

"We must institute security measures and capture that rogue zombie," said Director Z. "But I don't want the residents who have yet to be exposed to this dreadful sickness to know anything about it. They should be able to go about their daily lives—the better their moods, the stronger their lebensplasm will stay."

"I have an idea," I said. "Let's get them all into the theater for Ben's trivia. They love that stuff."

"Yeah," said Ben, "I could keep them distracted while you guys search for the zombie.

"They would all be safe in one place," said Director Z.

"Excellent!" I said. "So, I'll start the search for the rogue zombie with Shane . . ."

"WAIT," said a voice.

We all turned to see Gordon sitting up on his table.

"I'll go with you," said Gordon. "I'm a little amped up from my nap. Nap . . . wait, I was sleeping?"

"Gordon," said Ben. "Are you okay?"

"I feel GREAT," he said.

"Are you ready for your home game?" asked Shane.

"What!?" said Gordon. "I thought we were battling a rogue zombie."

"Welcome back, Gordon," said Director Z. "You and Chris should grab a half-dozen Nurses and execute a search for the rogue zombie. Ben will host Monster Trivia in the amphitheater, while Shane stands guard with a few of the karate-trained Nurses. First, however, please allow me to show you to your rooms. You could probably use a shower and a break."

I looked down to see my shirt caked with dried sea worm slime and wet with sweat. I took a whiff of my armpit and nearly passed out.

"Wow," Ben said, looking at his own clothes. "I almost forgot how I got here."

"How did we get here?" asked Gordon. "And where *is* here?"

Our break wasn't long—the Director gave us fifteen minutes. We met in the hallway.

"Whoa!" said Shane, as the door slammed behind him. "Did you see that view!? Amazing!"

"How can you think about the view when there's a deranged zombie on the loose?" asked Ben.

"Look, I know how to handle zombies," said Shane. "Maybe we should enjoy a nice fruit smoothie and kick it on the sand for a bit."

"I hate to break it to you," I said, "but we're not exactly on vacation."

We walked back down to the theater to meet with the Nurses. Shane pulled the karate-trained Nurses to the side.

"Now, this guy is fast, but with no arms and just stubs for feet, his center of gravity is off," said Shane. "Low sweeping kicks will be the easiest way to stop him."

Ben headed down to the stage with Horace. All the monsters gathered in the theater, dressed in relaxing beachwear. They all seemed happy, filled with energy, tanned, and fit. They were still old, but they didn't seem completely incapacitated anymore.

"Chris the Sussoroblat Wrecker! 'Sup, Duder?"

The voice came from behind me. I turned around swiftly and stared at an old but amazingly fit-looking zombie surfer, complete with a surfboard impaled through his body.

"Huh?" I said.

He reached out a rotten green hand that had seaweed strands stuck between its fingers. I gave it a shake.

"Yo," he said, "I'm Clive. Director Z asked me to show you around our facilities."

"I told you the zombies could talk!" Shane said.

"Some of us better than others," Clive said. "With all the sun and the sea here, and the relaxed lifestyle, I've been able to keep in pretty good shape. Maybe all the seawater has pickled my brains!"

"The zombie in the infirmary was talking," I said. "But, he was so old—how was he able to talk? And he said weird things, like we didn't matter because we were just young ones."

Before the zombie surfer could answer, Gordon jumped in.

"Cool," said Gordon. "Nice surfboard."

Gordon gave the board a knock and Clive winced.

"Yo, that's a little sore, dude!" he groaned.

"Sorry!"

"Wait," said Shane. "Why didn't you head to Raven Hill with the rest of the residents?"

"We got a pretty good run of waves," said Clive, "and I was so busy hanging ten that by the time I was done, everyone was gone! When a wipeout can't kill you, you could just surf forever!"

"But how do you surf with that thing sticking out of you?" asked Gordon.

"It ain't easy," said Clive.

"All right," I said. "Ben's about to start. Let's get going."

I grabbed a few Nurses, gave Shane a thumbs-up, and turned to Clive.

"Okay," I said. "Where should we start?"

"The resort towers are pretty well guarded," Clive said, "so I don't think that the rogue zombie got into those. He's either still in the jungle, on the beach, or at the aquarium."

"Aquarium?" I asked. "Director Z didn't say anything about an aquarium."

"Well, Directors are never going to tell you everything," Clive said. "They've always got something up their sleeves."

"What sort of aquarium?" Gordon asked.

"Aw, it's cool, man!" said Clive. "Like SeaWorld for sea monsters. With all the monster juice drainage, it's hard for some of these creatures to be out in the open ocean anymore."

"Wait, you call lebensplasm *monster juice*?" Gordon asked. "That's what we call it!"

"Yeah, my dude, it's gotta be monster juice! It just sounds so much cooler," said Clive, while high-fiving Gordon.

"Let's start at the aquarium," I said.

"You got it!" said Clive.

SeaMonsterWorld

I thought I knew everything about monsters working at Raven Hill, but then I visited the Paradise Island Aquarium and Sea Creature Rehabilitation Center. We stood in the main entrance glass walls towered ominously in front of us. Dark figures shifted in the tanks.

"This is freaking me out a little," I said. "How thick is that glass?"

"Forget about the tanks," said Gordon. "That freak could be hiding in here, and it's really dark."

"Yeah, most of these sea monsters prefer the dark," said Clive. "Except for the mermaids. They have a display with big rocks. They like to lay out and catch the rays."

The Nurses handed out flashlights and we turned them on. An ominous glow filled the massive room.

"How should we split up?" I asked Clive.

"Uhhh . . ." Clive scratched his head. A clump of hair and seaweed fell out. "Two Nurses should head down the west wing toward Moby Dick. Two should head toward the sea serpent display—make sure Hydra still has three heads. Two more should go talk with the mermaids and sirens, but DON'T get too close. The three of us will head toward the Kraken."

"You have a Kraken!?" Gordon yelled.

"Moby Dick is real?" I asked.

"Sure," replied Clive. "Vampires are real. I'm real. Why not Moby Dick—one of the fiercest sea monsters?"

"I wonder what other crazy monsters there are in the world," I gasped.

"We've got a couple of the craziest in our collection," Clive continued. "Have you ever seen a vampire squid?"

We headed deeper into the aquarium's main hall. Moans and groans came from the tanks. The hair on the back of my neck slowly rose. I swept my flashlight around the nooks and crannies, waiting for a rogue zombie to pounce, but there was nothing but shadow.

"Maybe we should have brought a Nurse," I said.

"Don't worry, dude," Clive said, "I'll be able to talk him down. Hey, check these guys out." He pointed at a tank to his right.

"What's in there?" Gordon asked.

In a flash, a huge, rotten shark flung itself at us.

THUNK!

"Whaa!" Gordon and I jumped back.

Another shark hit the glass and chomped at us.

The glass shook, but stayed in place.

"Coooool," said Clive. He clapped his hands together.

"What happened to those sharks?" I asked.

"Well, one day I was surfing, and a shark tried to bite me, so I bit him back."

"ZOMBIE SHARKS!?!" said Gordon. "That's amazing!"

"TOTALLY GNARLY, RIGHT!" Clive said, and then high-fived Gordon again. "The first guy went off and bit a few more. They act all aggro, but they're totally chill with humans—all you gotta do is growl at them, and they totally remember who made them zombies."

A long, low growl came from the end of the hallway.

"Whoa," said Clive, "the Kraken is angry. I guess we got too loud. Come on, let's check him out and see if our little rogue friend is down this way."

We walked to the very end of the hallway, and stood in front of the largest tank we had seen so far. Tentacles floated in and out of sight.

"No rogue zombies down here," said Gordon.

"Yeah," I said. "Let's go see if the Nurses found anything."

"Wait a second, dudes," said Clive, pointing to the tank.

A huge eye loomed in front of us, staring us down.

"What's up, big guy?" asked Clive.

The eye blinked once.

"This guy's heavy," Clive said. "He's the strongest sea monster we've got here. His jaw can crush a battleship. He's a little weak, like the rest of us, but he could still do some major damage. I'd like to take him for a ride, but I don't have a strong enough karate chop. One strong whack to the top of the head, and he'll listen to any instruction you give him."

We turned back down the hallway and headed to the entrance.

The Nurses didn't find anything in the aquarium, so we spent the rest of the day searching the jungle and found absolutely nothing. We returned to the resort, where we updated Director Z, Ben, and Shane in the dining room. A chef, who looked exactly like a Nurse except for his uniform, brought over a steaming tray of frog legs.

"Wait," said Ben. "Before I bite into this, I just have to ask: Is it even safe?"

"I assure you, it's been properly prepared," replied Director Z. "Our chefs are quite skilled at dezombification."

"Well, I'm hungry," said Gordon, and he started tearing at the leg meat.

"Eat up, gentlemen," said Director Z. "We have a long night ahead of us. We'll need to keep watch. Please break into shifts. I'll ask the Nurses to do the same, but they're not exactly big on details—they might miss something. I need your eyes out there."

"Well someone else can take the first shift, because I'm exhausted," I said. "I need to sleep for a few hours."

"I'm ON IT!" said Gordon.

"Wow," Shane said. "What did Griselda's spell do to you? You're pumped."

"Thanks, Gordon," I said.

I grabbed a pair of frog legs and stood up.

"I'm pooped. I'll just nibble these in my room, if you guys don't mind," I said.

"Of course," Director Z said. "Good night, Chris. I will also be turning in early tonight. I haven't slept in nearly three days. I'm so glad you gentlemen are here."

"Good night." I yawned.

I shuffled up to my room and passed out.

Romantically Rotten Dinners

"Dude," Gordon yelled, shaking me violently out of a deep sleep. It felt like the island was having an earthquake.

"I gotta sleep," I mumbled and turned over. "I'll pass out tomorrow if I don't."

"C'mon, wake up," he said, shaking me again.

I ignored him and drifted back to sleep. Moments later I awoke with a gasp. Something horribly putrid had filled my lungs. I tried to sit up to but something pinned me down on the bed. As hard as I struggled, I couldn't get to fresh air.

Then I heard what sounded like laughing. I recognized the voice. Gordon had pulled the sheet over my head, slid his butt under it, and farted, sealing me in. It was disgusting—I felt like I had been covered in a layer of fart sweat. My nostrils flared.

"You're sick, dude!" I yelled, finally able to peel the covers off of my face.

"Well, you should have just woken up when I told you to," Gordon said, giggling.

I tried to kick him, but he was already headed through my open door.

"You've got to see this!" he yelled. "This is hilarious."

With an angry grunt, I kicked off the stinky sheet and followed him outside.

I was happy to be breathing in the hot, heavy, moist air. In the starry, cloudless sky above, an almost-full moon shined. It was so clear, you could almost make out the moon's face—a combination of plains, highlands, and craters that made the moon look like it had eyes, a nose, and a mouth. I sighed, remembering how close I was to touching moon rock at Kennedy Space Center.

Still half asleep, I asked Gordon, "Are you showing me the moon?"

"Naw, stupid," he said. "What I'm about to show you, ya don't see every day. Keep walking. Shane and Ben are already there."

I shuffled down a shorter path than the one we had used earlier in the day, and came out on the beach. At the very end of the beach, up against the cliffs, loomed a massive dead whale.

"Ha-ha," I said, and yawned. "That beached whale is really funny, Gordon! The way its body has rotted and hollowed out to show its ribs. HILARIOUS!"

I turned around to leave, but Gordon grabbed me.

"Just wait until we get closer," he said, and chuckled.

We walked farther down the beach, and found Shane and Ben crouched behind a huge pile of driftwood.

"Get down," they hissed as we approached.

"They're too busy staring in each other's eyes to notice us," Gordon said.

"Who?!" I asked. Now I was really interested.

Gordon and I crouched down behind the driftwood with our friends. Our four heads peeked up over the wood and stared at the beached whale. It took a while for my eyes to adjust, but then I saw it.

"No way!" I said. "Clarice and Pietro are having dinner in the whale carcass."

"Yep, they sure are," said Gordon, and he had to put his hand over his mouth to stifle a giggle.

"I mean, this is serious," said Shane. "They must have snuck out after lights-out. They've got the checkered tablecloth and a nice candelabra. They've got really beautiful plates and silverware. Well done, Pietro!"

They sat at a small table inside the whale carcass. Pietro, the werewolf, picked up his fork, speared something on his plate, and then reached over to feed it to Clarice, the banshee.

She plucked the morsel off of the fork with her teeth, and began to chew delicately.

"What are they eating?" I asked.

"I think they're eating the whale," Ben said. "It must have washed up on the beach a few weeks ago. That thing is STINKY."

Just as Ben finished his statement, a strong wind blew up the beach, and we could smell the rotting sea creature.

"Ugggh," I said, and covered my nose.

"Wait, look," said Shane. "Ben is right!"

Pietro, huge butcher knife in hand, stood up, walked deeper into the whale, grabbed a nice rotten chunk, and sliced it off. He brought it down on the platter between their plates. He reached up and grabbed a scoop of the fat that was dripping off the rib cage above them, putting it on the whale meat like one would put whipped cream on an ice cream sundae.

"Banshees eat whale, huh? Who'd have known?" asked Gordon.

"Love makes you do strange things," said Ben with a sigh.

"Shut up, guys," I said. "I think they're talking."

It was hard to hear because of the shifting winds. We cupped our ears.

"When I first heard you screech at Raven Hill," said Pietro, "my ears perked right up. I knew that yours was the voice I always wanted howling at the moon with me."

"Oh, Pietro," purred the banshee, "you're just too kind. Well, I love that you actually still have all that hair on your head—most of the men around here are bald as babies!"

She reached up to his bushy head and started to twirl his hair.

His leg started twitching like a dog's.

"So silky," she said. "Do you use conditioner?"

"He most certainly does not," said Shane. "But he does like to roll around in dead things."

I started to laugh uncontrollably. Ben and Gordon soon followed.

We tried hard to stop, for fear of being heard, but it was too late.

Pietro stood up . . . and looked right at us.

"What are you doing here?" he asked.

We slunk lower behind the driftwood.

The vegetation next to us started to rustle, and out stepped another werewolf—I think his name was Howie. He held an accordion.

"What am I doing here?" he said. "You said ten o'clock, right?"

"Yes, and it's nine thirty," said Pietro. "We haven't even finished our main course."

"Forget it then," Howie said, "I'll just transform and

find something to roll around in for a while."

He was about to put the accordion down when Clarice stood up.

"No, wait," she said. "I'd love some music."

"Wonderful, then!" said Howie.

He started to play a crazy tune on the accordion, and the banshee nodded her head in appreciation. The song continued for a few seconds and then Howie started to sing.

"Awooo, awooo, aweeeeeeeooooo," Howie howled.

Pietro and Clarice joined in, their howls and screeches rattling the whale ribs.

"Man," said Gordon, "this is crazy."

We all plugged our ears while the three kept screeching and howling.

When the music was over, Clarice and Pietro began applauding wildly.

"Bravo, BRAVO!" she said.

"Well," Howie said with a bow, "I'll leave you two alone now. Have a wonderful evening!"

"Thanks, Howie," said Pietro. "I really, really appreciate it, my brother. Sorry I got snippy before."

Howie slunk back into the brush, leaving Pietro and Clarice in the moonlight.

"That was so romantic," said Clarice, and she put her head on Pietro's shoulder.

"Well," said Pietro, putting his hand around her back,

"now that we've had dinner and some entertainment, perhaps we should have a little dessert."

"Oh, my," she said. "What do you have for dessert?"

"Just your sweet, sweet lips," said Pietro.

"Oooh, not smooth," said Shane.

Clarice lifted her head in surprise.

The both moved in closer for a kiss.

"Ewww," said Gordon. "This is going to be gross."

They moved even closer . . .

. . . when a splash made us turn our heads. It sounded like something had flopped up onto the beach, but I couldn't see anything. Pietro and Clarice clearly didn't notice, as they were still lost in their kiss.

"Ewww," said Gordon again. "Old people kissing is just so gross."

"I think it's beautiful," said Shane. "Cross-monster relationships. We're entering a new era."

"Whatever," said Gordon.

"AAAAAHHHHHHHH!"

A screech pierced our ears.

"You bit me," said Clarice, jumping up from her seat. "And I thought you were a gentleman!"

She got up to leave, and Pietro got up to follow.

"Wait! I'm a werewolf, and you taste good! I had a moment of weakness! It will never happen again! Wait!"

"This was a huge mistake," she said.

Pietro suddenly dropped to the ground, shaking and drooling.

"Pietro?! PIETRO!?" Clarice yelled.

"Guurrrrgggglllyyyaaaaaah!" Pietro was struggling with something invisible, his arms pinned to his side, his head twisted back in agony.

"What the heck?" said Ben.

We jumped up and ran over toward Pietro.

Clarice saw us and said, "I have no idea what happened. It came on so quick!"

Shane leaned down to help Pietro up, but he thrashed around violently, frothing at the mouth.

"Pietro!" Shane yelled. "Relax!"

Pietro howled, and Shane jumped back.

"He won't bite you," I said.

"No, it's not that," said Shane. "Something's covering him. A thin skin."

"What!?" said Clarice.

Pietro thrashed and kicked the sand, fighting some invisible assailant. He growled and snapped his teeth.

"It's disappeared," said Shane, "but it was there when he howled."

"Howl again!" I yelled. "Pietro, howl again!"

"Aaaaarrrooooooooo!" Pietro howled, and the skin lifted off his body again, but sucked tight against him as soon as he was done howling.

"Again," Clarice yelled. "AAAAGGGAAIIINNNNN!"

"Your scream is helping," said Shane to Clarice.

"Arrrroooooooooooooooooaaaaahhhhh!" we all yelled as a clear skin peeled itself off Pietro, from his feet up to his forehead, with a wet, sticky sound.

The skin slowly rolled off of his head, and Pietro stopped struggling and started shaking. The skin was barely visible—almost completely see-through.

"Grab it," Ben yelled.

Gordon pounced, but by the time he hit the ground, all that was left was sand.

The skin zoomed back to the water, and with a splash it was gone.

"What *was* that thing?!" screeched Ben.

"Pietro, are you okay?" Clarice knelt down next to Pietro.

"He looks like he's twenty years older," I said.

"I . . . feel . . . twenty years . . . older," he said, and then turned into an old mangy dog.

Old mangy Pietro laid in the sand, sleeping and dreaming, his paws twitching uneasily.

"We should bring him back up to the facility," I said.

I've Got You Under My Skin

Gordon picked up the twitching dog and we all headed up the nearest path to the resort.

"It'll be all right, Pietro," said Gordon. "We're gonna get you some help."

Halfway to the resort, we ran into Director Z. His fine silk pajamas flapped in the ocean breeze.

"I heard screams and came as quickly as I could," he said. "What is it?"

"It's Pietro," I said. "He's been attacked by a weird sea skin."

"It covered him and drained him insanely fast," said Shane. "I think this is why the other residents are sick."

"Are you sure this skin is actually gone?" Director Z asked.

"Yeah, we heard it splash back into the ocean," said Gordon.

Two Nurses pounded down the path toward us.

"Nurse Inx," commanded Director Z, "take Pietro to the infirmary as swiftly as you can. Nurse Glick, raise the witches—we'll need special potions to be brewed tonight."

The Nurses ran off.

"Clarice," said the Director, "what on Earth were you doing outside? Why did you and Pietro violate our curfew?"

"I know, I know," said Clarice. "It was a very stupid thing to do."

"What is that on your lip?" asked Director Z. "Were you bitten by the sea skin?"

"Well . . . no." She hesitated. "It wasn't the sea skin . . ."

There was a long silence.

"Very well," said Director Z.

Clarice went back to her room. Director Z turned to us.

"Gentlemen, this is quite a development. We should all meet in my office. Please just give me fifteen minutes to ready myself, and do grab Clive. He's in room 345."

Director Z stormed back up the path.

Fifteen minutes later, we arrived at Director Z's office with Clive. A broken fish tank sat to the right of a huge desk. I walked over to the massive tank—the front of the tank was smashed in and the tank was completely dry. A small brass plate attached to the wood under the tank read PYGOCENTRUS NATTERERI.

I was about to ask Director Z what that meant when he sat down behind his desk. The desk still had a HERR DIREKTOR DETLEF nameplate sitting on it.

"Gentlemen," he said, "please do have a seat."

There was a leather couch and plush chairs surrounding a rug in front of the desk. We all chose a spot and sat down.

"Ummm, Boss . . ." Clive was halfway into his seat, and the board that ran through his body wouldn't let him go any further.

"I think I'll just stand," he said.

"That's quite fine," said Director Z. "Tell me, have you ever seen or heard about the bizarre skin creature that attacked Pietro?"

"No, I can't say that I have," replied Clive. "Totally new to me."

"I've been trying to ask Herr Direktor Detlef about it," said Director Z, "but I can't reach him at his number, and nobody seems to be picking up the phone at Raven Hill."

"Should we be worried?" Ben asked.

"Possibly," said Director Z, "but let's focus on the problem at hand. First, how can we be sure that this skin creature is responsible for all of the lebensplasm loss on the island?"

"I think it *has* to be," I said. "Each of the sick residents was drained extremely fast—just like Pietro."

"And," said Shane, "each of the sick residents was sealed in. We saw fluids from the monsters ooze out, but stay pressed against their bodies."

"And we couldn't even get lebensplasm levels," said Director Z. "But why do the victims act so strangely, so wild?"

"The skin must control them somehow," said Ben.

"What else do we know?" Director Z asked.

"Well," said Gordon, "it came from the ocean. We heard a splash as it came out of the water, and another splash when it went back in."

"We know it drained Pietro," said Shane, "but it was never able to control him. He was able to howl the skin off. Maybe it takes time to seal?"

"So, in essence, we're dealing with a deadly skin from the ocean that can seal itself perfectly onto its victim's body, drain the victim's lebensplasm, and control the victim. We're dealing with multiple skins, and the skins can't be removed by any means but howling."

"Yes," said Shane, "although I'm not sure how much time you would have to howl it off once it attacks. Maybe only ten or fifteen seconds."

"What else, gentlemen, what else?" asked a frustrated Director Z. "We must learn more about these beasts. But how?"

"We could ask the possessed monsters a series of questions," said Ben, "and see if we could get the right answers, or at least clues."

"I have a better idea," I said. "Let's follow the skin into the ocean and see where it goes—maybe learn something about it. Or catch it and bring it back to study it. Is this island equipped with a lab?"

"Yes, this island houses a premier lebensplasm research facility. But how are we going to get a skin to go back into the ocean?" Director Z asked.

"We just need to re-create the events of tonight," I replied.

"Clarice and Pietro need to kiss again?" Gordon asked. "Ewww."

"Clarice and Pietro were kissing?" Director Z asked.

"Well," said Ben, "they ended with a kiss. But there was a lot that lead up to it—a romantic candlelight dinner. An accordion song. And then there's the bite."

"The bite?" Director Z asked. "Oh . . . the mark on Clarice's lips . . ."

"If we re-create the date in every detail," I continued, "at the very same time it happened tonight, there may be a chance that the same skin will come for Pietro."

"Only this time when he howls it off," Shane said, "we go after it! Genius!"

"But how?" Gordon said. "Are we just going to throw on wet suits and swim really fast?"

"We've actually got some really gnarly scuba gear," said Clive. "And it's brand-new! None of the monsters use it, since most of them don't need to breathe underwater—or at all—but I think that should work."

"And do you have anything that could be used as transportation?" Director Z asked Clive.

"Yeah," Clive said. "Zombie sharks."

"Come again?" asked Director Z, eyebrow raised.

"Zombie sharks," Clive said, laughing. "They're a lot less deadly than they sound. In fact, zombie sharks are pretty chill around humans, because it was a human zombie that turned them into zombie sharks. *This* human zombie, to be precise."

"How do we get them to move?" asked Ben. "How do we steer them?"

"It's simple," said Clive. "You just dangle a little brain in front of them, and *zoom*, they're off. Need to turn right? Just dangle the brain a bit to the right. Need to turn left? Just—"

"We get the idea," Ben said. "But where are you

planning on getting the ... um ... brains for the mission?"

"Your friend Chris tells me that you're pretty smart," said Clive. "We could use your brains."

"See, this is what happens when you study," said Gordon.

"Naw, man," chuckled Clive. "I'm just kidding. We can just use some vegetable brain."

"Vegetable brain?" Shane asked.

"Yeah, man!" said Clive. "But it's really a fruit."

"Wait . . . ," I said, trying to clear my head. "Let me get this straight. The zombie sharks are going to chase down a fruit just because it's called *vegetable brain*?"

"They don't call it vegetable brain for nothin'!" said Clive.

"Vegetable brain . . . ," Ben mumbled as he pulled out his phone. "I really wish I could Google that, but there's no service on this island."

"Well, then, it's settled," said Director Z. "I'll send some nurses into the jungle to collect enough vegetable brain for the purpose. Chris, please work with Pietro and Clarice to make sure that tonight's date can be re-created. Clive, if you could please show the gentlemen how to work with the zombie sharks?"

Free Shark Rides for the Kids!

That next morning we waited nervously on top of the zombie sharks' tank for our riding lessons.

"I hope Clive's a no-show," said Ben. "I threw up on a plane; I don't think my stomach can handle riding a zombie shark. And what if they try to eat *our* brains?"

"I don't know," Gordon replied. "I'm kind of looking forward to it. This is like the ultimate extreme sport."

Gordon and Shane high-fived.

"Here he comes now," I said, and pointed to Clive dragging a bunch of scuba gear up the stairs to the top of the tank.

"Sorry I'm late, dudes," said Clive.

We all squeezed into our gear.

"Ummm . . ." Ben said. "Guys? I can't really see."

We looked over to see Ben's helmet fogged up.

"It's really hot in here," he said. "I'm not so worried about the zombie shark anymore. I'm worried I'm going to barf in *here* first. GUYS!?! ARE YOU THERE?!?"

"Deep breaths, dude," said Clive. "Just chill."

Gordon was stretching his suit out by running to the water's edge and back.

Suddenly the water at the top of the tank exploded and four rotten sharks flopped onto the platform right in front of Gordon.

"Ah!" yelled Ben as he fell over. "What the heck is going on?"

The sharks flopped and shook in the open air, but were able to turn teeth-side toward Gordon.

"Clive?" screamed Gordon, who was too stunned to move. "CLIVE?!"

The shark closest to Gordon used his fins to push himself forward. He opened his massive mouth wide, but before it could bite down on Gordon, Clive jumped into its mouth and . . .

CHOMP!

His surfboard pinned the shark's mouth open.

"Right on time, you stank fishies," yelled Clive. "Now, you better behave, or Daddy's gonna bite your nosies!"

The shark let Clive go and backed down. The other three started to whimper and shake.

"That's what I THOUGHT," yelled Clive. He grabbed the shark that had just bit him by the gill. "You! Stay here."

Clive turned to us. "Who's ready to rock?"

"CHRIS IS," my three friends said and pointed at me. They had clearly planned for this moment.

"Dude," said Clive, "come on over."

I slowly approached the shark. Its bloodshot eye turned toward me and it opened its mouth with a growl.

"Stop that!" yelled Clive, and gave the shark's nose a good slap.

Clive started the lesson. "All right, Chris. First thing you need to do is growl at the shark as you walk up to it. He needs to know you mean business."

"Grrr," I said.

"More," said Clive.

"GRRR," I said.

"Mean it," said Clive. "All you need to do is scare him, and he'll do whatever you want."

"GRRRRRRRRRRRRRR!"

The shark started to shake.

"Awesome, dude!" said Clive. "Now get on top of him and grab his fin!"

I looked at my friends.

"Go for it!" said Shane.

I mounted the shark, who growled and bucked below me.

"GRAB THE FIN, DUDE!" yelled Clive.

"Whoa," I said, clutching the fin. "Whoa, sharkie!"

"Kick his side!" yelled Clive. "Show him who's boss!"

I couldn't believe what I was doing. I thought of the rodeo I had seen a few years ago, and kicked the shark in the side while pulling back on his fin.

The shark stopped.

"Great!" Clive said. He dug around in a bag and pulled out a fishing pole. Hanging off the line was a piece of something yellowish-white and wrinkly. "Here's your vegetable brain. Just hold it in the direction you want to go, and go!"

I grabbed the fishing pole and dangled it in front of the shark. He started to creep forward, his fins flopping on the wet platform.

"Okay," I said, as the shark started to tip into the tank. I was frightened and excited. "Here I go! Yee-haw!"

The shark tipped over—SPLASH—and took off!

He was extremely fast, and extremely strong. I desperately clutched his fin with my left hand. I tried my best to wriggle the vegetable brain in a way that would get him to swim straight, but he was spiraling down to the bottom of the tank, shooting back up, swimming all over the place.

"Aaaahhhhhhh!" I screamed.

Only twenty seconds in the tank, and I didn't know which way was up. The shark jerked to the right and I felt the pole slip out of my hand. He bucked up, and I felt myself fly—first through the water, and then through air.

I landed with an OOF. Through my water-streaked helmet, I could see the other three sharks in front of me.

"Grr," I said weakly. The world spun before me. I felt like every part of my body was vibrating.

"You should be stoked," said Clive, who helped me up. "That was a great first run! We gotta work on some stuff here and there, but that was awesome! Who's next?"

I slowly made my way down the spiral staircase to the benches in front of the huge window looking into the tank. I sat down and closed my eyes to collect myself for a few minutes. I opened them up to see a zombie shark fling Shane against the window. He gave me a thumbs-up as he slowly slid down the glass.

This was going to take all day.

Date Night Re-do

Later that night, we were exhausted and sore, but ready to ride. Gordon, Shane, Ben, and I all stood behind the same piece of driftwood that we had the night before—this time in scuba gear. Just two hundred feet behind us, Clive held on tightly to the zombie sharks in preparation for our voyage.

"This is absolutely crazy," said Ben.

"I think that's why I like it," Shane said.

"You know who really thinks this is crazy?" I asked.

"Who?" asked Gordon.

"Clarice!" I replied. "The poor woman is sick of Pietro, but she's agreed to go through everything that happened last night, from appetizers to being bitten."

"She's getting nipped by an old werewolf," Gordon said. "We're riding zombie sharks into the deep. Now you tell me who's in for a crazier night."

A figure came shuffling up the beach to us. It was hard to tell who it was, even in the moonlight.

"Wait," the figure huffed, "I'm ready! Director Z said I should help you kids out!"

"Gil?" Ben asked, "Is that you?"

Sure enough, the old swamp creature shuffled up to us, huffing and puffing.

"I'm better at swimming than running," he said.

"Why are you wearing scuba gear?" asked Gordon. "Aren't you a fish?"

"I'm a freshwater fish," said the swamp creature. "This water is far too salty for me. But I know I'll be able to help you down there."

"Wow," said Shane, "a fish in scuba gear. Cool."

"All right," I said, "just crouch down with us behind this log, and stay quiet. No swamp gas."

"No swamp gas, got it," the swamp creature agreed.

Up ahead, Pietro and Clarice approached the whale carcass.

"Just get this straight," Clarice said to Pietro. "This is NOT going anywhere. I'm only doing this to help everyone out."

"Clarice, honey—" Pietro started.

"Don't 'honey' me!" Clarice yelled back.

I popped up from behind the driftwood, and yelled, "Guys! This is serious! You have to do everything exactly as you did before. You weren't yelling at each other!"

"Now *you're* yelling," pointed out Shane.

"Just this once," I hissed at him.

I crouched back down behind the driftwood with my friends and the swamp creature. Our five heads peeked up over the wood and stared at the beached whale. We waited five or ten minutes, while Clarice and Pietro ate their appetizers quietly.

"Okay, this is about the time we started talking," I said.

"I said something like, 'Wow, they snuck out. Pietro did a great job with the checkered tablecloth and plates and everything,'" said Shane.

Pietro picked up his fork, speared something on his plate, and then reached over to feed it to Clarice.

She grabbed the wad of whale flesh and stuffed it in her mouth.

"But you ate it off the fork before," Pietro whined.

"I'm telling you, thish ish going nowhere," said Clarice with a mouth full of whale flesh. "Thish ish absolutely dishgusting, by the way."

"I said something like, 'What are they eating,'" I said.

"And I said, 'They're eating the stinky whale, blah, blah, blah,'" said Ben.

"Blah, blah, blah," said Gordon.

"Blah, blah, blah," said Shane.

"Blah, blah, blah," said the swamp creature.

"Shush," I said to the swamp creature. "You weren't here."

The swamp creature shushed, and we all peeked over the log to Pietro and Clarice.

"When I first heard you screech at Raven Hill," said Pietro, "my ears perked right up. I knew that yours was the voice I always wanted howling at the moon with me."

"Oh, Pietro," said the banshee through clenched teeth. "You're. Just. Too. Kind. Ugh, I can't take this. Your hair is greasy and smells like cat turds. How you found a litter box to roll around in at Paradise Island is beyond me."

She reached up to his bushy head with a BLECH and started to twirl his hair.

His leg started twitching like a dog's.

"Then came Shane's joke and we started to laugh," I said.

"Har har har huh huh huh," we all fake-laughed.

Pietro stood up . . .

"What are you doing here?" he asked.

The vegetation next to us started to rustle, and out stepped Howie. He held his accordion.

"Yeah, what am I doing here?" he asked. "I thought

you said Clarice and you were through."

"And I think we still are," Pietro said. "But we still need to do this. I told you."

Howie played his crazy tune and the three of them howled. The whale's exposed ribs rattled again, though not quite as hard as the night before.

"I hope this works," I said.

When the music was over, Clarice and Pietro applauded.

"Bravo," she said, with no emotion at all.

"I'm outta here," said Howie.

"Thanks, Howie," said Pietro.

Howie slunk back into the brush, leaving Pietro and Clarice alone in the moonlight.

"I can't believe I'm doing this," said Clarice, and she put her head on Pietro's shoulder.

"Well," said Pietro putting his hand around her back, "now that we've had dinner—"

"Yeah, yeah," she said. "What do you have for dessert?"

"Just your sweet, sweet lips," said Pietro.

"Oooh, not smooth, Pietro," said Clarice.

Clarice lifted her head. They both moved in closer for the kiss.

"Ewww," mumbled Clarice. "This is going to be gross."

They moved even closer . . .

SPLASH!

"Yessss!" I hissed.

Gordon was still staring at the kiss.

"I've said it before, and I'll say it again," he said. "Old people kissing is gross."

"I think it's so sad it didn't work out," said Shane. "This could have been an amazing cross-monster relationship. Gil, are you currently looking for love? I hear Griselda's single."

"I've always been partial to Queen Hatshepsut," said the swamp creature.

"Ahhh, so you're a mummy man, eh?" said Shane.

"Shhhh," I said. "Get ready."

"AAAAAHHHHHHHH!"

The screech pierced our ears!

"I can't believe I let you bite me again," said Clarice, jumping up from her seat.

She got up to leave, and Pietro got up to follow.

"Wait! Wait! I really think we can work this out."

"This was a huge mistake," she said.

Pietro dropped to the ground, shaking and drooling.

"Goooooooo!" I yelled.

We ran down to the water and the zombie sharks.

"Take it easy down there," said Clive. "I wish I could come with you, but I do nothing but float with this surfboard crammed into me. Reserve your energy. Don't get gassed out too quick!"

We mounted our sharks and put on our helmets. Shane's shark had a small pouch strapped to it. Inside the pouch was a net.

"Let's hope we're lucky enough to catch this thing," I said.

Clive ran up to each shark and turned on the headlamps he had strapped on them. As he turned each light on, he yelled in the shark's ears.

"Don't try anything funny down there," he yelled, "or the humans riding on you will bite you into bits."

We all growled, and the sharks shuddered.

"Now, follow the brains!" Clive said, and we held up our vegetable brains.

Howling and screeching came from the whale carcass.

"There it is!" yelled Gordon.

In the moonlight, we could see the sea skin slink down to the water's edge.

"Goooooo!" I yelled.

We kicked our sharks and wiggled our vegetable brains.

The last thing I heard as we crashed under the waves was "Good luck!" from Clive.

Ripped from the Deep!

Our four zombie sharks swam deeper. The swamp creature kept pace alongside us. At first, I couldn't see anything through the murky water. Between the waves and trying to steer the zombie sharks in the open ocean, I was worried we had lost the skin.

I opened up my helmet communicator.

"Testing, testing, one, two, three," I said. "Are you getting this?"

"Copy," said Ben.

"Copy," said Gordon.

"Copy that," said Shane.

BLLLUUUURRRFFT!

"What was that?" Gordon asked.

"Sorry," said the swamp creature. "I held in a lot of swamp gas up on the beach." FFFFLLLLLAAAARRRT!

"Fine," I said. "We can't breathe it in down here, anyway."

We had finally got out of the murky water created by the waves, and could see a coral reef below us.

"Get your sharks to move their headlamps around," I said. "We have to find this thing!"

Fish shot out of the way of the zombie sharks as we skimmed the top of the coral reef. Crabs scuttled for shelter.

"This is beautiful," said Ben. "So many colors."

"Oh, suuuuuuuuuuuuure," said the swamp creature. "Everybody loves a coral reef. But a swamp . . . that's a beautiful thing."

We circled around the area where we though the skin had gone, and then circled around it again.

"I think we've lost it," said Shane.

"Wait!" said Gordon. "Follow me! I see something shimmering ahead."

Gordon kicked his zombie shark and shot forward. We followed.

"He's right," said Shane. "I can see it up there!"

"Whoa!" yelled Gordon and stopped his shark.

"What's going on?" I asked as we reached Gordon.

"Oh . . . ," said Ben, pointing down.

Gordon had stopped at the edge of a huge drop.

Behind us was the colorful, lively reef. Below us were dark, cloudy waters. We could see the skin slowly slink deeper and deeper until it was lost in the dark.

"I wonder how far down it goes?" Ben asked.

"I'm not sure," I replied, "but we *have* to go after it."

"All right, boss," said Shane.

"I dunno, guys," said Ben. "This is pretty creepy."

A high-pitched screech floated up from the deep.

"Let's go," said the swamp creature.

We headed down into the deep.

"I can barely see in front of me," Gordon said, "it's so murky."

"And fr-fr-freezing," stuttered Ben.

The sharks plodded ahead, and soon their headlamps gleamed off the skin.

"It's right in front of us," Gordon said.

"We've reached the bottom of this trench," I said, and shined my light along the lifeless sea floor. "Look."

"Oh, man," said Ben. "Take a look at this."

He shined his light on something white lying on the floor.

"Is that a skeleton?" I asked

"Yep," said Shane. "A human skeleton."

"Oh, man," I said. "This isn't good."

"Um, guys," said Gordon, "check this out."

He had stopped his zombie shark. The shark's headlamp shined on a wicked looking monster that bloomed out of a huge fleshy sea pod like a sick flower. Its face looked like an eel's, razor-sharp teeth lined its mouth, and its hands were massive crab claws. Huge bloody gills breathed in and out. Below the scaly, slimy neck, the creature's organs hung out freely, bobbing around in the shifting waters.

"What the heck?!" Ben said.

"Membranium!" said the swamp creature.

"What?" said Gordon.

"Just watch the skin," said the swamp creature.

The skin floated over to the disgusting creature, and covered it from head to toe. As it did, the skin went from translucent to the same green, scaly, slimy color of the rest of the creature.

"I've heard about these things," said the swamp creature, sounding a little scared now, "but I never knew they ate lebensplasm."

The skin sealed up with a nice PLOP, and the creature opened its eyes.

"Move your lights away," I hissed.

Everyone did as they were told, and swung their sharks around . . .

. . . to reveal an entire wall of membranium! Some had skin, and some did not. Their disgusting bodies swayed in the soft current.

"We've got to get out of here," said the swamp creature, "and we can if we just move fast enough."

"All right," I said. "Everybody—"

"Arrgghh! It's got me," yelled the swamp creature.

He thrashed in the water, screamed . . . and farted.

FRRRRRRRTTTTT!

He stopped thrashing.

"Gil?" I said, "Are you okay?"

"I think so," he said. "Look . . ."

Before the swamp creature could say anything else, my zombie shark bucked from under me. It must have caught a smell of the organs that were floating out in the water, because it headed for the nearest skinless membranium and . . .

CHOMP!!!

The entire wall erupted in screams. The skinless membranium floated in place, but the ones with skins pulled themselves slowly out of their sea pods, and slinked slowly toward us.

"They can only go so far," said the swamp creature. "They're attached by umbilical cords!"

My shark had been bitten by several membranium and was being munched on the wall. I grabbed on to the tail of Ben's zombie shark.

"Swim up, up, uuuuup!" I yelled.

The swamp creature floated up, and Ben, Shane, and Gordon jiggled their vegetable brains in front of their sharks.

But it was too late.

"Skins!" Gordon yelled.

"They're after the zombie sharks!" I said.

Within seconds, three skins had sealed themselves around our zombie sharks. The sharks struggled in the water. The membranium kept coming out of the wall, snarling and snapping, their razor teeth lashing in the water. Their bodies pulsated with anger in the deep water as they released more and more of their umbilical cords.

"We've got to get out of here!" I yelled. "Swim up as fast as you can—they're going to turn the zombie sharks on us!"

We swam as hard as we could, the zombie sharks struggling below us, lashing and snapping at the skin that was closing in on them.

"Grrrrr . . ." They growled and fought. We were halfway up the trench, gaining speed. Then, from the deep—

BLLLLUUUURRRFFFTTTT!

BRRRRRPPPFFFFFT!

SPPPLLUUUUUFFFFFTTTT!

"The sharks just farted," said Shane. "They're turning our way."

We neared the top of the trench, and the sharks were already halfway up. The swamp creature was nowhere to be seen.

"Gil!" I yelled. "We could really use your help!!!"

A huge boulder on the edge of the trench started to shimmy and shake.

"Hurrrrryyyyy," said the swamp creature.

"He's the one pushing the boulder!" yelled Ben.

We shot up past the boulder, and as soon as we leveled off to head for the coral, it tipped over the edge. There were scrapes and crunches as it headed down the side of the trench.

"Hurry," said the swamp creature. "It will just stun them momentarily. You've got to get to the shore. Pull off your gear, you'll float up faster!"

Before the swamp creature could even finish his statement, we each took huge breaths, pulled off our scuba gear, and raced to the surface of the water.

When we burst through the waves, it looked like the beach was at least a hundred yards away. We swam as fast as we could.

"I . . . ," gasped Ben, "I . . . can't do it . . ."

"Yeah," I gasped, "I think I'm done for."

The swamp creature popped up out of the water and grabbed Ben. Shane and Gordon each grabbed one of my arms.

"Let's goooooo!" screamed Gordon.

We swam like crazy, but there was a splash just behind us. The zombie sharks jumped out of the water, belly flopped, and headed for us.

"We're fish food!" yelled Ben.

"Not today!"

"Clive?" I asked.

Sure enough, Clive was using the surfboard lodged in his body to paddle out past us and toward the sharks.

"Hey, you overgrown guppies!" yelled Clive. "Stop this right now, or Daddy's gonna poke your eyes out!"

"Wait," I yelled. "Clive, they're possessed!"

But it was too late.

A shark picked Clive up by his surfboard and whipped his jaw back and forth. Clive flew right off and disappeared under the water. The sharks followed.

"No!!!!" I yelled.

I tried to swim back, but the swamp creature stopped me.

"Are you crazy?" he asked "Do you want to die, too?"

I stopped fighting, and we swam the last ten yards or so to the shore. We flopped up on the beach, breathing hard.

Two waves later, Clive's surfboard washed up next to us.

I passed out.

With a Little Help from an Enemy

I awoke to find myself lying on the cold, wet beach. Under the light of the moon, Director Z leaned over me. Behind him were Shane, Ben, Gordon, and the swamp creature. I looked up and down the beach, but it was just the four of them.

"Clive?" I asked.

"I'm sorry Chris, but we don't think he made it," Director Z said.

"Man, that stinks," I said.

"He totally saved us," said Shane. "He was a good zombie."

"How long was I out?" I asked, standing up.

"Just long enough for Director Z to get down here," Ben said.

"Gil tells me that he knows what's lurking down there," said Director Z.

"Well," said the swamp creature. "I heard rumors before. Rumors about the membranium. Disgusting, grotesque creatures, bound to the seafloor by their own flesh and unable to ever free themselves. To feed, they peel off their own skin, which is then sent to hunt down prey. Once it finds its meal, the skin wraps around the poor soul and slowly drains the life out it. I never knew it had a taste for lebensplasm. And I certainly never heard of the skin controlling its victims."

"So, basically, we now have our answer," said Director Z. "The reason that the residents have been so ill—and so possessed—is because of the hive of membranium that live just off the shore."

"Have you ever heard of these things?" Ben asked Director Z. "Do you know how to defeat them?"

"There is absolutely no research on membranium," said Director Z. "So, figuring out how to defeat them is not going to be easy."

A great gurgling interrupted our conversation. We looked to see the ocean frothing and bubbling at about the spot where the trench was. The water rippled and slowly headed toward the shore.

"Oh no," said the Director.

"The membranium!" said the swamp creature.

"They must be really angry," said Gordon.

The swamp creature farted again.

"I'm sorry," he said. "When I get frightened, I fart."

"Is there ever an occasion where you don't break wind?" asked Director Z, waving his hand in front of his nose. "Wait . . . why don't I smell anything?"

"Well," said the swamp creature, "I'm still locked into this skin. It's not doing anything to me. But, I'm stuck."

"Wait," I said, "it didn't just fall off when you farted in the ocean?"

"No, in fact it gave me the strength I needed to push that boulder onto the sharks."

"But you're not possessed?" asked Shane.

"Nope," said the swamp creature. "Feel great."

The pack of membranium skin was about fifty yards from the shore.

"Wait," Shane said. "Wait a minute. I think I've got a big idea here. I think farting is the answer."

"What do you mean!?" I said. "Shane, be quick and be clear. We don't have much time!"

"When did the zombie sharks fall under the control of the skin?" Shane asked, and then answered his own question, "Right after they farted. And when did the rogue zombie go rogue? Right after it farted."

"Okay, go on . . ." Gordon said. He looked nervously at the membranium skin, which was riding a wave on its way up to the shore.

Shane took in a big breath, and said, "I think that to control their victims, the membranium squeeze them so hard that they fart. That's how the skin knows it's got you! But when the victim farts before the membranium really has a grip on them, then it just stops and sits there."

"That's wonderful for someone like Gil," said Director Z, "but what about the residents who are already affected?"

The first of the skin creatures washed up on the shore, and started creeping up the beach.

"Wait! Remember when the rogue zombie was force-fed herbs?" I asked.

"Yes," everyone said in unison.

"The membranium lost control for just a little bit," I said. "The skin let loose for ten or fifteen seconds. If we could get the monsters to fart just then, they should be okay."

"All right," said Director Z, and then he called up the beach, "all Nurses, this is an ALARM! Please secure the residents in their rooms and await further instructions in the infirmary. Gil, I'll need your help with the victims—you'll make the perfect flatulence coach."

"How can we help? By stopping the line of membranium skin heading into the resort?" I asked.

"No," said Director Z. "I'd rather you remain worthless."

"Worthless!?" yelled Gordon. "We almost lost *our* skin down there."

"No, you misunderstand," said Director Z. "So far the membranium haven't paid you much notice—perhaps they've developed a taste for the residents. But now that you've snooped around their lair, they might have started noticing you."

"Got it," said Shane. "Just tell us what to do."

"I need you to figure out how we can defeat these nasty creatures. Getting the residents to fart, if we can even keep them conscious long enough to, is going to be tough. We need a real solution."

"Got it!" I said.

"For now," said Director Z, watching the last of the membranium head through the jungle, "I'll get Griselda to make as much herbal remedy as possible, and add a gas-producing ingredient. We'll have to hope that we can convince the residents to fart in the ten to fifteen seconds we have when they're released from the membranium's grip."

Director Z ran up the beach, as the sound of screams rose into the air once again.

"GET THEM IN THEIR ROOOOOOMMMS!" Director Z yelled up to the resort.

I shook my head, trying to stay conscious.

"I'm so overwhelmed," I said.

"We can think this through," said Ben.

Another scream tore through our ears. It started healthy and young, and ended old and garbled.

"Maybe we should let all of the membranium skins attach to monsters," said Gordon, "and then, while they're busy, lead the Kraken down there and POW!"

"It's a good idea," I said, "but did you see how many membranium there were down there? We'd need three or four times more monsters."

"Plus," added Shane, "what if they drained the monsters dry before the Kraken was able to finish the job? I guess we can hope that there are enough herbs, and the monsters fart so they're not harmed. But that's asking a lot of the monsters."

"No matter what," I said, "we need to make sure to tell all of the monsters to fart as much as they can if they're attacked. Then we won't even need herbs."

From the resort, we could hear the Nurses yell, "FAAAART! FAAAAART!"

"Looks like they already know," said Shane.

"But back to the Kraken," said Gordon. "What if he could take care of business even with the membranium's skin on?"

"It's too risky," I said. "We don't even know if we can control the Kraken. And the membranium will just get angrier and hungrier if we fail. We have to attack them when all of their skins are off. So, how do we get all of the skins off and keep them distracted?"

We all thought as hard as we could. It was hard with all the screaming.

"Wait!" yelled Ben. "I've got it! We just need to get Nabila out here."

"You're kidding, right?" said Gordon. "These guys are about to be sucked dry like a bowl of blood punch at a vampire prom, and all you can think about is your girlfriend?"

"She's not my girlfriend!" Ben yelled. "Hear me out! She showed us her machine that could make the sound of farting herring, right? If we could get her and her invention here, maybe she could attract a school of farting herring. She keeps the machine in her fanny pack, and she always has that on."

"But why would the membranium be interested in a school of farting herring?" I asked.

"We could wrangle the herring she attracts into a tank at the aquarium," Ben replied. "And then have the zombies bite all of them. Then, we'd have a school of zombified farting herring to lead down to the membranium hive with vegetable brain. We'd be able to lure ALL the skins *and* have a school of hungry fish to feast on the tender and delicious membranium organs!"

"Genius!" Shane yelled.

"All right," I said. "Let's tell Director Z and figure out how to get her here."

We all rushed back up to the resort. It was completely deserted. There was no steel drum music in the open-air theater. There was no zombie floating in the Jacuzzi.

"This is creepy," Ben said.

"If it wasn't for all of the screaming," Shane said, "I'd say that this place was abandoned."

We followed the screaming back to the infirmary.

"Oh man," Gordon said. "Look at that line."

A massive line had formed outside of the infirmary. It was filled with Nurses who each had a grip on a possessed old monster, waiting to get inside.

We ducked into the infirmary to see the Nurses and witches frantically running around, administering the herbal remedy to monsters that thrashed wildly. A few looked like they had farted successfully, and were calmly being checked out by Nurses. The others looked as if they were deep in the grip of membranium madness.

"Fart! Just fart as fast as you can!" yelled the swamp creature.

"Vhat do you mean?" croaked one weak-looking vampire. "I can't just faaaaaAAAARRGHHH!"

He writhed on his bed, went stiff as a board, and then farted.

"That's not the kind of fart we were hoping for," said Shane.

The vampire broke from his restraints, and grabbed the bag of herbs that was in the hand of the Nurse.

"These taste terrible!" yelled the vampire. "Let us eat in peace!"

He threw the bag of herbs in the fire that was built in the back of the infirmary to boil the cauldron. It burst into a purple flame.

The Nurse went to grab the vampire, but he jumped to the left and cackled wildly.

"We'll drain this one with one big slurp," the vampire yelled, and threw is head back. "Yummmmmmmm . . ."

As the YUM went on, the vampire wrinkled up in front of our eyes. We could hear him being dried up and eaten, but there was nothing we could do.

"Disgusting!" said Gordon. "He looks mummified."

The skin crawled off the vampire, and he was left gasping for air. He let out one last death rattle and fell into the arms of the Nurse. The skin shot out of the room.

As the Nurse dragged him to the back of the infirmary, Shane said, "He's not the only one. Just look!"

The Nurse gently laid the vampire on top of a pile of poor, mummified monsters.

Director Z walked over to us.

"This isn't the safest place to be at the moment," he said. "Things are getting dire. We've cured a few thanks to the herbs, but it's been very hard to get the monsters to fart in time. And we can't keep this up forever."

"Well, no worries," Shane said, "because we've got an idea that's going to solve all of this."

"Let's go to my office, where it's safer," the Director said.

With the doors to Director Z's office closed, the screams of the monsters were almost drowned out.

Almost.

"What do you think, gentlemen?" said Director Z. "How are you going to save the day this time?"

"Zombie herring," said Ben. "We need you to get one of the girls who was with us on our school trip. How quickly can we make that happen?"

"I can call Ms. Veracruz straight away," said Director Z. "But, what do we need this girl for?"

"She has a device that can be used to call a school of herring," said Ben. "Did you know that herring fart—constantly, in fact? It's their way of communicating. We'll call a school, zombify them, and then use them to distract all of the membranium skin that's not already feasting on the monsters."

"And then what?" asked Director Z.

"And then," said Shane, "when the skinless membranium's organs are all squishy and juicy hanging out in the ocean, the school of herring will swarm . . . and feast!"

"Excellent!" said Director Z. "A wonderful idea!"

He picked up the phone, but frowned once it was up to his ear.

"The line is dead," he said.

He got up from behind his desk.

"I must find out who has cut the phone line, and see if it can be repaired," he said.

He stormed toward the door, which was thrown open in his face.

Griselda stood in the door with a crazy look in her eye, holding several long cords in her hand.

"Looking for something, Zachary dear?" she cackled.

"Griselda!" Director Z gasped.

"I'm afraid your dear Griselda is no longer here," said the twisted figure in the door. "And I'm afraid that you will not be getting off of this island! Welcome to your doom!"

A huge explosion rattled the resort.

"That sounds like the boat depot!" said Director Z.

In response, Griselda cackled and ran back into the resort.

"This has certainly changed things," said Director Z. "We've just lost our chief witch and herbalist at a time when we're already running out of herbal remedy, the phone lines have been cut, and we now have no boats to get off of the island."

Calling All Farters! Calling All Farters!

"Well, now," said Director Z, "we have to think of another plan—we can't summon your friend."

"What about Gil?" I asked. "Can he call the herring?"

"I don't think Gil is actually communicating when he farts," said Director Z. "I think he is simply...farting."

"All right," Ben said. "Stick me back in my sea worm. I want to go home."

"Wait!" said Gordon. "Maybe Ben's onto something. Let's just send a sea worm to get Nabila!"

"I'm afraid we can't do that," said Director Z. "The only woman who knows how to create the correct smellgood and hibernation spells is under the control of the membranium."

"But Nabila doesn't have a sense of smell," said Ben. "Would she be able to make the trip then?"

"Hmmm . . . ," said Director Z. "The trip will be long for her. She'll be confused and disoriented. However, the chances of her perishing inside of the worm are very slim."

"Let's do it, then!" I said.

"Does the intercom still work?" Director Z asked himself. He walked over to the door, and pressed a button on the box there. "Calling Nurse Kook."

There was a short pause.

"Yes, Boss?" Nurse Kook said over the intercom.

"Oh, good, the intercom still works!" said Director Z. "Please send the swiftest sea worm over to my office, immediately."

"Your office?" asked Nurse Kook.

"Immediately," replied Director Z.

There was another pause. We listened to the crackle of the intercom and screams in the distance.

"Okay, Boss," said Nurse Kook. "Sea worm's on its way to you."

"How are things at the aquarium?" asked Director Z. "Have you had any problems guarding it?"

"So far, so good, Boss," said Nurse Kook. "Everyone seems to be fine here."

"Excellent!" said Director Z. "It looks like the membranium either can't get through the filtration system of the tanks, or are unaware of the aquatic residents. Thank you, Nurse Kook."

Director Z returned to his desk. Just as he sat down, there was a crash, and a sea worm head burst through the window.

"Oh, man!" said Gordon. "Not that smell again!"

"Ah," said Director Z to the sea worm. "Thank you for being so quick. We need you to head back to Cape Canaveral, as swiftly as you can."

The sea worm nodded its slimy head. Director Z turned to us.

"Whom does the sea worm seek?" he asked.

"Her name is Nabila," said Ben. "She's small with dark, beautiful eyes and—"

"Actually," I said, "she's really easy to find. She has the thickest glasses and the shiniest braces you've ever seen."

"You forgot the fanny pack," added Shane. "It's hot pink."

"Seek the bespectacled but beautiful bearer of the fluorescent fanny pack," boomed Director Z. "Be discreet. But most of all, be swift. And drop this message off with Ms. Veracruz. You will know her by her hairnet."

Director Z scribbled on a piece of paper and held it up. The sea worm slurped it up, leaving a bit of slime on his hand.

"What are you telling her?" asked Shane.

"To prepare more memory-erasing serum," Director Z replied.

The sea worm backed out of the window. When his head had fully cleared, the frame fell into the office with a CLUNK, and the stinky, cool air was replaced with fresh, warm air.

Director Z stuck his head out of the window, and called to the exiting sea worm.

"NEXT TIME, PLEASE USE THE DOOR!"

As the sun rose on Paradise Island, the situation had gone from bad to insane. We had gone over every detail of our plan twenty times, and all we needed now was for Nabila to arrive. We waited on the beach for her sea worm to come in. Ben, more nervous than usual, paced across the sand.

From behind us, the sound of broken glass filled the air. We turned our heads to see a monster sailing from the top floor of the resort.

"It looks like the membranium have figured out how to get into the rooms," I said.

"At least the skin will protect him from the fall," added Shane. "That's one positive thing."

"Why are we just sitting here waiting!?" groaned

Gordon. "I could be up there shoving herbs into monster mouths!"

He kicked a mound of sand.

"There aren't many herbs left," said Shane. "It's safest for us down here at the beach, and we need to be here when Nabila arrives, or she's going to be crazy confused."

"Gordon's right, though," I said. "We shouldn't *all* be down here. It's insane up at the resort! Sure, we saved a dozen monsters, but most of them are so weak they can't even help with the superpowered skin on. The dead monster pile was pretty deep when we left."

"Director Z is in control for now," said Ben. "We just have to hope he stays in control. Once the herbs run out, the membranium will drain the monsters *fast!*"

More membranium skin shimmied up the shore.

"Hurrrryyyyy!" I yelled out into the ocean.

As if in response, the sea worm crashed out of the ocean, and crawled up to the beach.

WHAAARRRFFF!

It barfed up Nabila, and then backed down into the water. We ran up to her with the towels we had brought, and surrounded her.

"Oh, man!" said Ben, waving a hand around in front of his face. "I can't imagine how bad that would have smelled."

She was curled up in a pile of goo, and we bent down

to clean her off. Shane reached to roll her over onto her back, and she sprang up in one fast jump.

"Aaaarrrrgh!" she yelled, and whipped something out of her fanny pack.

There was a crackle and Shane jumped back.

"It's a Taser!" Gordon yelled, and rushed at her.

"WAAAAAIT!" I yelled.

Everybody stopped.

"What. Is. Going. ON?" Nabila asked. She gripped the Taser, which was still crackling loudly.

"Nabila," I said. "We need your help with the . . ."

I hesitated, but then continued. "With the old monsters from Raven Hill. They're here on vacation."

She looked confused for a few seconds, and then she put the Taser back into her fanny pack.

"Oh, wow," she said. "This is AMAZING!"

She looked down at her clothes, which were still covered in sand and sea worm gunk.

"Was that a giant sea worm?" she asked. "It was so tight in there, I passed out after a few hours."

"We didn't mean to startle you," said Ben. "But it was the only way we could get you here quickly. Luckily for you, you can't smell. Those things smell terrible."

"Wait," she said, looking confused again, "how do you know I don't have a sense of smell? How do you even know my name? I was going to introduce myself on the science trip, but you guys didn't join us."

"Well, it's a long story and we don't have much time," I said, "but the short story is that you DID meet us on the trip to Cape Canaveral. Then, on the first night, *we* got taken away in sea worms to here: Paradise Island. You, and all the other students were given a memory-erasing serum to forget us."

"I thought breakfast that first morning tasted unusual," she said.

"What we really need to know," said Ben, "is if you have that fish-calling device in your fanny pack. We need your help to attract a group of farting herring, zombify them, and use them to lure the skin off a disgusting hive of sea creatures called the membranium."

"Wow, this is unbelievable. Yes, I've got it!" she said. "I've never tested the farting herring setting, but many of the others function well."

"Great," I said. "We have to work quickly—we don't have that much more time. Let me introduce you to—"

"Director Z?" she asked.

"Yep," said Shane. "It doesn't look like you forgot anything you heard us say at lunch!"

"We'll fill you in on the way up to Director Z's office," I said.

As we headed up the trail, the screams got louder and louder.

We stood in front of the door to Director Z's office.

"And that's why we need the farting herring," Ben finished explaining, with a smile.

"And why they need to be zombified," she said, and she smiled back. "Got it. I'm ready."

They stared into each other's eyes, grinning ear to ear.

"Great," I said, and shook her hand to break up the staring contest. "Welcome to the club. I'm really sorry about before."

"Before?" she asked.

"Never mind," Gordon said.

Gordon lifted his clenched fist to the door, about to knock, when . . .

WHOOOSH!

It swung open. A crazy-looking Director Z nearly knocked us over as he breezed past.

"Hey," I yelled. "Hold on a minute!"

He turned awkwardly in the hallway—first his head, and then his body.

He looked at us with a crooked grin for a moment, and then finally said, "Oh! Gentlemen! Just who I was looking for."

He clapped his hands together and shuffled us into the office. He closed the door behind him.

"Please, gentlemen," he said. "Have a seat. And who is your new friend?"

He sat down and put his feet up on his desk.

"This is—" Gordon started, but I cut him off.

"New? Nabila's been with us from the start," I said.

"Oh," Director Z's eyes searched the room, looking confused, but that same crooked grin stayed on his face. "Of course! Nabila. I'm so sorry, I've been quite busy fighting the membranium."

"Wait," she started to say, "I just—"

"—have been having a great time in the tropics?" asked Shane. "Us, too. In fact, let's hit the beach!"

Shane got up, and everyone followed. Everyone but Nabila.

"What is going on here?" Nabila asked. "I thought I had just figured everything out . . ."

Nabila was so confused, her eyebrows formed a *V*.

"Yes," said Director Z, "I would like to know the very same thing. What *is* going on here? I seem to remember us talking about a plan? Chris, you are my number one. Always by my side. I'm sure you remember us talking about it."

"Yeah," I said. "We're still planning to hike through the jungle tomorrow. Five a.m. Don't be late."

"Come on, Nabila," said Ben, and then in a whisper, *"Please!"*

She looked at him strangely, but got up.

We all headed to the door.

"WAIT," boomed Director Z. "ALL OF YOU WAIT."

RUN!!!

We turned around. Director Z was no longer smiling. His body was bent over slightly, and his face was red with anger.

"We're through being nice," he hissed.

"Leave these monsters alone!" I yelled.

"You might as well tell a lion to stop eating a gazelle," Evil Z growled. "We must feast. And feast we will."

"But why the monsters?" I asked as we backed toward the door. "Why now?"

"It is their will," Evil Z replied. "We must collect all the juice. And in return, we shall rule all the seas of the Earth."

"Not if we can help it," I said, and turned the doorknob.

It wouldn't budge.

"Looking for this?" Evil Z hissed, and held up a key.

"What is he doing?" screamed Nabila.

"The membranium have taken him over," Ben replied.

"Indeed we have," said Evil Z. "And if you tell me what I want to know, I just may spare you scrawny children. WHAT IS THE PLAN?"

"Plan?" Shane scoffed. "Plan!? Director Z has just spent the last day saying how you guys are completely invincible."

"Nice try," said Evil Z, "but we have tapped his mind, and know there is a plan to stop us. We just don't know what that plan is. But you're going to tell us."

"All right, you win," said Shane. "I'll tell you everything you want to know."

"Dude!" protested Gordon.

Shane walked over toward the desk, and stood between the leather couch and the broken fish tank.

"Where should we start?" asked Shane.

Evil Z came out from behind his desk, and stood between Shane and the fish tank.

"Very good, very good," said Evil Z. "We are very, very pleased that you've decided to tell us the plan. We will crush those lumbering Nurses!"

"Get ready for the plan," said Shane.

He turned his head back to us, winked, and then

345

turned back to Evil Z who was wringing his hands together.

"I dunno what Shane's doing," I whispered to the others, "but we should get ready."

"The plan is simple, really," said Shane. "I'm going to deliver a powerful roundhouse kick to your head, you'll fall back into the fish tank and get snagged by the razor coral and broken glass, and then, rather than waste time looking for the key in your pocket and exiting from the front door, we'll all jump out of the window."

"What?" screamed Evil Z. "How dare you sass us, you impudent little fool!"

Evil Z rushed at Shane, who landed a roundhouse kick square in his jaw. Evil Z flew back onto the fish tank with a crunch.

"Run!!!" I yelled, and we all rushed for the window.

"Arrrrgggh!" Evil Z yelled.

He tried to pull himself out of the fish tank, and though there was a loud RIP, his clothes stayed snagged by the coral that was secured inside.

"NOOOOOOO!" he struggled.

More tearing and screaming could be heard as we each jumped a few feet down onto the ground and ran for the aquarium.

"Let's hope that he stays stuck for long enough," I said.

We were out of breath when we hit the aquarium a few minutes later. Nurse Kook had sealed himself into the entrance. We ran up to the huge metal blockade and knocked as hard as we could. A few moments later, a door in the metal scraped to the side, and we were let in.

"The Director has been taken over," Gordon said to Nurse Kook. "We have to work quickly!"

We rushed over to a pile of scuba gear, and Nurse Kook helped us put it on.

We ran up to the top of an empty tank that was open to the ocean. Two old zombies waited for us there.

"Are you guys ready?" I asked them.

They each gave me a big thumbs-up, although one of them was missing a thumb.

"All right," I said. "Everyone take some of Griselda's gas elixir. Be careful, this is all that's left."

We each whipped out a vial that was in a small pouch on our wet suits.

"Ach," said Ben. "This tastes terrible! Are you sure it's not barf elixir?"

"Don't fart it all out at once," said Shane.

"Nabila, you know what to do!" I said.

"Got it!" she said.

She switched on the little black device she held in her hand.

PLIP, PLIP, PLIP, PLIP!

"Those don't sound like farts," said Gordon. "Are

you sure we shouldn't use mine?"

"I assure you," said Nabila, "that this is the actual sound of herring farts. Underwater farts sound different, you know."

She lowered her device into the tank.

FLURT, FLURT, FLURT, FLURT, FLURT!

"Ah," said Shane. "That's more like it."

"Now we wait," said Nabila.

We waited, and waited, and waited. Five minutes went by and it felt like five years.

"What if this doesn't work?" whined Ben.

"It has to work," said Gordon, "we don't have a Plan B."

"I really wish that Gil could speak Herring," said Shane.

"I'm starting to worry. I'm sure Evil Z has freed himself by now," I said. "And this tank is wide open! What if the skin is attracted to the farting?"

The water began to bubble and froth at the entrance of the tank.

"The herring!" Nabila yelled.

"YES!" I yelled.

Nabila's machine slowly drew the massive school of herring over to where we stood. The zombies shuffled over in preparation.

When they reached the edge of the tank, the four of us threw a large net over the herring, and jumped into the water.

As soon as we hit the water we could hear millions of tiny farts a second.

FLURT, FLURT, FLURT, FLURT, FLURT.

"Take it slow," I said through the radio communicator, "we don't want to spook them."

"The school is massive," said Shane. "There must be a thousand fish in there!"

"This is awesome!" Nabila said. "They're actually wolf herring, so they have loads of teeth. Farewell, organs!"

"All right," I said. "Let's pull the bottom of the net up so we can let the zombies in."

We got the net right where we wanted it, and I came up to the surface of the water to call the zombies . . .

. . . only to find Evil Z standing in a badly-shredded suit at the edge of the tank!

"Hello, children," he growled.

SWIM!!!

"We are very, very disappointed in you," said Evil Z. "But, in the end, your plan is of no consequence to us. You will be defeated, you weak little babies!!!"

He walked to the wall at the back of the tank platform and hit a large red button. An alarm sounded, and red lights flashed.

My friends surfaced around me.

"What's going on?" asked Ben.

I pointed at Evil Z, who approached the water's edge again.

"We have let all the sea monsters loose," cackled Evil Z. "If they don't get you—we will!"

He grabbed both zombies by the arm and turned to leave.

"Wait!" I yelled. "Whatever you do, please don't hurt them!"

"Oh," said Evil Z, "are these two juicy tidbits important to you? Then watch them DIE!"

He tossed the two zombies into the water and stormed off the platform.

"There's plenty of food back at the facility," he said, "and now WE'RE IN CONTROL. HA-HA-HA-HA! Let the feast begin!"

Evil Z stormed through the door to the main hall of the aquarium and locked us inside.

The zombies dog-paddled slowly toward me. The tank was soon filled with angry growls.

"The sea monsters!" Gordon yelled.

"Chris, get those zombies chompin'," Shane said. "I think I can give you some time, but I don't know how much, so HURRY!"

Shane dipped under the water and swam off.

"Wait!" I yelled, and ducked underwater to see where he was going. "Shane, what are you doing?"

"The Kraken," he said back. "I've got to get the Kraken—"

With a burst of static, his transmission cut off.

"Shane? Shane!?" I yelled into the communicator. "Argh! Guys—let's do this! Hold the netting tight."

I swam over to the struggling zombies, grabbed each by the arm, and brought them over to the opening in the net the others had created.

They leaned in and CHOMPED into a few herring. CHOMP, CHOMP, CHOMP!

Soon, the zombie's chomps were joined by smaller chomps.

"The first zombie herring are starting to bite the others," said Ben.

"That's good, guys," I said to the zombies.

They turned to slowly dog-paddle back to the platform. I swam ahead of them to get the vegetable brain.

Suddenly, one of them splashed in the water.

"Arrrrgggbbbbbwww!" he screamed into the water.

"Oh, no," said Ben. "A membranium!"

"Let's get these fish moving, now!" yelled Gordon.

"We can't yet!" I yelled. "We need the vegetable brain to lead them in the right direction."

I shot out of the water, and grabbed the platform edge.

The zombie under attack knocked me back in the water before I could grab the vegetable brain. He splashed around so violently I was pinned between him and the wall.

"He's right on top of you," yelled Ben. "Unless he farts, the membranium will grab you as soon as they have control. TELL HIM TO FART!"

"*OOF,*" I grunted as a zombie arm smashed into my stomach.

"I'm not taking any chances," said Nabila.

She broke away from her position at the net and swam toward me and the writhing zombie—backward!

"What are you doing?" screamed Ben.

"Trust me," she said.

She backed her backside right up against the writhing zombie and

PLRFFFTTTTTTT!

He stopped writhing.

"Get back!" yelled Gordon. "The membranium just squeezed him."

"Oh, no it didn't," she said.

The zombie began swimming up to the platform, faster now. I quickly helped him up and then grabbed the vegetable brain. Nabila helped the second zombie up and we headed back to the net.

"Did you just fart on him?" I asked.

"Yes," she said. "In fact, I did."

"Wait," said Gordon. "That works?"

Ben stared at his not-girlfriend in complete admiration.

"Wow," I said. "This girl is AWESOME!"

"Thanks, guys," said Nabila, "but let's get going."

I headed to the front of the net and waved the

vegetable brain in front of the herring. They slowly started to move forward.

"Nabila and Gordon," I said, "grab hold of the net just in case the zombie herring get any funny ideas. I want you to be able to put them back on the right course."

"Got it," said Nabila.

"Ben," I continued, "keep an eye out for membranium and sea monsters.

FURT, FLURT, FURT, PLURT, FUURT!

The zombie herring happily farted their way into the deep, following the vegetable brain. They picked up speed, but when we passed over the coral reef, they got a little distracted by some of the tastier sea creatures.

"Maybe they can smell fish brains?" Gordon wondered.

We reached the lip of the trench down to the membranium hive.

"Oh no," said Ben. "We can't get down there!"

The dark figure of Moby Dick, the monstrous white whale, loomed at the edge of the trench. He was soon joined by dozens of slimy sea serpents. Razor sharp teeth shined in the water.

We froze in place.

"What do we do?" screamed Nabila. "Never mind; I don't want to meet any more monsters! This is more than enough."

"Pull yourself together, Nabila!" I yelled.

But I was just as frightened as Nabila. Even the zombie fish were stunned.

With a great blast of snotty bubbles from Moby Dick, the sea monsters headed straight toward us.

"Back up, back up!" I yelled.

I swung around to the other side of the net, and waved the vegetable brain around like crazy.

But it was too late.

The sea monsters rose out of the trench, and surrounded us.

FAAAAART!!!

Great roars, squeals and moans sounded in the deep.
Mouths filled with razor-sharp teeth snapped. A hydra
moved closer, each head looking straight into each of
our eyes. Moby Dick opened his mouth wide and . . .

"Yahhoooooooo!"

There was a scream and a huge dark figure swooped
in from above us.

"It's the Kraken," yelled Ben.

"Look." Nabila pointed.

On top of the Kraken's head, holding on like a
crazed bull rider, was Shane.

"Yeeeeeeehaw!" Shane yelled.
"Catch us if you can!"

The Kraken turned back the way it came, and the sea monsters sped in its direction.

"Awesome!" said Ben. "Yeah, Shane!"

"Ben!" yelled Nabila. "Look out!"

One last sea serpent roared past us, smacking Ben in the head as it went. Ben was flung down onto the sea floor. With an OOF, his oxygen tanks crunched into the sharp coral.

"Are you okay?" Nabila squealed.

"I'm. S-so. D-dizzy," stammered Ben.

"That's all right, beautiful one," a voice shimmered in the deep.

"We'll take care of you," said another, equally magical voice.

"Whoa," said Gordon. "Mermaids!"

"Oh, I don't think so," said Nabila.

She swam down to Ben and grabbed one of his arms just as another was grabbed by the mermaid.

"I've got him," said Nabila

"Oh, but my dear, we're more than capable of taking care of him," a mermaid purred.

"I said *I've* got him," growled Nabila.

"It's okay," said Ben. "Let me go with the pretty mermaid."

"What?" gasped Nabila and let him go.

"Oh, you're such a cute little one," said another mermaid. "We're going to have so much fun."

The mermaids swam off with Ben.

"He's MY cute one," yelled Nabila, and followed the exiting mermaids.

"Nabila," I yelled. "NABILA! We don't have much time now. I'm sure Ben will be fine with the mermaids. But we need you. Gordon and I can't do this alone."

Nabila turned around.

"Fine," she said. "Ben can take care of himself. I'm ready."

I moved the back over the trench with the vegetable brain. We had just picked up speed again when . . .

"Chris," Gordon yelled. "Look out! To your right!"

I turned just in time to see the shimmer of skin as it quickly enveloped me from head to toe.

"Arrrrgggh!" I yelled.

It was surprisingly fast, and surprisingly strong. Every single inch of me was squeezed. Pain flashed like lightning in my eyes. My brain felt like it was being taken over, and words rushed into my head and made me dizzy.

You are ours now! Submit! Open your mind to us!

"Fart!" yelled Nabila, and I snapped out of it.

I was in so much pain, I was barely able to do it, but I finally let out a BLLLLURP.

"Whoa!" I yelled, catching my breath.

"Faaaarrt!" yelled Gordon.

"I just did!" I yelled back.

"No, you didn't," Gordon said. "All you did was yell, 'Cheesecake whoa!'"

But I must have farted. I could still feel the skin on me, but it was no longer pressing me. In fact, it made me feel even stronger.

"No, he farted," said Nabila. "Now, let's hurry up and get down there so we can get out of here."

I went over the side of the ridge into the darkness. The farting zombie herring followed.

Two more skins shimmered past.

"Look out!" I yelled, but soon Nabila and Gordon were thrashing and dealing with the insane pain.

"Fart, fart, faaaart!" I yelled so hard that my ears hurt inside my scuba gear.

BLLLLLAARRRP!

"Easy-peasy lemon squeezy," said Gordon, coughing.

"Fart, Gordon!" I yelled. "Fart!"

"He farted," said Nabila.

"No, he didn't," I said. "He just said—"

"We can talk about it later," said Gordon, pointing forward.

We had arrived at the hive.

"We need one last push to get these herring into the hive," I said.

"Got it," they said.

"This is it, guys!" I said.

"Let's do it!" said Gordon.

I swam ahead with the vegetable brain, while Nabila and Gordon grabbed the top of the net, and the first of the zombie herring made their way out.

"Build up some speed, guys," I yelled.

We all kicked as hard as we could.

"All right," I yelled. "I'm letting go of the vegetable brain in three . . . two . . . one . . . GO!"

I flung the brain into the hive and swam back toward Nabila and Gordon. They slowly peeled the net off the school and headed back up toward the ridge. As I swam past the school, there was a shimmer of skin, and three zombie herring were suddenly wrapped around me.

"AHHHH!" I shrieked.

They chomped my body like crazy, and it sounded like they were farting directly into my ears.

"Chris!" Gordon yelled, and he began to swim back toward me.

"Wait," I said. "The skin I have on is protecting me. Let's get out of here."

I swam toward Gordon and away from the hive, which awoke with the appearance of the zombie herring.

But soon I was being pulled backward! The zombie herring had created a layer of fart under the skin, and were no longer pressed against my body. They headed back to the school.

"Chris!" yelled Nabila.

"Forget it!" I yelled back. "Just go!"

I turned around and saw the school follow the vegetable brain into the very center of the hive. The membranium came a little farther out of their sea pods, hissing and growling in excitement at their tasty new visitors. Their moldy claws cracked, and they drooled a blue cloud out of the sides of their mouths. Their tongues lashed behind their razor-sharp shark teeth.

This better work, I thought, *or I'll be membranium meat.*

Slowly, disgustingly, all of the membranium peeled off their skins like slimy T-shirts. The ocean was filled with a wet, tearing sound, as hundreds of nasty, green, scaly skins peeled off of ugly bodies, and turned clear as they headed for the fish.

FURT, PLURT, FLART, PLIP, PLOP!

The herring farted as the skin overtook them.

"It's working!" I yelled. "Go, guys, goooooo!"

"All right, all right," said Gordon, "but keep us updated with the communicator. We're going to try to find Shane and the Kraken. Maybe they can help."

Entire walls of membranium were now exposed, their organs pulsating in the cold water, giving off heat waves.

"The herring have noticed the organs," I yelled.

A few of the herring had broken off from the rest, and were chomping at the organs of the membranium. Soon they were thrashing, which got the others' attentions.

"It's a feeding frenzy!" I said.

My three zombie herring brought me up against the wall to join the feast, and I was pulled in all sorts of different directions, scraping up against the wall and squishing into sea pods.

The sounds of scraping and squishing mixed with the bloodcurdling screams of the membranium as they were devoured.

The water began to cloud with blood as organs were chewed up in seconds. Entire walls of the hideous beasts were taken down by the frantic fish, who were farting even faster and stronger now.

"I'm getting pummeled by all of the fish," I said. "They're not hurting me, but I'm dizzy, and—"

My helmet was knocked off the side of my head, with a large scrape, as we bounced off the wall and joined the rest of the school.

"Chris," Nabila said, "can you hear us? Chris?"

I held my breath, struggling to put my helmet back on. Meanwhile, the three zombie herring trapped in our bubble started chewing into anything they could, still hungry after all of the tasty organs.

"Chris?" asked Gordon.

I finally got my helmet on and then CHOMP, one of the zombie herring bit into the air hose feeding my helmet.

"Uh, oh," I said. "Oh . . ."

I gagged on the next breath. The bubble of skin

expanded with the green and brown gas of the zombie herring that were trapped with me.

"Oh, it's terrible," I said.

"What's going on down there?" asked Gordon.

"My skin. Is filling up. With gas," I said between coughs.

Sure enough, the entire school was slowly becoming separated as bubbles of gas formed in what used to be the membranium skin. And I was in the middle of it all.

"We're coming down there," said Gordon.

I coughed and gagged. It smelled a million times worse than being trapped under a sheet with Gordon's fart.

The herring, frightened by being trapped in their own gas, began farting even harder. We started to rise in the water, slowly at first, and then picking up speed as the bubbles expanded even further.

The bubble I was in popped with a loud BANG. We jiggled the hundreds of other bubbles, most of which were filled by one or two fish.

"No!" I yelled, still coughing in the green/brown fart stew. "Turn back!"

COUGH, GAG, COUGH!

"The skins," I screamed between coughs, "ARE GOING TO EXPLODE!"

But it was too late. The gas bubbles were expanding at amazing rates, and the frantic school rose up the side of the trench.

The entire mass of bubbles began to jiggle and vibrate, until, suddenly.

POW! POP! BAM! BLORP!

All the bubbles burst violently and shot us to the surface of the water. I flew up out of the water fifteen feet and then landed on top of a huge wave that had formed by the explosion. It crashed over the beach, over the jungle, and smashed into the resort!

When I finally stopped spinning, I found myself facedown in the Jacuzzi!

Gordon and a mermaid washed up nearby, in the infinity pool. I scanned the horizon for Ben, Nabila, and Shane, but all I could see were zombie herring flip-flopping everywhere. A few wet Nurses looked around confused, and waved their hands at the horrendous odor that had washed up with the wave.

"Do you see the others?" I asked Gordon.

"Ben and Nabila, sitting in a tree . . . ," Gordon said, and pointed up.

"Just so you know, we are NOT k-i-s-s-i-n-g," came Nabila's voice from above.

I looked up to see Ben and Nabila tangled up in the fronds of a palm tree.

"Woooo-hooo," Ben yelled. "And I didn't even barf in my helmet!"

Gordon turned to the mermaid in the pool.

"So," he cooed, "what are you doing later?"

The Sweet Stench of Success

I laid in the Jacuzzi for a few minutes, and let the bubbles blurp at my backside.

"Ahhh," I sighed.

"Can someone get me out of here?" asked Ben from his perch.

"Relax and enjoy the view," scolded Nabila. "Or are you still trying to get away from me?"

"No, I'm not. But, how can you enjoy the view, when—oh, riiiiiiight," said Ben. "You can't smell the massive fartbomb that just exploded."

A zombie herring flopped out of the palm tree above Ben and smacked him in the head on its way down.

"I think it smells like victory!" said Shane, who ran up to the infinity pool and jumped in.

"I don't want to know what losing smells like," quipped Gordon, floating in the pool.

"Shane!" I yelled. "How were you able to ride the Kraken? That was amazing!"

"I just remember what Gordon told me Clive had said," Shane said. "And gave him one swift karate chop to the top of his head."

"Works every time, brah," a weak voice came from the pool.

"Hey, what's that?" Gordon said.

I lifted my head out of the relaxing Jacuzzi and looked to see Gordon pointing to something bobbing up and down in the water.

"Is that Clive?" Gordon asked.

"WHAT!?" I yelled, and jumped out of the Jacuzzi.

Shane ducked underwater, and swam up to the surface a few seconds later with . . .

"CLIVE!" I yelled. "You're alive! I mean, you're not dead. I mean . . . it's great to see you!"

Shane lifted him up to the side of the pool, and I dragged out the old zombie surfer.

"Hey, buddy," he gurgled, water pouring out of his mouth. "I think I'm a little waterlogged here. Get me in some sun!"

"What happened?" I asked. "I thought we lost you!"

Shane walked over to Clive and me. Gordon swam up to the side of the pool. Ben waved from the palm tree.

"Hey, I think I tweaked my right ear," Clive said. "Is it still there?"

I turned his head to have a look, and a crab scurried out of his ear and into the jungle.

"I think it's fine now," Shane said. "So, what happened?"

"Well, I was able to hide in a small crevice under the coral where the sharks couldn't reach me," he said, "but when they finally left, I realized I was stuck. How did I get here?"

"It's a long story," I said, "but the short version is—"

Before I could start, Director Z, a dozen Nurses, and almost all of the residents showed up poolside. Some of them looked like they were about to fall over, and were held up by other residents, or by the Nurses.

"Chris," said Director Z, "you and your friends have done it again! I'm so very, very pleased."

The crowd burst into applause, the monsters laughing and smiling.

"Aw, thanks!" I said. "We had a lot of help. Gil, your farts are amazing! Clive, you saved our lives! And, Nabila! We never could have done it without you."

The swamp creature walked out of the crowd and I gave him such a hard hug that he farted . . . of course! Then I shook the Director's hand.

"Don't forget to thank Ms. Veracruz," said Director Z. "If it weren't for the rare zombie piranha she fed you, you wouldn't have been quite so agile in the water."

"Zombie," Gordon choked, "piranha?"

A shower of vomit fell from the palm tree. Poor Ben.

"Yes, twice actually," Director Z said. "Once at school—"

"The Mac 'n' Sneeze!" Shane yelled. "I *knew* it tasted fishy!"

"And again during the barbecue in Cape Canaveral," finished Director Z.

"Aw, man," said Gordon, "my stomach is cramping."

Gordon grunted and little bubbles rose to the surface of the pool. As each one popped we heard:

"POP—Oh—POP—man—POP—I—POP—ate—PLIP—zombie—PLUP—piranha!"

"Interesting," Director Z said. "The zombie piranha was meant to help you swim faster in case you ended up in the water. But apparently, a side effect is that you can fartspeak."

Shane lifted his leg and farted a single word: "AWESOME."

"Everyone that still has skin on them is fine," Director Z said, "although they no longer have superstrength. If it wasn't for that superstrength, I don't think we would have made it through the day. I'm told a werewolf and Gil personally held me down to keep me from wreaking havoc on the facility. I want to apologize for my actions. I couldn't fight the mind control."

"It wasn't your fault," said Shane, "but I apologize for kicking you in the noggin."

"Not a problem," said Director Z, rubbing his jaw. "Now, how do we get out of this skin? Any ideas?"

"Get to fartin'!" said Gordon. "You've got to pop it like a balloon!"

"That's what caused the fartsunami," I said. "All the zombie herring popped their skin bubbles at once."

"Fartsunami!" Ben called down from the palm tree. "That's awesome!"

"Well, it looks like we have a lot to fartspeak about," said Director Z.

Shane looked at Director Z strangely.

"I ate zombie piranha as well," Director Z said.

"Ohhhhhhh," we all said.

Grigore walked forward and stood next to the swamp creature.

"Chris," said Grigore, "I just vant to apologize on behalf of all the residents. You saved us from the sussuroblats, cleaned up our messes, wiped blood soup off our mouths, made our coffins, and ve returned the favor by treating you like servants. Ve're very sorry—ve've not quite been ourselves. Ve vere cooped up and getting crazy in Raven Hill. It vas hard *not* to be cranky. But ve'll try to be better. Ve'll try our best to vork as a team."

"Hear, hear!" screamed the crowd.

"Now," yelled Director Z, "let's soak up some sun, eat a few zombie frogs, relax, and build up our lebensplasm!"

Gordon jumped out of the pool and walked over to Director Z.

"I was just wondering if I could ask you one thing," said Gordon.

"Please," said Director Z, "anything you need."

"Can you just call it *monster juice*? It sounds so much more fun than lebensplasm."

"MONSTER JUICE!" yelled Clive from his seat.

"All right," said Director Z, "*monster juice* it is!"

The crowd cheered.

We spent the next few days at Paradise Island, enjoying the sun, sand, and sea. The swamp creature and I took a trip down to the membranium hive to make sure it was completely destroyed. It was. Clive gave us surfing lessons. Shane finally got his fruit smoothie. And when the zombie sharks returned to the aquarium, we made them special vegetable-brain smoothies.

It was the vacation we had desperately needed.

A Nurse fixed the telephone lines and we called in transportation. We returned to Cape Canaveral, where Lunch Lady made all the preparations for folks to think we had been there the whole time.

Then it was back home!

I walked into my house completely relaxed, but before I could say, "Hello," my mother attacked me.

"Chrissy!" she screeched. "You have A LOT of explaining to do!"

"Huh?" I asked. "What's going on?"

"THAT'S WHAT I WANT TO KNOW!" she screeched even louder.

"Whoa, Mom," I said, "calm down."

"I will not calm down!" she said. "I can't even count how many times I called you, and you never called back! You always call back! What's going on?"

"I was just hanging out with my friends," I replied.

"Oh, really?" she asked. "I saw all sorts of pictures from parents of their kids, and you're not in any of them. We always talk about how much you love space, and you didn't even text me a photo of Kennedy Space Center!"

"Mom, I was busy," I said, starting to get nervous.

What if she knows about my trip to Paradise Island? I wondered.

"Yeah, you're always busy these days," she replied. "Ever since you started volunteering at Raven Hill, you've been so busy . . . and acting so *strange*."

"It's . . . hard work," I stammered. "Really tiring. Sorry if I'm a little out of it and just wanted to relax on vacation."

"Chris, I know you too well. Something's wrong. What's going on at Raven Hill? You always stay there so late. I've been e-mailing your father about it, and he's just as worried."

"All right, Mom, all right!" I said, not really knowing what to say. "Everything is fine. Nothing is wrong."

"I think it's about time I spoke with the Director of Raven Hill," she said. "In fact, I think I would like to speak with him IMMEDIATELY. RIGHT NOW."

"All right," I said, not knowing what to do. "I guess I'll go and get him."

"Go and get him?" Mom said. "I don't want you go anywhere until I speak with him—just give me his number."

"I . . . don't have his number," I said.

"Well," she said, grabbing her purse, "I'll go up there myself."

"No, wait," I said. "Everything's fine, and there's nothing to worry about. I need . . . um . . . I need to get my volunteer form anyway! Trust me."

"FINE," she yelled. "But if you come back here without the Director, you're going to be sorry."

I biked up to Raven Hill as quickly as I could. My

mind was buzzing. *What are we going to tell my mother? We have to tell her something!*

But soon my mind was buzzing even more. When I reached the top of the hill, there was nothing there but a smoldering pile of rubble. The Nurses were erecting large tents behind the burned remains of Raven Hill. Director Z stood in front of the building with his head down.

"Director Z!" I yelled. "What happened?"

"Chris!" he replied. "It's terrible. The ravens—and there are only three of them now—report that Herr Direktor Detlef was a tool of the membranium this whole time. He never intended to bring his residents to Raven Hill. They were all sucked dry by the membranium shortly before we arrived. We were lured to Paradise Island by the membranium! Herr Direktor Detlef destroyed our facility—and himself."

He paused, then said, quietly, "There's something bigger going on here. Why would the membranium want to destroy Raven Hill?"

"When you were possessed," I said, "you said that someone was making the membranium collect all the monster juice."

"Yes, I seem to remember that now . . . ," said Director Z. "And 'they' look to be collecting even more than monster juice. Herr Direktor Detlef's pendant can't be found anywhere."

"Pendant?" I asked.

Director Z loosened his tie and pulled a necklace out from under his shirt. A sliver of bloodstone hung off the bottom.

"Every Director has one, and Herr Direktor Detlef's is gone. This is all very troubling," said the Director.

A Nurse approached with a slightly-charred painting. He held it up to Director Z.

"I told you so," said Lucinda B. Smythe.

The Nurse carried the painting away.

"What are you going to do?" I asked.

"We don't have the resources to rebuild," he said, sadly. "So we'll have to seek shelter somewhere else. I'm not sure where yet."

"Well," I said, "we have another problem."

"What?" he said.

"My mother knows something's going on at Raven Hill."

"We'll just have the witches whip up a batch of memory-erasing serum."

"No, it's not that simple. My father's in Afghanistan with the Air Force Reserve, and she's already e-mailed him about it. We can't erase his memory—unless you have a facility in Afghanistan, and can find him. His mission is classified—but there are e-mail records, and the US government doesn't destroy e-mail records. She's asked to speak with you right away."

"All right." He sighed.

We both looked at the smoldering rubble, and at the same time, said:

"We should have just stayed on Paradise Island."

ABOUT THE AUTHOR . . .

M. D. Payne is a mad scientist who creates monsters by stitching together words instead of dead body parts. After nearly a decade in multimedia production for public radio, he entered children's publishing as a copywriter and marketer. Monster Juice is his debut series. He lives in the tiny village of New York City with his wife and baby girl, and hopes to add a hairy, four-legged monster to his family soon.